# Cleopatra's Nights

# One of Cleopatra's Nights

THEOPHILE GAUTIER

TRANSLATED BY
LAFCADIO HEARN

Wildside Press
Berkeley Heights, NJ · 1999

**ONE OF CLEOPATRA'S NIGHTS,**

**by Theophile Gautier**

**Translated by Lafcadio Hearn**

Published by:

Wildside Press
PO Box 45
Gillette, NJ 07933-0045

ISBN: 1-880448-59-9

# CONTENTS

*The love that caught strange light from death's*
*own eyes,*
*And filled death's lips with fiery words and sighs,*
*And half asleep, let feed from veins of his,*
*Her close red warm snake's-mouth, Egyptian-*
*wise:*

*And that great night of love more strange than*
*this,*
*When she that made the whole world's bale and*
*bliss*
*Made king of the whole world's desire a*
*slave*
*And killed him in mid-kingdom with a kiss.*

SWINBURNE.

*"Memorial verses on the death of Theophile Gautier."*

# TO THE READER.

The stories composing this volume have been selected for translation from the two volumes of romances and tales by Théophile Gautier, respectively entitled, *Nouvelles* and *Romans et Contes.* They afford in the original many excellent examples of that peculiar beauty of fancy and power of painting with words, which made Gautier the most brilliant literary artist of his time. No doubt their warmth of coloring has been impoverished and their fantastic enchantment weakened by the process of transformation into a less voluptuous tongue; yet enough of the original charm remains, we trust, to convey a just idea of the French author's rich imaginative power and ornate luxuriance of style.

The verses of Swinburne referring to the witchery of the novelette which opens the volume, and to the peculiarly sweet and strange romance which follows, sufficiently indicate the extraordinary art of these tales. At least three of the stories we have attempted to translate rank among the most remarkable literary productions of the century.

These little romances are characterized, however, by merits other than those of mere literary workmanship:—they are further remarkable for a wealth of erudition—picturesque learning, we might say,—which often lends them an actual archæologic value, like the paintings of some scholarly artist, some Alma Tadema, who with fair magic of color-blending evokes for us eidolons of ages vanished and civilizations passed away.

Thus one finds in the delightful fantasy of *Arria Marcella* not only a dream of "Pompeiian Days," pictured with an idealistic brilliancy beyond the art of Coomans, but a rich knowledge, likewise, of all that fascinating lore gleaned by antiquarian research amid the ashes of the sepultured city—a knowledge enriched in no small degree by local study, and presented with a descriptive power finely strengthened by personal observation. It is something more than the charming imagination of a poetic dreamer which paints for us the blue sea "unrolling its long volutes of foam" upon a beach as black and smooth as sifted charcoal; the fissured summit of Vesuvius, out-pouring white threads of smoke from its crannies "as from the orifices of a perfuming pan;"—and the far-purple hills "with outlines voluptuously undulating, like the hips of a woman."

And throughout these romances one finds the same evidences of archæologic study, of artistic observation, of imagination fostered by picturesque fact. The glory of the Greek kings of Lydia glows goldenly again in the pages of *Le Roi Candaule;* the massive gloom and melancholy weirdness of ancient Egypt is reflected as in a necromancer's mirror throughout *Une Nuit de Cleopatre.* It is in the Egyptian fantasies, perhaps, that the author's peculiar descriptive skill appears to most advantage; the still-fresh hues of the hierophantic paintings, the pictured sarcophagi and the mummy-gilding, seem to meet the reader's eye with the gratification of their bright contrasts; a faint perfume of unknown balm seems to hover over the open pages; and mysterious sphinxes appear to look on "with that undefinable rose-granite smile that mocks our modern wisdom."

Excepting *Omphale* and *La Morte Amoreuse*, the stories selected for translation are mostly antique in composition and coloring, the former being Louis-Quinze, the latter medieval rather than aught else. But all alike frame some exquisite delineation of young love-fancies—some admirable picture of what Gautier in the *Histoire du Romantisme* has prettily termed "the graceful *succubi* that haunt the happy slumbers of youth."

And what dreamful student of the Beautiful has not been once enamored of an Arria Marcella, and worshiped on the altar of his heart those ancient gods "who loved life and youth and beauty and pleasure"?—how many a lover of medieval legend has in fancy gladly bartered the blood of his veins for some phantom Clarimonde?—what true artist has not at some time been haunted by the image of a Nyssia, fairer than all daughters of men, lovelier than all fantasies realized in stone—a Pygmalion-wrought marble transmuted by divine alchemy to a being of opalescent flesh and ichor-throbbing veins?

Gautier was an artist in the common acceptation of the term, as well as a poet and a writer of romance; and in those pleasant fragments of autobiography scattered through the *Histoire du Romantisme* we find his averment that at the commencement of the Romantic movement of 1830 he was yet undecided whether to adopt literature or art as a profession; but, finding it "easier to paint with words than with colors," he finally decided upon the pen as his weapon in the new warfare against "the hydra of classicism with its hundred peruked heads." As a writer, however, he remained the artist still: his pages were pictures, his sentences touches of color; he learned indeed to "paint with words" as no other writer of the century has done, and created a powerful impression not only upon the literature of his day, but even, it may be said, upon the language of his nation.

Possessed of an almost matchless imaginative power, and a sense of beauty as refined as that of an antique sculptor, Gautier so perfects his work as to leave nothing for the imagination of his readers to desire. He insists that they should behold the author's fancy precisely as the author himself fancied it with all its details:—the position of objects, the effects of light, the disposition of shadow, the material of garments, the texture of stuffs, the interstices of stonework, the gleam of a lamp upon sharp angles of furniture, the whispering sound of trailing silk, the tone of a voice, the expression of a face, —all is visible, audible, tangible. You can find nothing in one of his picturesque scenes which has not been treated with a studied accuracy of minute detail that leaves no vacancy for the eye to light upon,—no hiatus for the imagination to supply. This is the art of painting carried to the highest perfection in literature. It is not wonderful that such a man should at times sacrifice style to description; and he has himself acknowledged an occasional abuse of violent coloring.

Naturally a writer of this kind pays small regard to the demands of prudery. His work being that of the artist, he claims the privilege of the sculptor and the painter in delineations of the beautiful. A perfect human body is to him the most beautiful of objects: he does not seek to vail its loveliness with cumbrous drapery; he delights to behold it and depict it in its "divine nudity"; he views it with the eyes of the Corinthian statuary or the Pompeiian fresco-painter; he idealizes even the ideal of beauty: under his treatment flesh becomes diaphanous, eyes are transformed to orbs of prismatic light, features take tints of celestial loveliness. Like the Hellenic sculptor, he is not satisfied with beauty of form alone, but must add a vital glow of delicate coloring to the white limbs and snowy bosom of marble.

It is the artist, therefore, who must judge of Gautier's creations. To the lovers of the loveliness of the antique world, the lovers of physical beauty and artistic truth,—of the charm of youthful dreams and young passion in its blossoming,—of poetic ambitions and the sweet pantheism that finds all Nature vitalized by the Spirit of the Beautiful,—to such the first English version of these graceful fantasies is offered in the hope that it may not be found wholly unworthy of the original.

NEW ORLEANS, 1882. L. H.

THEOPHILE GAUTIER

# ONE OF CLEOPATRA'S NIGHTS.

## CHAPTER I.

Nineteen hundred years ago from the date of this writing, a magnificently gilded and painted cangia was descending the Nile as rapidly as fifty long flat oars, which seemed to crawl over the furrowed water like the legs of a gigantic scarabæus, could impel it.

This cangia was narrow, long, elevated at both ends in the form of a new moon, elegantly proportioned, and admirably built for speed; the figure of a ram's head, surmounted by a golden globe, armed the point of the prow, showing that the vessel belonged to some personage of royal blood.

In the center of the vessel arose a flat-roofed cabin,—a sort of *naos*, or tent of honor, colored and gilded, ornamented with palm-leaf moldings, and lighted by four little square windows.

Two chambers, both decorated with hieroglyphic paintings, occupied the horns of the crescent. One of them, the larger, had a second story of lesser height built upon it—like the *chateaux gaillards* of those fantastic galleys of the sixteenth century, drawn by Della-Bella; the other and smaller chamber, which also served as a pilot-house, was surmounted with a triangular pediment.

In lieu of a rudder, two immense oars, adjusted upon stakes decorated with stripes of paint, which served in place of our modern rowlocks,—extended into the water in rear of the vessel like the webbed feet of a swan; heads crowned with *pshents* and bearing the allegorical horn upon their chins, were sculptured upon the handles of these huge oars, which were manœuvred by the pilot as he stood upon the deck of the cabin above.

He was a swarthy man, tawny as new bronze, with bluish surface gleams playing over his dark skin, long oblique eyes, hair deeply black and all plaited into little cords, full lips, high cheekbones, ears standing out from the skull—the Egyptian type in all its purity. A narrow strip of cotton about his loins, together with five or six strings of glass beads, and a few amulets, comprised his whole costume.

He appeared to be the only one on board the cangia; for the rowers bending over their oars, and concealed from view by the gunwales, made their presence known only through the symmetrical movements of the oars themselves, which spread open alternately on either side of the vessel, like the ribs of a fan, and fell regularly back into the water after a short pause.

Not a breath of air was stirring; and the great triangular sail of the cangia, tied up and bound to the lowered mast with a silken cord, testified that all hope of the wind rising had been abandoned.

The noonday sun shot his arrows perpendicularly from above; the ashen-hued slime of the river banks reflected the fiery glow; a raw light, glaring and blinding in its intensity, poured down in torrents of flame; the azure of the sky whitened in the heat as a metal whitens in the furnace; an ardent and lurid fog smoked in the horizon. Not a cloud appeared in the sky—a sky mournful and changeless as Eternity.

The water of the Nile, sluggish and wan, seemed to slumber in its course, and slowly extend itself in sheets of molten tin. No breath of air wrinkled its surface, or bowed down upon their stalks the cups of the lotus-flowers, as rigidly motionless as though sculptured; at long intervals the leap of a bechir or fabaka expanding its belly, scarcely caused a silvery gleam upon the current; and the oars of the cangia seemed with difficulty to tear their way through the fuliginous film of that curdled water. The banks were desolate, a solemn and mighty sadness weighed upon this land, which was never aught else than a vast tomb, and in which the living appeared to be solely occupied in the work of burying the dead. It was an arid sadness, dry as pumice stone, without melancholy, without reverie, without one pearly grey cloud to follow toward the horizon, one secret spring wherein to lave one's dusty feet; the sadness of a sphinx weary of eternally gazing upon the desert, and unable to detach herself from the granite socle upon which she has sharpened her claws for twenty centuries.

So profound was the silence that it seemed as though the world had become dumb, or that the air had lost all power of conveying sound. The only noises which could be heard at intervals were the whisperings and stifled "chuckling" of the crocodiles, which, enfeebled by the heat, were wallowing among the bullrushes by the river banks; or the sound made by some ibis, which—tired of standing with one leg doubled up against its stomach, and its head sunk between its shoulders, — suddenly abandoned its motionless attitude, and brusquely whipping the blue air with its white wings, flew off to perch upon an obelisk or a palm-tree.

The cangia flew like an arrow over the smooth river-water, leaving behind it a silvery wake which soon disappeared; and only a few foam-bubbles rising to break at the surface of the stream bore testimony to the passage of the vessel, then already out of sight.

The ochre-hued or salmon-colored banks unrolled themselves rapidly like scrolls of papyrus between the double azure of water and sky — so similar in tint that the slender tongue of earth which separated them, seemed like a causeway stretching over an immense lake, and that it would have been difficult to determine whether the Nile reflected the sky, or whether the sky reflected the Nile.

The scene continually changed: at one moment were visible gigantic propylæa, whose sloping walls, painted with large panels of fantastic figures, were mirrored in the river; pylons with broad-bulging capitals; stairways guarded by huge crouching sphinxes, wearing caps with lappets of many folds, and crossing their paws of black basalt below their sharply projecting breasts; palaces, immeasurably vast, projecting against the horizon the severe horizontal lines of their entablatures, where the emblematic globe unfolded its mysterious wings like an eagle's vast-extending pinions; temples with enormous columns thick as towers, on which were limned processions of hieroglyphic figures against a back ground of brilliant white; all the monstrosities of that Titanic architecture. Again the eye beheld only landscapes of desolate aridity:—hills formed of stony fragments from excavations and building works,—crumbs of that gigantic debauch of granite which lasted for more than thirty centuries; mountains exfoliated by heat, and mangled and striped with black lines which seemed like the cauterizations of a conflagration; hillocks humped and deformed, squatting like the criocephalus of the tombs, and projecting the outlines of their misshapen attitude against the sky-line; expanses of greenish clay, reddle, flour-white tufa, and from time to time some steep cliff of dry rose-colored granite, where yawned the black mouths of the stone quarries.

This aridity was wholly unrelieved; no oasis of foilage refreshed the eye; green seemed to be a color unknown to that nature; only some

THE SPHINX AND THE PYRAMIDS, EGYPT.

meagre palm-tree, like a vegetable crab, appeared from time to time in the horizon,—or a thorny fig-tree brandished its tempered leaves like sword blades of bronze,—or a carthamus-plant, which had found a little moisture to live upon in the shadow of some fragment of a broken column, relieved the general uniformity with a speck of crimson.

After this rapid glance at the aspect of the landscape, let us return to the cangia with its fifty rowers, and without announcing ourselves, enter boldly into the *naos* of honor.

The interior was painted white with green arabesques, bands of vermillion, and gilt flowers fantastically shaped; an exceedingly fine rush matting covered the floor; at the further end stood a little bed, supported upon griffin's feet—having a back resembling that of a modern lounge or sofa, a stool with four steps to enable one to climb into bed, and (rather an odd luxury according to our ideas of comfort!) a sort of hemicycle of cedar wood, supported upon a single leg, and designed to fit the nape of the neck so as to support the head of the person reclining.

Upon this strange pillow reposed a most charming head,—one look of which once caused the loss of half-a-world,—an adorable, a divine head; the head of the most perfect woman that ever lived,— the most womanly and most queenly of all women; an admirable type of beauty which the imagination of poets could never invest with any new grace, and which dreamers will find forever in the depths of their dreams: it is not necessary to name Cleopatra.

Beside her stood her favorite slave Charmion, waving a large fan of ibis feathers; and a young girl was moistening with scented water the little reed blinds attached to the windows of the naos, so that the air might only enter impregnated with fresh odors.

Near the bed of repose, in a striped vase of alabaster with a slender neck and a peculiarly elegant, tapering shape—vaguely recalling the form of a heron,—was placed a bouquet of lotus-flowers, some of a celestial blue, others of a tender rose-color, like the finger-tips of Isis, the great goddess.

Either from caprice or policy, Cleopatra did not wear the Greek dress that day: she had just attended a panegyris,* and was returning to her

* *Panegyris;* pl., *panegyreis,*—from the Greek πανήγυρις,—signifies the meeting of a whole people to worship at a common sanctuary or participate in a national religious festival. The assemblies at the Olympic, Pythian, Nemean, or Isthmian games were in this sense *panegyreis.* See Smith's Dict. Antiq.—[TRANS.

summer palace still clad in the Egyptian costume she had worn at the festival.

Perhaps our fair readers will feel curious to know how Queen Cleopatra was attired on her return from the Mammisi of Hermonthis whereat were worshiped the holy triad of the god Mandou, the goddess Ritho, and their son, Harphra: luckily we are able to satisfy them in this regard.

For headdress Queen Cleopatra wore a kind of very light helmet of beaten gold, fashioned in the form of the body and wings of the sacred partridge: the wings, opening downward like fans, covered the temples, and extending below almost to the neck, left exposed on either side through a small aperture, an ear rosier and more delicately curled than the shell whence arose that Venus whom the Egyptians named Athor;—the tail of the bird occupied that place where our women wear their chignons: its body, covered with imbricated feathers, and painted in variegated enamel, concealed the upper part of the head; and its neck, gracefully curving forward over the forehead of the wearer, formed together with its little head a kind of horn-shaped ornament, all sparkling with precious stones;—a symbolic crest designed like a tower, completed this odd but elegant headdress. Hair dark as a starless night, flowed from beneath this helmet, and streamed in long tresses over the fair shoulders whereof the commencement only, alas! was left exposed by a collerette or gorget adorned with many rows of serpentine stones, azodrachs, and chrysoberyls; a linen robe diagonally cut,—a mist of material, of woven air, *ventus textilis* as Petronius says,—undulated in vapory whiteness about a lovely body, whose outlines it scarcely shaded with the softest shading. This robe had half-sleeves, tight at the shoulder, but widening toward the elbows like our *manches-à-sabot*, and permitting a glimpse of an adorable arm and a perfect hand;—the arm being clasped by six golden bracelets, and the hand adorned with a ring representing the sacred scarabæus. A girdle whose knotted ends hung down in front, confined this free-floating tunic at the waist; a short cloak adorned with fringing completed the costume; and if a few barbarous words will not frighten Parisian ears, we might add that the robe was called *schenti* and the short cloak *calisiris*.

Finally we may observe that Queen Cleopatra wore very thin light sandals, turned up at the toes, and fastened over the instep, like the *souliers-à-la-poulaine* of the mediæval *chatelaines*.

But Queen Cleopatra did not wear that air of satisfaction which becomes a woman conscious of being perfectly beautiful and perfectly well dressed: she tossed and turned in her little bed;

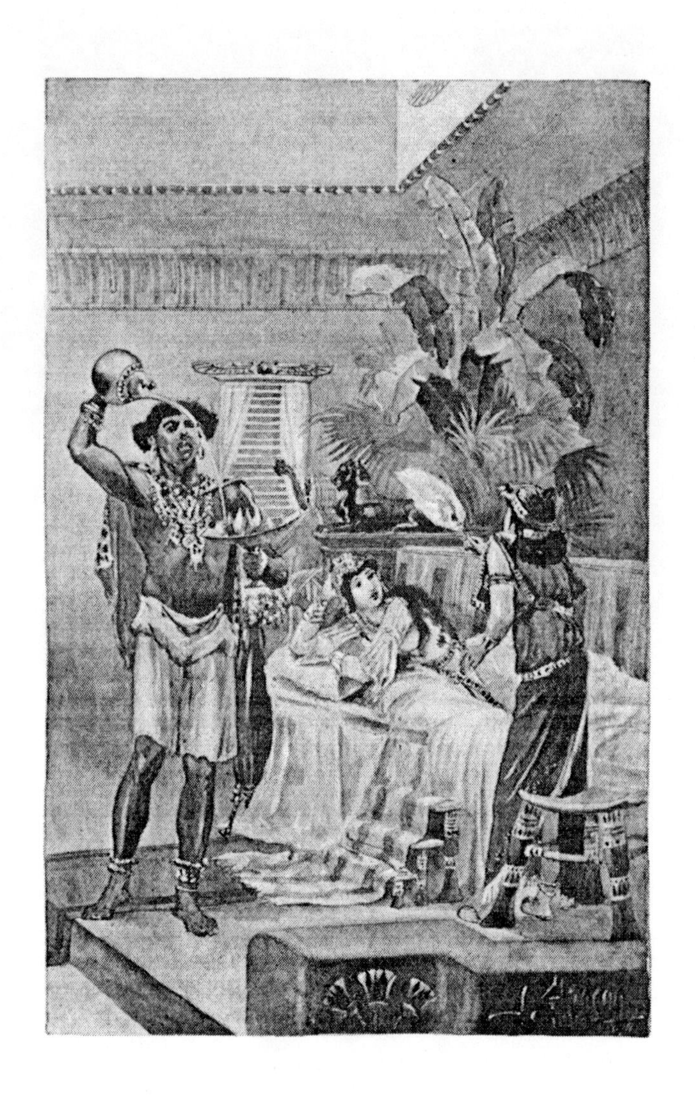

and her rather sudden movements momentarily disarranged the folds of her gauzy *conopeum* which Charmion as often rearranged with inexhaustible patience, and without ceasing to wave her fan.

"This room is stifling," said Cleopatra;—"even if Pthah the God of Fire established his forges in here, he could not make it hotter: the air is like the breath of a furnace!" And she moistened her lips with the tip of her little tongue; and stretched out her hand like a feverish patient seeking an absent cup.

Charmion, ever attentive, at once clapped her hands; a black slave clothed in a short tunic hanging in folds like an Albanian petticoat, and a panther-skin thrown over his shoulders, entered with the suddenness of an apparition; with his left hand balancing a tray laden with cups and slices of water-melon, and carrying in his right a long vase with a spout like a modern teapot.

The slave filled one of these cups,—pouring the liquor into it from a considerable height with marvelous dexterity,—and placed it before the queen. Cleopatra merely touched the beverage with her lips, laid the cup down beside her, and turning upon Charmion her beautiful liquid black eyes, lustrous with living light, exclaimed:

"O, Charmion, I am weary unto death!"

## CHAPTER II.

Charmion, at once anticipating a confidence, assumed a look of pained sympathy, and drew nearer to her mistress.

"I am horribly weary!" continued Cleopatra, letting her arms fall like one utterly discouraged; —"this Egypt crushes, annihilates me; this sky with its implacable azure is sadder than the deep night of Erebus,—never a cloud! never a shadow, and always that red sanguine sun which glares down upon you like the eye of a Cyclops. Ah, Charmion, I would give a pearl for one drop of rain! From the inflamed pupil of that sky of bronze no tear has ever yet fallen upon the desolation of this land; it is only a vast covering for a tomb,—the dome of a necropolis,—a sky dead and dried up like the mummies it hangs over; it weighs upon my shoulders like an over-heavy mantle; it constrains and terrifies me; it seems to me that I could not stand up erect without striking my forehead against it. And, moreover, this land is truly an awful land;—all things in it are gloomy, enigmatic, incomprehensible! Imagination has produced in it only monstrous chimeræ and monuments immeasurable; this architecture and this art fill me with fear; those colossi, whose stone-entangled limbs compel them to remain eternally sitting with their hands upon their knees, weary me with their stupid immobility,—they trouble my eyes and my horizon. When indeed shall the giant come who is to take them by the hand and relieve them from their long watch of twenty centuries? For even granite itself must grow weary at last! Of what master, then, do they await the coming, to leave their mountain-seats and rise in token of respect? of what invisible flock are those huge sphinxes the guardians, crouching like dogs on the watch, that they never close their eye-lids and forever extend their claws in readiness to seize? why are their stony eyes so obstinately fixed upon eternity and infinity? what weird secret do their firmly locked lips retain within their breasts? On the right hand, on the left, whithersoever one turns, only frightful monsters are visible,—dogs with the heads of men; men with the heads of dogs; chimæras begotten of hideous couplings in the shadowy depths of the labyrinths; figures of Anubis, Typhon, Osiris; partridges with great yellow eyes that seem to pierce through you with their inquisitorial gaze, and see beyond and behind you things which one dare not speak of,—a family of animals and horrible gods with scaly wings, hooked beaks, trenchant claws,—ever ready to seize and devour you should you venture to cross the threshhold of the temple, or lift a corner of the veil.

"Upon the walls, upon the columns; on the ceilings, on the floors; upon palaces and temples; in the long passages and the deepest pits of the necropoli,—even within the bowels of the earth where light never comes, and where the flames of the torches die for want of air; for ever and everywhere are sculptured and painted interminable hieroglyphics, telling in language unintelligible of things which are no longer known, and which belong, doubtless, to the vanished creations of the past;—prodigious buried works wherein a whole nation was sacrificed to write the epitaph of one king! Mystery and granite!—this is Egypt; truly a fair land for a young woman, and a young queen!

"Menacing and funereal symbols alone meet the eye,—the emblems of the *pedum*, the *tau*, allegorical globes, coiling serpents, and the scales in which souls are weighed,—the Unknown, death, nothingness! In the place of any vegetation only *stelæ* limned with weird characters; instead of avenues of trees avenues of granite obelisks; in lieu of soil vast pavements of granite for which whole mountains could each furnish but one slab; in place of a sky ceilings of granite;—eternity made palpable,—a bitter and everlasting sarcasm upon the frailty and brevity of life! —stairways built only for the limbs of Titans, which the human foot cannot ascend save by the aid of ladders; columns that a hundred arms cannot encircle; labyrinths in which one might travel for years without discovering the termination!—the vertigo of enormity,—the drunkenness of the gigantic,—the reckless efforts of that pride which would at any cost engrave its name deeply upon the face of the world!

"And, moreover, Charmion, I tell you a thought haunts me which terrifies me:—in other lands of the earth, corpses are burned, and their ashes soon mingle with the soil. Here, it is said that the living have no other occupation than that of preserving the dead; potent balms save them from destruction; the remains endure after the soul has evaporated;—beneath this people lie twenty peoples;—each city stands upon twenty layers of necropoli;—each generation which passes away leaves a population of mummies to a shadowy city; beneath the father you find the grandfather and the great-grandfather in their gilded and painted boxes, even as they were during life; and should you dig down forever, forever you would still find the underlying dead.

"When I think upon those bandage-swathed myriads,—those multitudes of parched specters who fill the sepulchral pits and who have been there for two thousand years, face to face in their own silence which nothing ever breaks, not even the noise which the graveworms make in crawling, and who will be found intact after yet another two thousand years with their crocodiles, their cats, their ibises, and all things that lived in their lifetime,—then terrors seize me, and I feel my flesh creep! What do they mutter to each other?—for they still have lips; and every ghost would find its body in the same state as when it quitted it, if they should all take the fancy to return!

"Ah, truly is Egypt a sinister kingdom, and little suited to me, the laughter-loving and merry one!—everything in it encloses a mummy: that is the heart and the kernel of all things. After a thousand turns you must always end there;—the pyramids themselves hide sarcophagi. What nothingness and madness is this! Disembowel the sky with gigantic triangles of stone,—you cannot thereby lengthen your corpse an inch. How can one rejoice and live in a land like this, where the only perfume you can respire is the acrid odor of the naphtha and bitumen which boil in the caldrons of the embalmers, where the very flooring of your chamber sounds hollow because the corridors of the hypogea and the mortuary pits extend even under your alcove? To be the queen of mummies,—to have none to converse with but statues in constrained and rigid attitudes,—this is in truth a cheerful lot! Again: if I only had some heartfelt passion to relieve this melancholy—some interest in life; if I could but love somebody or something—if I were even loved! but I am not!

"This is why I am weary, Charmion: with love this grim and arid Egypt would seem to me fairer than even Greece with her ivory gods, her temples of snowy marble, her groves of laurel and fountains of living water. There I should never dream of the weird face of Anubis, and the ghastly terrors of the cities under ground."

Charmion smiled incredulously: "That ought not, surely, to be a source of much grief to you, O queen; for every glance of your eyes transpierces hearts, like the golden arrows of Eros himself."

"Can a queen," answered Cleopatra, "ever

know whether it is her face or her diadem that is loved? The rays of her starry crown dazzle the eyes and the heart:—were I to descend from the height of my throne, would I even have the celebrity or the popularity of Bacchis or Archianassa?—of the first courtesan from Athens or Miletus? A queen is something so far removed from men,—so elevated, so widely separated from them,—so impossible for them to reach! What presumption dare flatter itself in such an enterprise? It is not simply a woman: it is an august and sacred being that has no sex, and that is worshiped kneeling without being loved. Who was ever really enamoured of Hera, the snowy-armed, or Pallas of the sea-green eyes?—who ever sought to kiss the silver feet of Thetis or the rosy fingers of Aurora?—what lover of the divine beauties ever took unto himself wings that he might soar to the golden palaces of heaven? Respect and fear chill hearts in our presence; and in order to obtain the love of our equals, one must descend into those necropoli of which I have just been speaking!"

Although she offered no further objection to the arguments of her mistress, a vague smile which played about the lips of the handsome Greek slave, showed that she had little faith in the inviolability of the royal person.

"Ah," continued Cleopatra, "I wish that something would happen to me,—some strange unexpected adventure! The songs of the poets; the dances of the Syrian slaves; the banquets, rose garlanded, and prolonged into the dawn; the nocturnal races; the Laconian dogs; the tame lions; the humpbacked dwarfs; the brotherhood of the Inimitables; the combats of the arena; the new dresses; the byssus robes; the clusters of pearls; the perfumes from Asia; the most exquisite of luxuries, the wildest of splendors—nothing any longer gives me pleasure; everything has become indifferent to me—everything is insupportable to me!"

"It is easily to be seen," muttered Charmion to herself, "that the queen has not had a lover, nor had anyone killed for a whole month."

Fatigued with so lengthy a tirade, Cleopatra once more took the cup placed beside her, moistened her lips with it; and putting her head beneath her arm, like a dove putting its head under its wing, composed herself for slumber as best she could. Charmion unfastened her sandals, and commenced to gently tickle the soles of her feet with a peacock's feather; and Sleep soon sprinkled his golden dust upon the beautiful eyes of Ptolemy's sister.

While Cleopatra sleeps, let us ascend upon deck and enjoy the glorious sun-set view. A broad band of violet color, warmed deeply with ruddy tints toward the west, occupies all the lower portion of the sky; encountering the zone of azure above, the violet shade melts into a clear lilac, and fades off through half-rosy tints, into the blue beyond: afar, where the sun, red as a buckler fallen from the furnace of Vulcan casts his burning reflection, the deeper shades turn to pale citron hues, and glow with turquoise tints. The water rippling under an oblique beam of light, shines with the dull gleam of the quicksilvered side of a mirror, or like a damascened blade: the sinuosities of the bank, the reeds, and all objects along the shore are brought out in sharp black relief against the bright glow. By the aid of this crepuscular light you may perceive afar off, like a grain of dust floating upon quicksilver, a little brown speck trembling in the net work of luminous ripples. Is it a teal diving?—a tortoise lazily drifting with the current?—a crocodile raising the tip of his scaly snout above the water to breathe the cooler air of evening?—the belly of a hippopotamus gleaming amid-stream; or, perhaps a rock left bare by the falling of the river: for the ancient Opi-Mou, Father of Waters, sadly needs to replenish his dry urn from the solstitial rains of the Mountains of the Moon.

It is none of these.—By the atoms of Osiris so deftly resewn together! it is a man, who seems to walk, to skate upon the water!—now the frail bark which sustains him becomes visible,—a very nutshell of a boat,—a hollow fish!—three strips of bark fitted together, (one for the bottom and two for the sides) and strongly fastened at either end by cord well smeared with bitumen. The man stands erect with one foot on either side of this fragile vessel, which he impels with a single oar that also serves the purpose of a rudder;—and although the royal cangia moves rapidly under the efforts of the fifty rowers, the little black bark visibly gains upon it.

Cleopatra desired some strange adventure, something wholly unexpected; this little bark which moves so mysteriously, seems to us to be conveying an adventure, or at least an adventurer. Perhaps it contains the hero of our story;—the thing is not impossible.

At any rate he was a handsome youth of twenty, with hair so black that it seemed to own a tinge of blue, a skin blonde as gold, and a form so perfectly proportioned that he might have been taken for a bronze statue by Lysippus;—although he had been rowing for a very long time he betrayed no sign of fatigue, and not a single drop of sweat bedewed his forehead.

The sun half sank below the horizon; and against his broken disk figured the dark silhouette of a far-distant city, which the eye could not have distinguished but for this accidental effect of light; his radiance soon faded altogether away; and the stars,—fair night-flowers of heaven,—opened their chalices of gold in the azure of the firmament. The royal cangia closely followed by the little bark, stopped before a huge marble stairway, whereof each step supported one of those sphinxes that Cleopatra so much detested. This was the landing place of the summer palace.

Cleopatra, leaning upon Charmion, passed swiftly like a gleaming vision between a double line of lantern-bearing slaves.

The youth took from the bottom of his little boat, a great lion-skin, threw it across his shoulders, drew the tiny shell upon the beach, and wended his way toward the palace.

## CHAPTER III.

Who is this young man, balancing himself upon a fragment of bark, who dares to follow the royal cangia, and is able to contend in a race of speed against fifty strong rowers from the land of Kush, all naked to the waist, and anointed with palm-oil? what secret motive urges him to this swift pursuit? That, indeed, is one of the many things we are obliged to know in our character of the intuition-gifted poet, for whose benefit all men, and even all women (a much more difficult matter) must have in their breasts that little window which Momus of old demanded.

It is not a very easy thing to find out precisely what a young man from the land of Kemi,—who followed the barge of Cleopatra, queen and goddess Evergetes, on her return from the Mammisi of Hermonthis two thousand years ago,—was then thinking of. But we shall make the effort notwithstanding.

Meïamoun, son of Mandouschopsch, was a youth of strange character; nothing by which ordinary minds are affected made any impression upon him; he seemed to belong to some loftier race, and might well have been regarded as the offspring of some divine adultery. His glance had the steady brilliancy of a falcon's gaze; and a serene majesty sat on his brow as upon a pedestal of marble; a noble pride curled his upper lip, and expanded his nostrils like those of a fiery horse;—although owning a grace of form almost maidenly in its delicacy, and though the bosom of the fair and effeminate god Dionysos was not more softly rounded or smoother than his, yet beneath this soft exterior were hidden sinews of steel, and the strength of Hercules—a strange privilege of certain antique natures to unite in themselves the beauty of woman with the strength of man!

As for his complexion, we must acknowledge that it was of a tawny orange color,—a hue little in accordance with our white-and-rose ideas of beauty, but which did not prevent him from being a very charming young man, much sought after by all kinds of women,—yellow, red, copper-colored, sooty-black, or golden skinned; and even by one fair white Greek.

Do not suppose from this that Meïamoun's lot was altogether enviable;—the ashes of aged Priam, the very snows of Hippolytus, were not more insensible or more frigid; — the young white-robed neophyte preparing for the initiation into the mysteries of Isis led no chaster life; — the young maiden benumbed by the icy shadow of her mother was not more shyly pure.

Nevertheless, for so coy a youth, the pleasures of Meïamoun were certainly of a singular nature: — he would go forth quietly some morning with his little buckler of hippopotamus hide, his *harpe* or curved sword, a triangular bow and a snake-skin quiver, filled with barbed arrows; then he would ride at a gallop far into the desert upon his slender-limbed, small-headed, wild-maned mare, until he could find some lion-tracks: — he especially delighted in taking the little lion-cubs from underneath the belly of their mother. In all things he loved the perilous or the unachievable; he preferred to walk where it seemed impossible for any human being to obtain a foothold, or to swim in a raging torrent; and he had accordingly chosen the neighborhood of the cataracts for his bathing place in the Nile: the Abyss called him!

Such was Meïamoun, son of Mandouschopsh.

For some time his humors had been growing more savage than ever: during whole months he buried himself in the Ocean of Sands, returning only at long intervals. Vainly would his uneasy mother lean from her terrace, and gaze anxiously down the long road with tireless eyes. At last after weary waiting, a little whirling cloud of dust would become visible in the horizon; and finally the cloud would open to allow a full view of Meïamoun, all covered with dust, riding upon a mare gaunt as a wolf with red and blood-shot eyes, nostrils trembling, and huge scars along her flanks,—scars which certainly were not made by spurs!

After having hung up in his room some hyena or lion skin, he would start off again.

And yet no one might have been happier than Meïamoun: he was beloved by Nephthe, daughter of the priest Afomouthis, and the loveliest woman of the Nome Arsinoïtes. Only such a being as Meïamoun could have failed to see that Nephthe had the most charmingly oblique and indescribably voluptuous eyes, a mouth sweetly illuminated by ruddy smiles; little teeth of wondrous whiteness and transparency: arms exquisitely round, and feet more perfect than the jasper feet of the statue of Isis:—assuredly there was not a smaller hand nor longer hair than hers in all Egypt. The charms of Nephthe could have been eclipsed only by those of Cleopatra. But who could dare to dream of loving Cleopatra? Ixion, enamoured of Juno, strained only a cloud to his bosom, and must forever roll the wheel of his punishment in hell.

It was Cleopatra whom Meïamoun loved.

He had at first striven to tame this wild passion; he had wrestled fiercely with it: but love cannot be strangled even as a lion is strangled; and the strong skill of the mightiest athlete avails nothing in such a contest. The arrow had remained in the wound, and he carried it with him everywhere;—the radiant and splendid image of Cleopatra with her golden-pointed diadem and her imperial purple, standing above a nation on their knees, illumined his nightly dreams and his waking thoughts: like some imprudent man who has dared to look at the sun and forever thereafter beholds an impalpable blot floating before his eyes,—so Meïamoun ever beheld Cleopatra. Eagles may gaze undazzled at the sun; but what diamond eye can with impunity fix itself upon a beautiful woman—a beautiful queen?

He commenced at last to spend his life in wandering about the neighborhood of the royal dwelling, that he might at least breathe the same air as Cleopatra,—that he might sometimes kiss the almost imperceptible print of her foot upon the sand (a happiness, alas! rare indeed): he attended the sacred festivals and *panegyreis* striving to obtain one beaming glance of her eyes—to catch in passing one stealthy glimpse of her loveliness in some of its thousand varied aspects. At other moments filled with sudden shame of this mad life, he gave himself up to the chase with redoubled ardor, and sought by fatigue to tame the ardor of his blood and the impetuosity of his desires.

He had gone to the panegyris of Hermonthis; and in the vague hope of beholding the queen again for an instant as she disembarked at the summer palace, had followed her cangia in his boat,—little heeding the sharp stings of the sun,—through a heat intense enough to make the panting sphinxes melt in lava-sweat upon their reddened pedestals.

And then he felt that the supreme moment was nigh,—that the decisive instant of his life was at hand; and that he could not die with his secret in his breast.

It is a strange situation, truly, to find one's self enamored of a queen; it is as though one loved a star,—yet she, the star, comes forth nightly to sparkle in her place in heaven: it is a kind of mysterious rendezvous;—you may find her again, you may see her; she is not offended at your gaze! O, misery! to be poor, unknown, obscure, seated at the very foot of the ladder,—and to feel one's heart breaking with love for something glittering, solemn, and magnificent,—for a woman whose meanest female attendant would scorn you!—to gaze fixedly and fatefully upon one who never sees you, who never will see you;—one to whom you are no more than a ripple on the sea of humanity, in nowise differing from the other ripples; and who might a hundred times encounter you without once recognizing you!—to have no reason to offer, should an opportunity for addressing her present itself, in excuse for such mad audacity; neither poetical talent, nor great genius, nor any superhuman qualification,—nothing but love; and to be able to offer in exchange for beauty, nobility, power, and all imaginable splendor, only one's passion and one's youth,—rare offerings, forsooth!

Such were the thoughts which overwhelmed Meïamoun; lying upon the sand, supporting his chin on his palms, he permitted himself to be lifted and borne away by the inexhaustible current of reverie;—he sketched out a thousand projects, each madder than the last. He felt convinced that he was seeking after the unattainable; but he lacked the courage to frankly renounce his undertaking; and a perfidious hope came to whisper some lying promises in his ear.

"Athor, mighty goddess," he murmured in a

deep voice,—"what evil have I done against thee that I should be made thus miserable?—art thou avenging thyself for my disdain of Nephthe, daughter of the priest Afomouthis?—hast thou afflicted me thus for having rejected the love of Lamia, the Athenian hetaira, or of Flora, the Roman courtesan? Is it my fault that my heart should be sensible only to the matchless beauty of thy rival, Cleopatra? Why hast thou wounded my soul with the envenomed arrow of unattainable love? What sacrifice, what offerings dost thou desire? Must I erect to thee a chapel of the rosy marble of Syene with columns crowned by gilded capitals, a ceiling all of one block, and hieroglyphics deeply sculptured by the best workmen of Memphis and of Thebes? Answer me!"

Like all gods or goddesses thus invoked, Athor answered not a word; and Meïamoun resolved upon a desperate expedient.

Cleopatra, on her part, likewise invoked the goddess Athor; she prayed for a new pleasure, for some fresh sensation: as she languidly reclined upon her couch, she thought to herself that the number of the senses was sadly limited; that the most exquisite refinements of delight soon yielded to satiety; and that it was really no small task for a queen to find means of occupying her time. To test new poisons upon slaves; to make men fight with tigers, or gladiators with each other; to drink pearls dissolved; to swallow the wealth of a whole province: all these things had become commonplace and insipid!

Charmion was fairly at her wit's end; and knew not what to do for her mistress.

Suddenly a whistling sound was heard; and an arrow buried itself, quivering, in the cedar wainscoting of the wall.

Cleopatra well-nigh fainted with terror. Charmion ran to the window, leaned out, and beheld only a flake of foam on the surface of the river. A scroll of papyrus encircled the wood of the arrow; it bore only these words written in Phœnician characters: "I love you!"

## CHAPTER IV.

"I love you," repeated Cleopatra, making the serpent-coiling strip of papyrus writhe between her delicate white fingers; "those are the words I longed for; what intelligent spirit, what invisible genius has thus so fully comprehended my desire?"

And thoroughly aroused from her languid torpor, she sprang out of bed with the agility of a cat which has scented a mouse, placed her little ivory feet in her embroidered *tatbebs*, threw a byssus tunic over her shoulders, and ran to the window from which Charmion was still gazing.

The night was clear and calm; the risen moon outlined with huge angles of light and shadow the architectural masses of the palace, which stood out in strong relief against a background of bluish transparency; and the waters of the river wherein her reflection lengthened into a shining column, was frosted with silvery ripples: a gentle breeze, such as might have been mistaken for the respiration of the slumbering sphinxes, quivered among the reeds and shook the azure bells of the lotus flowers; the cables of the vessels moored to the Nile's banks groaned feebly; and the rippling tide moaned upon the shore like a dove lamenting for its mate. A vague perfume of vegetation, sweeter than that of the aromatics burned in the *anschir* of the priests of Anubis, floated into the chamber. It was one of those enchanted nights of the Orient, which are more splendid than our fairest days; for our sun can ill compare with that Oriental moon.

"Do you not see far over there, almost in the middle of the river, the head of a man swimming? See! he crosses that track of light, and passes into the shadow beyond!—he is already out of sight!" And supporting herself upon Charmion's shoulder she leaned out, with half of her fair body beyond the sill of the window, in the effort to catch another glimpse of the mysterious swimmer. But a grove of Nile acacias, dhoum-palms, and sayals flung its deep shadow upon the river in that direction, and protected the flight of the daring fugitive. If Meïamoun had but had the courtesy to look back, he might have beheld Cleopatra, the sidereal queen, eagerly seeking him through the night gloom,—he, the poor obscure Egyptian! the miserable lion-hunter!

"Charmion! Charmion! send hither Phrehipephbour, the chief of the rowers; and have two boats dispatched in pursuit of that man!"—cried Cleopatra, whose curiosity was excited to the highest pitch.

Phrehipephbour appeared,—a man of the race of Nahasi, with large hands and muscular arms; wearing a red cap not unlike a Phrygian helmet in form, and clad only in a pair of narrow drawers diagonally striped with white and blue. His huge torso, entirely nude, black and polished like a globe of jet, shone under the lamplight. He received the commands of the queen and instantly retired to execute them.

Two long narrow boats so light that the least inattention to equilibrium would capsize them, were soon cleaving the waters of the Nile with hissing rapidity under the efforts of the twenty vigorous rowers; but the pursuit was all in vain. After searching the river banks in every direction, and carefully exploring every patch of reeds, Phrehipephbour returned to the palace; having only succeeded in putting to flight some solitary heron which had been sleeping on one leg, or in troubling the digestion of some terrified crocodile.

So intense was the vexation of Cleopatra at being thus foiled, that she felt a strong inclination to condemn Phrehipephbour either to the wild beasts, or to the hardest labor at the grindstone. Happily Charmion interceded for the trembling unfortunate who turned pale with fear despite his black skin. It was the first time in Cleopatra's life that one of her desires had not been gratified as soon as expressed; and she experienced in consequence a kind of uneasy surprise, — a first doubt, as it were, of her own omnipotence.

She, Cleopatra, wife and sister of Ptolemy, — she who had been proclaimed goddess Evergetes, living queen of the regions Above and Below, Eye of Light, Chosen of the Sun (as may still be read within the cartouches sculptured on the walls of the temples), — she to find an obstacle in her path! to have wished aught that failed of accomplishment! to have spoken and not been obeyed! As well be the wife of some wretched Paraschistes, — some corpse-cutter, — and melt natron in a caldron! It was monstrous, preposterous! — and none but the most gentle and clement of queens could have refrained from crucifying that miserable Phrehipephbour!

You wished for some adventure, something strange and unexpected: your wish has been gratified. You find that your kingdom is not so dead as you deemed it. It was not the stony arm of a statue which shot that arrow; —it was not from a mummy's heart that came those three words which have moved even you,— you who smilingly watched your poisoned slaves dashing their heads and beating their feet upon your beautiful mosaic and porphyry pavements, in the convulsions of death-agony!—you who even applauded the tiger which boldly buried its muzzle in the flank of some vanquished gladiator!

You could obtain all else you might wish for: chariots of silver starred with emeralds; griffin-quadrigeræ; tunics of purple thrice-dyed; mirrors of molten steel, so clear that you might find the charms of your loveliness faithfully copied in them; robes from the land of Serica so fine and subtly light that they could be drawn through the ring worn upon your little finger; orient pearls of wondrous color; cups wrought by Myron or Lysippus; Indian paroquets that speak like poets:—all things else you could obtain, even should you ask for the Cestus of Venus or the *pshent* of Isis; but most certainly you cannot this night capture the man who shot the arrow which still quivers in the cedar wood of your couch.

The task of the slaves who must dress you to-morrow will not be a grateful one; they will hardly escape with blows: the bosom of the unskillful waitingmaid will be apt to prove a cushion for the golden pins of the toilette; and the poor hairdresser will run great risk of being suspended by her feet from the ceiling.

"Who could have had the audacity to send me this avowal upon the shaft of an arrow? Could it have been the Nomarch Amoun-Ra who fancies himself handsomer than the Apollo of the Greeks?—what think you, Charmion?—or perhaps Cheâpsiro, commander of Hermothybia, who is so boastful of his conquests in the land of Kush? Or is it not more likely to have been young Sextus, that Roman debauchee who paints his face, lisps in speaking, and wears sleeves in the fashion of the Persians?"

"Queen, it was none of those: though you are indeed the fairest of women, those men only flatter you; they do not love you. The Nomarch Amoun-Ra has chosen himself an idol to which he will be forever faithful; and that is his own person: the warrior Cheâpsiro thinks of nothing save the pleasure of recounting his victories;—as for Sextus, he is so seriously occupied with the preparation of a new cosmetic that he cannot dream of anything else. Besides he had just purchased some Laconian dresses, a number of yellow tunics embroidered with gold, and some Asiatic children which absorb all his time. Not one of those fine lords would risk his head in so daring and dangerous an undertaking;—they do not love you well enough for that.

"Yesterday in your cangia, you said that men dared not fix their dazzled eyes upon you; that they knew only how to turn pale in your presence,—to fall at your feet and supplicate your mercy; and that your sole remaining resource would be to awake some ancient, bitumen-perfumed Pharoah from his gilded coffin. Now here is an ardent and youthful heart that loves you: what will you do with it?"

Cleopatra that night sought slumber in vain. she tossed feverishly upon her couch, and long and vainly invoked Morpheus the brother of Death;—she incessantly repeated that she was the most unhappy of queens,—that everyone sought to persecute her,—and that her life had become insupportable: woeful lamentations which had little effect upon Charmion, although she pretended to sympathize with them.

Let us for a while leave Cleopatra to seek fugitive sleep, and direct her suspicions successively upon each noble of the court;—let us return to Meïamoun;—and as we are much more sagacious than Phrehipephbour, chief of the rowers, we shall have no difficulty in finding him.

Terrified at his own hardihood Meïamoun had thrown himself into the Nile, and had succeeded in swimming the current and gaining the little grove of dhoum-palms, before Phrehipephbôur had even launched the two boats in pursuit of him.

When he had recovered breath, and brushed back his long black locks, all damp with river foam, behind his ears, he began to feel more at ease, — more inwardly calm. Cleopatra possessed something which had come from him; some sort of communication was now established between them: Cleopatra was thinking of him, — Meïamoun! Perhaps that thought might be one of wrath; but then he had at least been able to awake some feeling within her, — whether of fear, anger, or pity: he had forced her to the consciousness of his existence. It was true that he had forgotten to inscribe his name upon the papyrus scroll; but what more of him could the queen have learned from the inscription, — *Meïamoun, Son of Mandouschopsh?* In her eyes the slave or the monarch were equal. A goddess, in choosing a peasant for her lover, stoops no lower than in choosing a patrician or a king: the Immortals from a height so lofty can behold only love in the man of their choice.

The thought which had weighed upon his breast like the knee of a colossus of brass, had at last departed: it had traversed the air; it had even reached the queen herself,—the apex of the triangle,—the inaccessible summit! It had aroused curiosity in that impassive heart—a prodigious advance, truly, toward success!

Meïamoun indeed never suspected that he had so thoroughly succeeded in this wise; but he felt more tranquil,—for he had sworn unto himself by that mystic Bari who guides the souls of the dead to Amenthi, by the sacred birds Bermou and Ghenghen, by Typhon and by Osiris and by all things awful in Egyptian mythology, that he should be the accepted lover of Cleopatra though it were but for a single night,—though for only a single hour,—though it should cost him his life, and even his very soul.

If we must explain how he had fallen so deeply in love with a woman whom he had beheld only from afar off, and to whom he had hardly dared to raise his eyes—even he who was wont to gaze fearlessly into the yellow eyes of the lion,—or how the tiny seed of love, chance-fallen upon his heart, had grown there so rapidly and extended its roots so deeply, we can answer only that it is a mystery which we are unable to explain: — we have already said of Meïamoun, — The Abyss called him.

Once assured that Phrehipephbour had returned with his rowers, he again threw himself into the current and once more swam toward the palace of Cleopatra, whose lamp still shone through the window curtains like a painted star. Never did Leander swim with more courage and vigor toward the tower of Sestos; yet for Meïamoun no Hero was waiting, ready to pour vials of perfume upon his head to dissipate the briny odors of the sea, and banish the sharp kisses of the storm.

A strong blow from some keen lance or *harpe* was certainly the worst he had to fear; and in truth he had but little fear of such things.

He swam close under the walls of the palace which bathed its marble feet in the river's depths, and paused an instant before a submerged archway into which the water rushed downward in eddying whirls. Twice, thrice, he plunged into the vortex unsuccessfully; — at last, with better luck, he found the opening and disappeared.

This archway was the opening to a vaulted canal, which conducted the waters of the Nile into the baths of Cleopatra.

## CHAPTER V.

Cleopatra found no rest until morning, at the hour when wandering dreams reënter the Ivory Gate. Amidst the illusions of sleep she beheld all kinds of lovers swimming rivers and scaling walls in order to come to her; and, through the vague souvenirs of the night before, her dreams appeared fairly riddled with arrows bearing declarations of love. Starting nervously from time to time in her troubled slumbers, she struck her little feet unconsciously against the bosom of Charmion, who lay across the foot of the bed to serve her as a cushion.

When she awoke a merry sunbeam was playing through the window curtain, whose woof it penetrated with a thousand tiny points of light, and thence came familiarly to the bed; flitting like a golden butterfly over her lovely shoulders, which it lightly touched in passing by with a luminous kiss. Happy sunbeam, which the Gods might well have envied!

In a faint voice, like that of a sick child, Cleopatra asked to be lifted out of bed; two of her women raised her in their arms and gently laid her on a tiger skin stretched upon the floor, of which the eyes were formed of carbuncles and the claws of gold. Charmion wrapped her in a *calasiris* of linen whiter than milk; confined her hair in a net of woven silver threads; tied to her little feet cork *tatbebs* upon the soles of which were painted in token of contempt two grotesque figures representing two men of the races of Nahasi and Nahmou, bound hand and foot:—so that Cleopatra literally deserved the epithet, "Conculcatrix of Nations"* which the royal cartouche-inscriptions bestow upon her.

It was the hour for the bath; Cleopatra went to bathe accompanied by her women.

The baths of Cleopatra were built in the midst of immense gardens filled with mimosas, aloes, carob-trees, citron-trees, and Persian apple-trees, whose luxuriant freshness afforded a delicious contrast to the arid appearance of the neighboring vegetation: there, too, vast terraces uplifted masses of verdant foliage, and enabled flowers to climb almost to the very sky upon gigantic stairways of rose-colored granite;—vases of Pentelic marble bloomed at the end of each

* *Conculcatrice des peuples.* From the Latin *conculcare*, to trample under foot:—therefore the epithet literally signifies the "Trampler of nations."—[TRANS.

step like huge lily-flowers; and the plants they contained seemed only their pistils; — chimeras caressed into form by the chisels of the most skillful Greek sculptors, and less stern of aspect than the Egyptian sphinxes, with their grim mien and moody attitudes, softly extended their limbs upon the flower-strewn turf, like shapely white leverettes upon a drawing-room carpet. These were charming feminine figures, — with finely chiseled nostrils, smooth brows, small mouths, delicately dimpled arms, breasts fair-rounded and daintily formed; wearing earrings, necklaces, and all the trinkets suggested by adorable caprice, — whose bodies terminated in bifurcated fishes' tails, like the women described by Horace, or extended into birds' wings, or rounded into lions' haunches, or blended into volutes of foliage according to the fancies of the artist or in conformity to the architectural position chosen. A double row of these delightful monsters lined the alley which led from the palace to the bathing halls.

At the end of this alley was a huge fountain-basin, approached by four porphyry stairways; through the transparent depths of the diamond-clear water the steps could be seen descending to the bottom of the basin, which was strewn with gold-dust in lieu of sand; — here figures of women terminating in pedestals like Caryatides * spirted from their breasts slender jets of perfumed water, which fell into the basin in silvery dew, pitting the clear watery mirror with wrinkle-creating drops. In addition to this task these Caryatides had likewise that of supporting upon their heads an entablature decorated with Nereids and Tritons in bas-relief, and furnished with rings of bronze to which the silken cords of a velarium might be attached. From the portico was visible an extending expanse of freshly humid, bluish-green verdure and cool shade, — a fragment of the Vale of Tempe transported to Egypt. The famous gardens of Semiramis would not have borne comparison with these.

We will not pause to describe the seven or eight other halls of various temperature, with their hot and cold vapors, perfume boxes, cosmetics, oils, pumice stone, gloves of woven horse-hair, and all the refinements of the antique balneatory art brought to the highest pitch of voluptuous perfection.

Hither came Cleopatra, leaning with one hand upon the shoulder of Charmion; she had taken

* The Greeks and Romans usually termed such figures Hermæ or Termini. Caryatides were, strictly, entire figures of women. — [TRANS.

at least thirty steps all by herself—mighty effort! —enormous fatigue! A tender tint of rose commenced to suffuse the transparent skin of her cheeks, refreshing their passionate pallor;—a blue network of veins relieved the amber blondness of her temples; her marble forehead—low like the antique foreheads, but full and perfect in form,—united by one faultless line with a straight nose finely chiseled as a cameo, with rosy nostrils which the least emotion made palpitate like the nostrils of an amorous tigress; the lips of her small, rounded mouth, slightly separated from the nose, wore a disdainful curve; but an unbridled voluptuousness,—an indescribable vital warmth,—glowed in the brilliant crimson and humid luster of the under lip. Her eyes were shaded by level eyelids and eyebrows slightly arched and delicately outlined. We cannot attempt by description to convey an idea of their brilliancy; it was a fire, a languor, a sparkling limpidity which might have made even the dog-headed Anubis giddy; every glance of her eyes was in itself a poem richer than aught of Homer or Mimnermus. An imperial chin, replete with force and power to command, worthily completed this charming profile.

She stood erect upon the upper step of the

basin, in an attitude full of proud grace; her figure slightly thrown back, and one foot in suspense, like a goddess about to leave her pedestal, whose eyes still linger on heaven: her robe fell in two superb folds from the peaks of her bosom to her feet, in unbroken lines. Had Cleomenes been her cotemporary and enjoyed the happiness of beholding her thus, he would have broken his Venus in despair.

Before entering the water, she bade Charmion, for a new caprice, to change her silver hair-net;—she preferred to be crowned with reeds and lotos-flowers, like a water divinity. Charmion obeyed; and her liberated hair fell in black cascades over her shoulders, and shadowed her beautiful cheeks in rich bunches like ripening grapes.

Then the linen tunic, which had been confined only by one golden clasp, glided down over her marble body, and fell in a white cloud at her feet, like the swan at the feet of Leda. . . . .

And Meïamoun, where was he?

O cruel lot, that so many insensible objects should enjoy the favors which would ravish a lover with delight! The wind which toys with a wealth of perfumed hair, or kisses beautiful lips with kisses which it is unable to appreciate; the water which envelopes an adorably beautiful body in one universal kiss, and is yet notwithstanding indifferent to that exquisite pleasure; the mirror which reflects so many charming images; the buskin or *tatbeb* which clasps a divine little foot: — oh, what happiness lost!

Cleopatra dipped her pink heel in the water and descended a few steps: the quivering flood made a silver belt about her waist, and silver bracelets about her arms, and rolled in pearls like a broken necklace over her bosom and shoulders; her wealth of hair, lifted by the water, extended behind her like a royal mantle: — even in the bath she was a queen. She swam to and fro, dived and brought up handfuls of gold dust with which she laughingly pelted some of her women; — again, she clung suspended to the balustrade of the basin, concealing or exposing her treasures of loveliness, — now permitting only her lustrous and polished back to be seen, — now showing her whole figure, like Venus Anadyomene, and incessantly varying the aspects of her beauty.

Suddenly she uttered a cry as shrill as that of Diana surprised by Actæon: she had seen gleaming through the neighboring foliage a burning eye, yellow and phosphoric as the eye of a crocodile or lion.

It was Meïamoun who, crouching behind a tuft

J. Gleeson

of leaves, and trembling like a fawn in a field of wheat, was intoxicating himself with the dangerous pleasure of beholding the queen in her bath. Though brave even to temerity, the cry of Cleopatra passed through his heart, coldly-piercing as the blade of a sword: a death-like sweat covered his whole body; his arteries hissed through his temples with a sharp sound;—the iron hand of anxious fear had seized him by the throat, and was strangling him.

The eunuchs rushed forward lance in hand: Cleopatra pointed out to them the group of trees, where they found Meïamoun crouching in concealment. Defence was out of the question: he attempted none, and suffered himself to be captured. They prepared to kill him with that cruel and stupid impassibility characteristic of eunuchs; but Cleopatra, who in the interim had covered herself with her calasiris, made signs to them to stop and bring the prisoner before her.

Meïamoun could only fall upon his knees and stretch forth suppliant hands to her, as to the altars of the gods.

"Are you some assassin bribed by Rome?—or for what purpose have you entered these sacred precincts from which all men are excluded?"—demanded Cleopatra with an imperious gesture of interrogation?

"May my soul be found light in the balance of Amenti, and may Tmeï, daughter of the Sun and goddess of Truth, punish me if I have ever entertained a thought of evil against you, O queen!" answered Meïamoun, still upon his knees.

Sincerity and loyalty were written upon his countenance in characters so transparent, that Cleopatra immediately banished her suspicions, and looked upon the young Egyptian with a look less stern and wrathful:—she saw that he was beautiful.

"Then what motive could have prompted you to enter a place where you could only expect to meet death?"

"I love you!" murmured Meïamoun in a low but distinct voice; for his courage had returned, as in every desperate situation when the odds against him could be no worse.

"Ah!" cried Cleopatra, bending toward him, and seizing his arm with a sudden brusque movement,—"so then it was you who shot that arrow with the papyrus scroll!—by Oms, the Dog of Hell, you are a very foolhardy wretch! . . . . I now recognize you: I long observed you wandering like a complaining Shade about the places where I dwell. . . . You were at the Procession of Isis,—at the Panegyris of Hermonthis:

you followed the royal cangia. Ah! — you must have a queen? . . . . You have no mean ambitions; you expect without doubt to be well paid in return! . . . . Assuredly I am going to love you! . . . . Why not?"

"Queen," returned Meïamoun with a look of deep melancholy, "do not rail! I am mad, it is true; I have deserved death, — that is also true: be humane; — bid them kill me!"

"No: I have taken the whim to be clement to-day: I will give you your life."

"What would you that I should do with life? — I love you!"

"Well, then, you shall be satisfied; — you shall die," answered Cleopatra: "you have indulged yourself in wild and extravagant dreams; in fancy your desires have crossed an impassible threshold: — you imagined yourself to be Cæsar or Mark Antony — you loved the queen! In some moment of delirium, you have been able to believe that — under some condition of things which takes place but once in a thousand years, — Cleopatra might some day love you. Well, what you thought impossible is actually about to happen — I will transform your dream into a reality; — it pleases me, for once, to secure the accomplishment of a mad hope. I am willing to inundate you with glories and splendors and lightnings: I intend that your good fortune shall be dazzling in its brilliancy. You were at the bottom of the ladder:—I am about to lift you to the summit, abruptly, suddenly, without a transition. I take you out of nothingness; I make you the equal of a God; and I plunge you back again into nothingness: that is all;—but do not presume to call me cruel or to invoke my pity,—do not weaken when the hour comes. I am good to you: I lend myself to your folly;—I have the right to order you to be killed at once; but since you tell me that you love me I will have you killed to-morrow instead: your life belongs to me for one night. I am generous: I will buy it from you;—I could take it from you. But what are you doing on your knees at my feet! Rise; and give me your arm, that we may return to the palace."

## CHAPTER VI.

Our world of to-day is puny indeed beside the antique world: our banquets are mean, niggardly, compared with the appalling sumptuousness of the Roman patricians and the princes of ancient Asia;—their ordinary repasts would in these days be regarded as frenzied orgies; and a whole modern city could subsist for eight days upon the leavings of one supper given by Lucullus to a few intimate friends. With our miserable habits, we find it difficult to conceive of those enormous existences, realizing everything vast, strange, and most monstrously impossible that imagination could devise. Our palaces are mere stables in which Caligula would not quarter his horse;—the retinue of our wealthiest constitutional king is as nothing compared with that of a petty satrap, or a Roman proconsul. The radiant suns which once shone upon the earth are forever extinguished in the nothingness of uniformity; above the dark swarm of men no longer tower those Titanic colossi, who bestrode the world in three paces, like the steeds of Homer;

—no more towers of Lylacq; no giant Babel scaling the sky with its infinity of spirals; no temples immeasurable, builded with the fragments of quarried mountains; no kingly terraces for which successive ages and generations could each erect but one step, and from whence some dreamfully-reclining prince might gaze on the face of the world as upon a map unfolded; no more of those extravagantly vast cities of cyclopean edifices, inextricably piled upon one another,—with their mighty circumvallations,—their circuses roaring night and day,—their reservoirs filled with ocean-brine and peopled with whales and leviathans,—their colossal stairways,—their super-imposition of terraces,—their tower-summits bathed in clouds,—their giant palaces,—their aqueducts,—their multitude-vomiting gates,—their shadowy necropoli. Alas! henceforth only plaster hives upon chessboard pavements!

One marvels that men did not revolt against such confiscation of all riches and all living forces for the benefit of a few privileged ones; and that such exorbitant fantasies should not have encountered any opposition on their bloody way. It was because those prodigious lives were the realizations by day of the dreams which haunted each man by night,—the personifications of the common ideal which the nations beheld living symbolized under one of those meteoric names that flame inextinguishably through the night of ages. To-day, deprived of such dazzling spectacies of omnipotent will,—of the lofty contemplation of some human mind, whose least wish makes itself visible in actions unparalleled,—in enormities of granite and brass,—the world becomes irredeemably and hopelessly dull: man is no longer represented in the realization of his imperial fancy.

The story which we are writing, and the great name of Cleopatra which appears in it, have prompted us to these reflections,—so ill-sounding, doubtless, to modern ears. But the spectacle of the antique world is something so crushingly discouraging, even to those imaginations which deem themselves exhaustless, and those minds which fancy themselves to have conceived the utmost limits of fairy magnificence, that we cannot here forbear recording our regret and lamentation that we were not cotemporaries of Sardanapalus,—of Teglathphalazar,—of Cleopatra, queen of Egypt,—or even of Elagabalus, emperor of Rome and priest of the Sun.

It is our task to describe a supreme orgie,—a banquet compared with which the splendors of

Belshazzar's feast must pale,—one of Cleopatra's nights! How can we picture forth in this French tongue, so chaste, so icily prudish, that unbounded transport of passions,—that huge and mighty debauch which feared not to mingle the double purple of wine and blood,—those furious outbursts of insatiate pleasure, madly leaping toward the Impossible with all the wild ardor of senses as yet untamed by the long fast of Christianity?

The promised night should well have been a splendid one; for all the joys and pleasures possible in a human lifetime were to be concentrated into the space of a few hours;—it was necessary that the life of Meïamoun should be converted into a powerful elixir, which he could imbibe at a single draught. Cleopatra desired to dazzle her voluntary victim, and plunge him into a whirlpool of dizzy pleasures,—to intoxicate and madden him with the wine of orgie; so that death, though freely accepted, might come invisibly and unawares.

Let us transport our readers to the banquet-hall!

Our existing architecture offers few points for comparison with those vast edifices whose very ruins resemble the crumblings of mountains rather than the remains of buildings. It needed all the exaggeration of the antique life to animate and fill those prodigious palaces, whose halls were too lofty and vast to allow of any ceiling save the sky itself, — a magnificent ceiling, and well worthy of such mighty architecture!

The banquet-hall was of enormous and Babylonian dimensions; the eye could not penetrate its immeasurable depth: monstrous columns — short, thick and solid enough to sustain the pole itself, — heavily expanded their broad-swelling shafts upon socles variegated with hieroglyphics, and sustained upon their bulging capitals gigantic arcades of granite rising by successive tiers, like vast stairways reversed. Between each two pillars a colossal sphinx of basalt, crowned with the *pschent*, bent forward her oblique-eyed face and horned chin, and gazed into the hall with a fixed and mysterious look. The columns of the second tier, receding from the first, were more elegantly formed, and crowned in lieu of capitals with four female heads addorsed, wearing caps of many folds and all the intricacies of the Egyptian headdress: instead of sphinxes bull-headed idols, — impassive spectators of nocturnal frenzy and the furies of orgie, — were seated upon thrones of stone, like patient hosts awaiting the opening of the banquet.

A third story constructed in a yet different style of architecture—with elephants of bronze spouting perfume from their trunks—crowned the edifice: above the sky yawned like a blue gulf; and the curious stars leaned over the frieze.*

Prodigious stairways of porphyry, so highly polished that they reflected the human body like a mirror, ascended and descended on every hand, and bound together these huge masses of architecture.

We can only make a very rapid sketch here, in order to convey some idea of this awful structure, proportioned out of all human measurements. It would require the pencil of Martin,†—the

* Does not this suggest the lines which DeQuincey so much admired:—

> "A wilderness of building, sinking far,
> And self-withdrawn into a wondrous depth,
> Far sinking into splendor,—without end!
> Fabric it seemed of diamond, and of gold,
> With alabaster domes and silver spires,
> And blazing terrace upon terrace, high
> Uplifted: here serene pavilions bright,
> In avenues disposed; their towers begirt
> With *battlements that on their restless fronts*
> *Bore stars.*"

† John Martin, the English painter, whose creations were unparalleled in breadth and depth of composition. His pictures seem to have made a powerful impression upon the highly imaginative author of these Romances. There is something in these descriptions of antique architecture that suggests the influence of such pictured fantasies as Martin's "Seventh Plague;" "The Heavenly City;" and perhaps especially the famous "Pandemonium," with its infernal splendor, in Martin's illustrations to "*Paradise Lost.*"—[TRANS.

great painter of enormities passed away; and we can present only a weak pen-picture in lieu of the Apocalyptic depth of his gloomy style: but imagination may supply our deficiencies;—less fortunate than the painter and the musician, we can only present objects and ideas separately in slow succession. We have as yet spoken of the banquet-hall only, without referring to the guests; and yet we have but barely indicated its character. Cleopatra and Meïamoun are waiting for us: we see them drawing near. . . . . .

Meïamoun was clad in a linen tunic constellated with stars, and a purple mantle, and wore a fillet about his locks, like an Oriental king. Cleopatra was appareled in a robe of pale green, open at either side, and clasped with golden bees: two bracelets of immense pearls gleamed around her naked arms; upon her head glimmered the golden-pointed diadem. Despite the smile on her lips, a slight cloud of preoccupation shadowed her fair forehead; and from time to time her brows became knitted in a feverish manner. What thoughts could trouble the great queen? As for Meïamoun, his face wore the ardent and luminous look of one in ecstasy or vision,—light beamed and radiated from his brow and temples, surrounding his head with a golden nimbus like one of the twelve great gods of Olympus.

A deep, heartfelt joy illumined his every feature: he had embraced his restless-winged chimera; and it had not flown from him;—he had reached the goal of his life. Though he were to live to the age of Nestor or Priam,—though he should behold his veined temples hoary with locks whiter than those of the high priest of Ammon, he could never know another new experience,—never feel another new pleasure. His maddest hopes had been so much more than realized that there was nothing in the world left for him to desire.

Cleopatra seated him beside her upon a throne with golden griffins on either side, and clapped her little hands together. Instantly lines of fire, bands of sparkling light, outlined all the projections of the architecture: the eyes of the sphinxes flamed with phosphoric lightnings;—the bull-headed idols breathed flame;—the elephants, in lieu of perfumed water, spouted aloft bright columns of crimson fire;—arms of bronze, each bearing a torch, started from the walls; and blazing aigrettes bloomed in the sculptured hearts of the lotos flowers.

Huge blue flames palpitated in tripods of brass; giant candelabras shook their disheveled light in the midst of ardent vapors: everything sparkled, glittered, beamed. Prismatic irises crossed and shattered each other in the air: the facets of the cups, the angles of the marbles and jaspers, the chiseling of the vases, — all caught a sparkle, a gleam, or a flash as of lightning. Radiance streamed in torrents, and leaped from step to step like a cascade over the porphyry stairways; it seemed the reflection of a conflagration on some broad river; — had the Queen of Sheba ascended thither she would have caught up the folds of her robe, and believed herself walking in water, as when she stepped upon the crystal pavements of Solomon. Viewed through that burning haze, the monstrous figures of the colossi, the animals, the hieroglyphics, seemed to become animated and to live with a factitious life; the black marble rams bleated ironically, and clashed their gilded horns; the idols breathed harshly through their panting nostrils.

The orgie was at its height: the dishes of phenicopters' tongues, and the livers of scarus fish; the eels fattened upon human flesh, and cooked in brine; the dishes of peacock's brains; the boars stuffed with living birds; — and all the marvels of the antique banquets were heaped upon the three table-surfaces of the gigantic triclinium. The wines of Crete, of Massicus, and of Falernus foamed up in cratera wreathed with roses, and filled by Asiatic pages whose beautiful flowing hair served the guests to wipe their hands upon. Musicians playing upon the sistrum, the tympanum, the sambuke, and the harp with one-and-twenty strings, filled all the upper galleries, and mingled their harmonies with the tempest of sound that hovered over the feast: even the deep-voiced thunder could not have made itself heard there.

Meïamoun, whose head was lying on Cleopatra's shoulder, felt as though his reason were leaving him: the banquet-hall whirled around him like a vast architectural nightmare; — through the dizzy glare he beheld perspectives and colonnades without end; — new zones of porticoes seemed to uprear themselves upon the real fabric, and bury their summits in heights of sky to which Babel never rose. Had he not felt within his hand the soft, cool hand of Cleopatra, he would have believed himself transported into an enchanted world by some witch of Thessaly or Magian of Persia.

Toward the close of the repast, hump-backed dwarfs and mummers engaged in grotesque dances and combats: then young Egyptian and Greek maidens representing the black and white Hours danced with inimitable grace a voluptuous dance after the Ionian manner.

Cleopatra herself arose from her throne, threw aside her royal mantle, replaced her starry diadem with a garland of flowers, attached golden *crotali* * to her alabaster hands, and began to dance before Meïamoun, who was ravished with delight. Her beautiful arms, rounded like the handles of an alabaster vase, shook out bunches of sparkling notes; and her *crotali* prattled with ever-increasing volubility. Poised on the pink tips of her little feet, she approached swiftly to graze the forehead of Meïamoun with a kiss:—then she recommenced her wondrous art, and flitted around him; now backward-leaning, with head reversed, eyes half closed, arms lifelessly relaxed, locks uncurled and loose-hanging like a Bacchante of Mount Mænalus; now again, active, animated, laughing, fluttering—more tireless and capricious in her movements than the pilfering bee. Heart-consuming love,—sensual pleasure,—burning passion,—youth inexhaustible and ever-fresh,—the promise of bliss to come: she expressed all! . . .

The modest stars had ceased to contemplate the scene: their golden eyes could not endure

* Antique castanets.—[TRANS.

such a spectacle: the heaven itself was blotted out; and a dome of flaming vapor covered the hall.

Cleopatra seated herself once more by Meïamoun. Night advanced: the last of the black Hours was about to take flight;—a faint blue glow entered with bewildered aspect into the tumult of ruddy light as a moonbeam falls into a furnace;—the upper arcades became suffused with pale azure tints: day was breaking.

Meïamoun took the horn vase which an Ethiopian slave of sinister countenance presented to him, and which contained a poison so violent that it would have caused any other vase to burst asunder. Flinging his whole life to his mistress in one last look, he lifted to his lips the fatal cup in which the envenomed liquor boiled up, hissing.

Cleopatra turned pale, and laid her hand on Meïamoun's arm to stay the act. His courage touched her;—she was about to say,—"Live to love me yet: I desire it! . . . ." when the sound of a clarion was heard. Four heralds-at-arms entered the banquet-hall on horseback; they were officers of Mark Antony, and rode but a short distance in advance of their master. Cleopatra silently loosened the arm of

Meïamoun. A long ray of sunlight suddenly played upon her forehead, as though trying to replace her absent diadem.

"You see the moment has come: it is daybreak; it is the hour when happy dreams take flight," said Meïamoun. Then he emptied the fatal vessel at a draught; and fell as through struck by lightning. Cleopatra bent her head; and one burning tear,—the only one she had ever shed,—fell into her cup to mingle with the molten pearl.

"By Hercules, my fair queen! I made all speed in vain,—I see I have come too late," cried Mark Antony, entering the banquet-hall,—"the supper is over. But what signifies this corpse upon the pavement?"

"Oh, nothing!" returned Cleopatra with a smile;—"only a poison I was testing with the idea of using it upon myself should Augustus take me prisoner.—My dear lord, will you not please to take a seat beside me, and watch those Greek buffoons dance?"

# CLARIMONDE.*

Brother, you ask me if I have ever loved: yes! My story is a strange and terrible one; and, though I am sixty-six years of age, I scarcely dare even now to disturb the ashes of that memory. To you I can refuse nothing; but I should not relate such a tale to any less experienced mind. So strange were the circumstances of my story, that I can scarcely believe myself to have ever actually been a party to them. For more than three years I remained the victim of a most singular and diabolical illusion. Poor country priest though I was, I led every night in a dream,—would to God it had been all a dream!—a most worldly life, a damning life, a life of Sardanapalus. One single look too freely cast upon a woman well-nigh caused me to lose my soul; but finally by the grace of God and the assistance of my patron saint, I succeeded in casting out the evil spirit that possessed me. My daily life was long interwoven with a nocturnal life of a totally different character. By day I was a priest of the

* "*La Morte Amoureuse.*"

Lord, occupied with prayer and sacred things:— by night,—from the instant that I closed my eyes I became a young nobleman,—a fine connoisseur in women, dogs, and horses; gambling, drinking, and blaspheming: and when I awoke at early day-break, it seemed to me on the other hand that I had been sleeping, and had only dreamed that I was a priest. Of this somnambulistic life there now remains to me only the recollection of certain scenes and words which I cannot banish from my memory; but although I never actually left the walls of my presbytery one would think to hear me speak that I were a man who, weary of all worldly pleasures, had become a religious, seeking to end a tempestuous life in the service of God,—rather than an humble seminarist who has grown old in this obscure curacy situated in the depths of the woods and even isolated from the life of the century.

Yes: I have loved as none in the world ever loved,—with an insensate and furious passion,—so violent that I am astonished it did not cause my heart to burst asunder. Ah! what nights!—what nights!

From my earliest childhood I had felt a vocation to the priesthood, so that all my studies were directed with that idea in view; up to the age of twenty-four, my life had been only a prolonged novitiate. Having completed my course of theology I successively received all the minor orders; and my superiors judged me worthy, despite my youth, to pass the last awful degree. My ordination was fixed for Easter week.

I had never gone into the world: my world was confined by the walls of the college and the seminary. I knew in a vague sort of a way that there was something called Woman; but I never permitted my thoughts to dwell on such a subject; and I lived in a state of perfect innocence. Twice a year only I saw my infirm and aged mother; and in those visits were comprised my sole relations with the outer world.

I regretted nothing: I felt not the least hesitation at taking the last irrevocable step;—I was filled with joy and impatience. Never did a betrothed lover count the slow hours with more feverish ardor;—I slept only to dream that I was saying mass;—I believed there could be nothing in the world more delightful than to be a priest: I would have refused to be a king or a poet in preference. My ambition could conceive of no loftier aim.

I tell you this in order to show you that what happened to me could not have happened in the natural order of things; and to enable you to understand that I was the victim of an inexplicable fascination.

At last the great day came: I walked to the church with a step so light that I fancied myself sustained in air, or that I had wings upon my shoulders: I believed myself an angel, and wondered at the somber and thoughtful faces of my companions,—for there were several of us. I had passed all the night in prayer, and was in a condition well-nigh bordering on ecstacy. The bishop, a venerable old man, seemed to me God the Father leaning over his Eternity, and I beheld Heaven through the vault of the temple.

You well know the details of that ceremony,—the benediction, the communion under both forms, the anointing of the palms of the hands with the Oil of Catechumens, and then the holy sacrifice offered in concert with the bishop.

Ah! truly spake Job when he declared that the imprudent man is one who hath not made a covenant with his eyes!—I accidentally lifted my head, which until then I had kept down, and beheld before me, so close that it seemed that I could have touched her—although she was actually a considerable distance from me and on the further side of the sanctuary railing,—a young woman of extraordinary beauty, and attired with royal magnificence. It seemed as though scales had suddenly fallen from my eyes: I felt like a blind man who unexpectedly recovers his sight. The bishop, so radiantly glorious but an instant before, suddenly vanished away; the tapers paled upon their golden candlesticks like stars in the dawn; and a vast darkness seemed to fill the whole church. The charming creature appeared in bright relief against the background of that darkness, like some angelic revelation: she seemed herself radiant and radiating light rather than receiving it.

I lowered my eyelids, firmly resolved not to again open them, that I might not be influenced by external objects; for distraction had gradually taken possession of me until I hardly knew what I was doing.

In another minute nevertheless I reopened my eyes; for through my eyelashes I still beheld her, all sparkling with prismatic colors, and surrounded with such a purple penumbra as one beholds in gazing at the sun.

Oh! how beautiful she was! The greatest painters, who followed ideal beauty into heaven itself, and thence brought back to earth the true portrait of the Madonna, never in their delineations even approached that wildly beautiful reality which I saw before me. Neither the verses of the poet nor the palette of the artist could convey any conception of her. She was rather tall, with the form and bearing of a goddess: her hair, of a soft blond hue, was parted in the midst and flowed back over her temples in two rivers of rippling gold; — she seemed a diademed queen: her forehead, bluish-white in its transparency, extended its calm breadth above the arches of her eyebrows, which by a strange singularity were almost black, and admirably relieved the effect of sea-green eyes of unsustainable vivacity and brilliancy. What eyes! — with a single flash they could have decided a man's destiny: they had a life, a limpidity, an ardor, a humid light which I have never seen in human eyes; — they shot forth rays like arrows, which I could distinctly *see* enter my heart. I know not if the fire which illumined them came from heaven or from hell; but assuredly it came from one or the other. That woman was either an angel or a demon, perhaps both: assuredly she never sprang from the flank of Eve, our common mother. Teeth of the most lustrous pearl gleamed in her ruddy smile, and at every inflection of her lips little dimples appeared in the satiny rose of her adorable cheeks. There was a delicacy and pride in the regal outline of her nostrils, bespeaking noble blood. Agate gleams played over the smooth lustrous skin of her half-bare shoulders; and strings of great blonde pearls — almost equal to her neck in beauty of color — descended upon her bosom. From time to time she elevated her head with the undulating grace of a startled serpent or peacock, thereby imparting a quivering motion to the high lace ruff which surrounded it like a silver trellis-work.

She wore a robe of orange-red velvet; and from her wide ermine-lined sleeves there peeped forth patrician hands of infinite delicacy, and so ideally transparent that, like the fingers of Aurora, they permitted the light to shine through them.

All these details I can recollect at this moment as plainly as though they were of yesterday; for notwithstanding I was greatly troubled at the time nothing escaped me: — the faintest touch of shading, — the little dark speck at the point of the chin, — the imperceptible down at the corners of the lips, — the velvety floss upon the brow, the quivering shadows of the eyelashes upon the cheeks, — I could notice everything with astonishing lucidity of perception.

And gazing I felt opening within me gates that had until then remained closed; vents long obstructed became all clear, permitting glimpses of unfamiliar perspectives within;—life suddenly made itself visible to me under a totally novel aspect: I felt as though I had just been born into a new world and a new order of things. A frightful anguish commenced to torture my heart as with red-hot pincers: every successive minute seemed to me at once but a second and yet a century. Meanwhile the ceremony was proceeding; and I shortly found myself transported far from that world of which my newly-born desires were furiously besieging the entrance. Nevertheless I answered "Yes" when I wished to say "No,"—though all within me protested against the violence done to my soul by my tongue. Some occult power seemed to force the words from my throat against my will. Thus it is, perhaps, that so many young girls walk to the altar firmly resolved to refuse in a startling manner, the husband imposed upon them; and that yet not one ever fulfills her intention. Thus it is, doubtless, that so many poor novices take the veil, though they have resolved to tear it into shreds at the moment when called upon to utter the vows. One dares not thus cause so great a scandal to all present, nor deceive the expectation of so many people: all those eyes, — all those wills seem to weigh down upon you like a cope of lead; and moreover measures have been so well taken, — everything has been so thoroughly arranged beforehand and after a fashion so evidently irrevocable, that the will yields to the weight of circumstances, and utterly breaks down.

As the ceremony proceeded, the features of the fair unknown changed their expression. Her look had at first been one of caressing tenderness: it changed to an air of disdain and of mortification, as though at not having been able to make itself understood.

With an effort of will sufficient to have uprooted a mountain, I strove to cry out that I would not be a priest; but I could not speak; my tongue seemed nailed to my palate, and I found it impossible to express my will by the least syllable of negation. Though fully awake, I felt like one under the influence of a nightmare, who vainly strives to shriek out the one word upon which life depends.

She seemed conscious of the martyrdom I was undergoing; and, as though to encourage me, she gave me a look replete with divinest promise.

Her eyes were a poem: their every glance was a song.

She said to me:—

"If thou wilt be mine, I shall make thee happier than God himself in his paradise: the angels themselves will be jealous of thee. Tear off that funeral shroud in which thou art about to wrap thyself; I am Beauty,—I am Youth,—I am Life,—come to me!—together we shall be Love. Can Jehovah offer thee aught in exchange? Our lives will flow on like a dream,—in one eternal kiss.

"Fling forth the wine of that chalice; and thou art free. I will conduct thee to the Unknown Isles; thou shalt sleep in my bosom upon a bed of massy gold under a silver pavilion:—for I love thee and would take thee away from thy God, before whom so many noble hearts pour forth floods of love which never reach even the steps of His throne!"

These words seemed to float to my ears in a rhythm of infinite sweetness;—for her look was actually sonorous; and the utterances of her eyes were reëchoed in the depths of my heart as though living lips had breathed them into my life. I felt myself willing to renounce God; and yet my tongue mechanically fulfilled all the formalities of the ceremony. The fair one gave me another look,—so beseeching, so despairing that keen blades seemed to pierce my heart; and I felt my bosom transfixed by more swords than those of Our Lady of Sorrows.

All was consummated: I had become a priest.

Never was deeper anguish painted on human face than upon hers:—the maiden who beholds her affianced lover suddenly fall dead at her side; the mother bending over the empty cradle of her child; Eve seated at the threshold of the gate of Paradise; the miser who finds a stone substituted for his stolen treasure; the poet who accidentally permits the only manuscript of his finest work to fall into the fire, could not wear a look so despairing, so inconsolable. All the blood had abandoned her charming face, leaving it whiter than marble; her beautiful arms hung lifelessly on either side of her body as though their muscles had suddenly relaxed; and she sought the support of a pillar, for her yielding limbs almost betrayed her. As for myself, I staggered towards the door of the church, livid as death, my forehead bathed with a sweat bloodier than that of Calvary;—I felt as though I were being strangled;—the vault seemed to have flattened down upon my shoulders; — and it seemed to me that my head alone sustained the whole weight of the dome.

As I was about to cross the threshold a hand suddenly caught mine, — a woman's hand! I had never till then touched the hand of any woman. It was cold as a serpent's skin; and yet its impress remained upon my wrist, burnt there as though branded by a glowing iron. It was she. "Unhappy man! — unhappy man! — what hast thou done?" she exclaimed in a low voice, and immediately disappeared in the crowd.

The aged bishop passed by: he cast a severe and scrutinizing look upon me. My face presented the wildest aspect imaginable; I blushed and turned pale alternately; dazzling lights flashed before my eyes. A companion took pity on me: he seized my arm and led me out; — I could not possibly have found my way back to the seminary unassisted. At the corner of a street, while the young priest's attention was momentarily turned in another direction, a negro page, fantastically garbed, approached me; and without pausing on his way slipped into my hand a little pocket-book with gold-embroidered corners, at the same time giving me a sign to hide it. I concealed it in my sleeve, and there kept it until I found myself alone in my cell. Then I opened the clasp;—there were only two leaves within, bearing the words:—"Clarimonde: At the Concini Palace." So little acquainted was I at that time with the things of this world that I had never heard of Clarimonde, celebrated as she was; and I had no idea as to where the Concini Palace was situated. I hazarded a thousand conjectures, each more extravagant than the last; but, in truth, I cared little whether she were a great lady or a courtesan, so that I could but see her once more.

My love, although the growth of a single hour, had taken imperishable root: I did not even dream of attempting to tear it up, so fully was I convinced such a thing would be impossible. That woman had completely taken possession of me,—one look from her had sufficed to change my very nature: she had breathed her will into my life, and I no longer lived in myself, but in her, and for her. I gave myself up to a thousand extravagancies;—I kissed the place upon my hand which she had touched, and I repeated her name over and over again for hours in succession. I only needed to close my eyes in order to see her distinctly as though she were actually present; and I reiterated to myself the words she had uttered in my ear at the church porch: "Unhappy man! — unhappy man! — what hast thou done?" I comprehended at last the full horror of my situation; and the funereal and awful restraints of the state into which I had just entered became clearly revealed to me. To be a priest! — that is, to be chaste, — to never love, — to observe no distinction of sex or age, — to turn from the sight of all beauty, — to put out one's own eyes, — to hide forever crouching in the chill shadows of some church or cloister, — to visit none but the dying, — to watch by unknown corpses, and ever bear about with one the black soutan as a garb of mourning for one's self — so that your very dress might serve as a pall for your coffin.

And I felt life rising within me like a subteranean lake, expanding and overflowing; my blood leaped fiercely through my arteries; my long-restrained youth suddenly burst into active being, like the aloe which blooms but once in a hundred years, and then bursts into blossom with a clap of thunder.

What could I do in order to see Clarimonde once more? I had no pretext to offer for desiring to leave the seminary, not knowing any person in the city: I would not even be able to remain there but a short time, and was only waiting my assignment to the curacy which I must thereafter occupy. I tried to remove the bars of the window; but it was at a fearful height from the ground, and I found that as I had no ladder it would be useless to think of escaping thus. And furthermore I could descend thence only by night in any event; and afterwards how should I be able to find my way through the inextricable labyrinth of streets? All these difficulties, which to many would have appeared altogether insignificant, were gigantic to me, a poor seminarist who had fallen in love only the day before for the first time, — without experience, without money, without attire.

"Ah!" cried I to myself in my blindness, — "were I not a priest I could have seen her every day; I might have been her lover, her spouse: instead of being wrapped in this dismal shroud of mine, I would have had garments of silk and velvet, golden chains, a sword, and fair plumes like other handsome young cavaliers. My hair, instead of being dishonored by the tonsure, would flow down upon my neck in waving curls; I would have a fine waxed moustache; — I would be a gallant." But one hour passed before an altar, a few hastily articulated words, had forever cut me off from the number of the living; and I had myself sealed down the stone of my own tomb,—I had with my own hand bolted the gate of my prison!

I went to the window:—the sky was beautifully blue; the trees had donned their spring robes; nature seemed to be making parade of an ironical joy. The *Place* was filled with people, some going, others coming; young beaux and young beauties were sauntering in couples toward the groves and gardens;—merry youths passed by, cheerily trolling refrains of drinking songs:—it was all a picture of vivacity, life, animation, gaiety, which formed a bitter contrast with my mourning and my solitude. On the steps of the gate sat a young mother, playing with her child: she kissed its little rosy mouth still impearled with drops of milk; and performed in order to amuse it a thousand divine little puerilities such as only mothers know how to invent. The father standing at a little distance smiled gently upon the charming group, and with folded arms seemed to hug his joy to his heart. I could not endure that spectacle: I closed the window with violence, and flung myself on my bed, my heart filled with frightful hate and jealousy; and gnawed my fingers and my bedcovers like a tiger that has passed ten days without food.

I know not how long I remained in this condition; but at last while writhing on the bed in a fit of spasmodic fury, I suddenly perceived the Abbé Sérapion, who was standing erect in the center of the room, watching me attentively. Filled with shame of myself, I let my head fall upon my breast and covered my face with my hands.

"Romuald, my friend, something very extraordinary is transpiring within you," observed Sérapion, after a few moments' silence; "your conduct is altogether inexplicable! You,—always so quiet, so pious, so gentle,—you to rage in your cell like a wild beast! Take heed, brother! —do not listen to the suggestions of the devil: the Evil Spirit, furious that you have consecrated yourself forever to the Lord, is prowling around you like a ravening wolf and making a last effort to obtain possession of you. Instead of allowing yourself to be conquered, my dear Romuald, make to yourself a cuirass of prayers,—a buckler of mortifications; and combat the enemy like a valiant man: you will then assuredly overcome him. Virtue must be proved by temptation; and gold comes forth purer from the hands of the assayer. Fear not!—never allow yourself to become discouraged: the most watchful and steadfast souls are at moments liable to such temptation. Pray, fast, meditate; and the Evil Spirit will depart from you."

The words of the Abbé Sérapion restored me to myself; and I became a little more calm. "I came," he continued, "to tell you that you have been appointed to the curacy of C . . . : the priest who had charge of it has just died; and Monseigneur the Bishop has ordered me to have you installed there at once. Be ready, therefore, to start to-morrow." I responded with an inclination of the head, and the Abbé retired. I opened my missal and commenced reading some prayers; but the letters became confused and blurred under my eyes; the thread of the ideas entangled itself hopelessly in my brain; and the volume at last fell from my hands without my being aware of it.

To leave to-morrow without having been able to see her again!—to add yet another barrier to the many already interposed between us!—to lose forever all hope of being able to meet her, except, indeed, through a miracle! Even to write her, alas! would be impossible; for by whom could I despatch my letter? With my sacred character of priest, to whom could I dare unbosom myself?—in whom could I confide? I became a prey to the bitterest anxiety.

Then suddenly recurred to me the words of the Abbé Sérapion regarding the artifices of the devil: and the strange character of the adventure, —the supernatural beauty of Clarimonde, the phosphoric light of her eyes, the burning imprint of her hand, the agony into which she had thrown me, the sudden change wrought within me when all my piety vanished in a single instant,—these and other things clearly testified to the work of the Evil One; and perhaps that satiny hand was but the glove which concealed his claws. Filled with terror at these fancies, I again picked up the missal which had slipped from my knees and fallen upon the floor, and once more gave myself up to prayer.

Next morning Sérapion came to take me away: two mules freighted with our miserable valises awaited us at the gate;—he mounted one, and I the other as well as I knew how.

As we passed along the streets of the city, I gazed attentively at all the windows and balconies in the hope of seeing Clarimonde; but it was yet early in the morning, and the city had hardly opened its eyes. Mine sought to penetrate the blinds and window-curtains of all the palaces before which we were passing. Sérapion doubtless attributed this curiosity to my admiration of the architecture; for he slackened the pace of his animal in order to give me time to look around me. At last we passed the city gates and commenced to mount the hill beyond. When we arrived at its summit I turned to take a last look at the place where Clarimonde dwelt. The shadow of a great cloud hung over all the city; the contrasting colors of its blue and red roofs were lost in the uniform half-tint, through which here and there floated upward, like white flakes of foam, the smoke of freshly kindled fires. By a singular optical effect, one edifice, which surpassed in height all the neighboring buildings that were still dimly veiled by the vapors, towered up, fair and lustrous with the gilding of a solitary beam of sunlight: although actually more than a league away it seemed quite near. The smallest details of its architecture were plainly distinguishable, — the turrets, the platforms, the window-casements, and even the swallow-tailed weather vanes.

"What is that palace I see over there, all lighted up by the sun?" — I asked of Sérapion. He shaded his eyes with his hand, and having looked in the direction indicated, replied: "It is the ancient palace which the Prince Concini has given to the courtesan Clarimonde: awful things are done there!"

At that instant, — I know not yet whether it was a reality or an illusion, — I fancied I saw gliding along the terrace, a shapely white figure, which gleamed for a moment in passing and as quickly vanished. It was Clarimonde.

Oh, did she know, that at that very hour, all feverish and restless, — from the height of the rugged road which separated me from her and which, alas! I could never more descend, — I was directing my eyes upon the palace where she dwelt, and which a mocking beam of sunlight seemed to bring nigh to me, as though inviting me to enter therein as its lord? Undoubtedly she must have known it; for her soul was too sympathetically united with mine not to have felt its least emotional thrill; and that subtle sympathy it must have been which prompted her to climb, — although clad only in her night-dress — to the summit of the terrace, amid the icy dews of the morning.

The shadow gained the palace; and the scene became to the eye only a motionless ocean of roofs and gables, amid which one mountainous undulation was distinctly visible. Sérapion urged his mule forward; my own at once followed at the same gait: and a sharp angle in the road at last hid the city of S * * forever from my eyes, as I was destined never to return thither. At the close of a weary three-days' journey through dismal country fields, we caught sight of the cock upon the steeple of the church which I was to take charge of, peeping above the trees; and after having followed some winding roads fringed with thatched cottages and little gardens, we found ourselves in front of the façade, which certainly possessed few features of magnificence. A porch ornamented with some mouldings, and two or three pillars rudely hewn from sandstone; a tiled roof with counterforts of the same sandstone as the pillars,—that was all: to the left lay the cemetery overgrown with high weeds, and having a great iron cross rising up in its center; to the right stood the presbytery, under the shadow of the church. It was a house of the most extreme simplicity and frigid cleanliness. We entered the enclosure: a few chickens were picking up some oats scattered upon the ground; —accustomed, seemingly, to the black habit of ecclesiastics, they showed no fear of our presence and scarcely troubled themselves to get out of our way. A hoarse, wheezy barking fell upon our ears; and we saw an aged dog running toward us.

It was my predecessor's dog: he had dull bleared eyes, grizzled hair, and every mark of the greatest age to which a dog can possibly attain. I patted him gently; and he proceeded at once to march along beside me with an air of satisfaction unspeakable. A very old woman, who had been the housekeeper of the former curé also came to meet us; and after having invited me into a little back parlor, asked whether I intended to retain her. I replied that I would take care of her, and the dog, and the chickens, and all the furniture her master had bequeathed her at his death. At this she became fairly transported with joy, and the Abbé Sérapion at once paid her the price which she asked for her little property.

As soon as my installation was over, the Abbé Sérapion returned to the seminary. I was, therefore, left alone, with no one but myself to look to for aid or counsel. The thought of Clarimonde again began to haunt me; and in spite of all my endeavors to banish it, I always found it present in my meditations. One evening while promenading in my little garden along the walks bordered with box-plants, I fancied that I saw through the elm trees the figure of a woman, who followed my every movement, and that I beheld two sea-green eyes gleaming through the foliage: but it was only an illusion; and on going round to the other side of the garden, I could find nothing except a footprint on the sanded walk, — a footprint so small that it seemed to have been made by the foot of a child. The garden was enclosed by very high walls: I searched every nook and corner of it, but could discover no one there. I have never succeeded in fully accounting for this circumstance, which after all was nothing compared with the strange things which happened to me afterward.

For a whole year, I lived thus, filling all the duties of my calling with the most scrupulous exactitude; praying and fasting; exhorting and lending ghostly aid to the sick; and bestowing alms even to the extent of frequently depriving myself of the very necessaries of life. But I felt a great aridness within me; and the sources of grace seemed closed against me. I never found that happiness which should spring from the fulfillment of a holy mission; my thoughts were far away; and the words of Clarimonde were ever upon my lips, like an involuntary refrain. O, brother, meditate well on this! Through having but once lifted my eyes to look upon a woman, — through one fault apparently so venial, — I have for years remained a victim to the most miserable agonies, and the happiness of my life has been destroyed forever.

I will not longer dwell upon those defeats, or on those inward victories invariably followed by yet more terrible falls; but will at once proceed to the facts of my story. One night my door bell was long and violently rung. The aged housekeeper arose and opened to the stranger; and the figure of a man, whose complexion was deeply bronzed, and who was richly clad in a foreign costume, with a poniard at his girdle, appeared under the rays of Barbara's lantern. Her first impulse was one of terror; but the stranger reassured her, and stated that he desired to see me at once on matters relating to my holy calling. Barbara invited him up stairs, where I was on the point of retiring. The stranger told me that his mistress, a very noble lady, was lying at the point of death, and desired to see a priest. I replied that I was prepared to follow him, took with me the sacred articles necessary for extreme unction; and descended in all haste. Two horses black as the night itself stood without the gate, pawing the ground with impatience, and veiling their chests with long streams of smoky vapor exhaled from their nostrils. He held the stirrup and aided me to mount upon one; then, merely laying his hand upon the pummel of the saddle, he vaulted on the other, pressed the animal's

sides with his knees, and loosened rein. The horse bounded forward with the velocity of an arrow; mine of which the stranger held the bridle, also started off at a swift gallop, keeping up with his companion. We devoured the road: the ground flowed backward beneath us in a long streaked line of pale grey; and the black silhouettes of the trees seemed fleeing by us on either side like an army in rout. We passed through a forest so profoundly gloomy that I felt my flesh creep in the chill darkness with superstitious fear. The showers of bright sparks which flew from the stony road under the ironshod feet of our horses, remained glowing in our wake like a fiery trail; and had any one at that hour of the night beheld us both — my guide and myself, — he must have taken us for two spectres riding upon night-mares. Witch-fires ever and anon flitted across the road before us; and the night-birds shrieked fearsomely in the depth of the woods beyond, where we beheld at intervals glow the phosphorescent eyes of wild cats. The manes of the horses became more and more disheveled: the sweat streamed over their flanks; and their breath came through their nostrils hard and fast. But when he found them slacking pace, the guide reanimated them by uttering a strange, guttural, unearthly cry; and the gallop recommenced with fury. At last the whirlwind race ceased: a huge black mass pierced through with many bright points of light suddenly rose before us; the hoofs of our horses echoed louder upon a strong wooden drawbridge; and we rode under a great vaulted archway which darkly yawned between two enormous towers. Some great excitement evidently reigned in the castle: servants with torches were crossing the courtyard in every direction; and, above, lights were ascending and descending from landing to landing. I obtained a confused glimpse of vast masses of architecture, —columns, arcades, flights of steps, stairways: a royal voluptuousness and elfin magnificence of construction worthy of Fairyland. A negro page,—the same who had before brought me the tablet from Clarimonde, and whom I instantly recognized,—approached to aid me in dismounting; and the major-domo, attired in black velvet with a gold chain about his neck, advanced to meet me, supporting himself upon an ivory cane. Large tears were falling from his eyes and streaming over his cheeks and white beard. "Too late!" he cried, sorrowfully shaking his venerable head: "too late, sir priest!—but if you have not been able to save the soul, come at least to watch by the poor body."

He took my arm and conducted me to the death chamber: I wept not less bitterly than he; for I had learned that the dead one was none other than that Clarimonde whom I had so deeply and so wildly loved. A *prie-dieu* stood at the foot of the bed; a blueish flame flickering in a bronze patera filled all the room with a wan, deceptive light, here and there bringing out in the darkness at intervals some projection of furniture or cornice. In a chiseled urn upon the table, there was a faded white rose, whose leaves,—excepting one that still held,—had all fallen, like odorous tears, to the foot of the vase: a broken black mask, a fan, and disguises of every variety, which were lying on the arm chairs, bore witness that death had entered suddenly and unannounced into that sumptuous dwelling. Without daring to cast my eyes upon the bed, I knelt down and commenced to repeat the Psalms for the Dead with exceeding fervor: thanking God that he had placed the tomb between me and the memory of this woman, so that I might thereafter be able to utter her name in my prayers as a name forever sanctified by death. But my fervor gradually weakened; and I fell insensibly into a reverie. That chamber bore no semblance to a chamber of death. In lieu of the fœtid and cadaverous odors which

I had been accustomed to breathe during such funereal vigils,—a languorous vapor of Oriental perfume,—I know not what amorous odor of woman,—softly floated through the tepid air. That pale light seemed rather a twilight gloom contrived for voluptuous pleasure, than a substitute for the yellow-flickering watch-tapers which shine by the side of corpses. I thought upon the strange destiny which enabled me to meet Clarimonde again at the very moment when she was lost to me forever; and a sigh of regretful anguish escaped from my breast. Then it seemed to me that some one behind me had also sighed; and I turned round to look. It was only an echo. But in that moment my eyes fell upon the bed of death which they had till then avoided. The red damask curtains, decorated with large flowers worked in embroidery, and looped up with gold bullion, permitted me to behold the fair dead, lying at full length, with hands joined upon her bosom. She was covered with a linen wrapping of dazzling whiteness, which formed a strong contrast with the gloomy purple of the hangings, and was of so fine a texture that it concealed nothing of her body's charming form, and allowed the eye to follow those beautiful outlines,—undulating like the neck of a swan,—which even death had not robbed of their supple grace. She seemed an alabaster statue executed by some skillful sculptor to place upon the tomb of a queen; or rather, perhaps, like a slumbering maiden over whom the silent snow had woven a spotless veil.

I could no longer maintain my constrained attitude of prayer: — the air of the alcove intoxicated me; that febrile perfume of half-faded roses penetrated my very brain; — and I commenced to pace restlessly up and down the chamber, pausing at each turn before the bier to contemplate the graceful corpse lying beneath the transparency of its shroud. Wild fancies came thronging to my brain: — I thought to myself that she might not, perhaps, be really dead, — that she might only have feigned death for the purpose of bringing me to her castle, and then declaring her love. At one time I even thought I saw her foot move under the whiteness of the coverings, and slightly disarrange the long, straight folds of the winding sheet.

And then I asked myself: "Is this indeed Clarimonde? — what proof have I that it is she? Might not that black page have passed into the service of some other lady? Surely, I must be going mad, — to torture and afflict myself thus!"

But my heart answered with a fierce throbbing: "It is she; it is she indeed!" I approached the bed again, and fixed my eyes with redoubled attention upon the object of my incertitude. Ah! must I confess it?—that exquisite perfection of bodily form, although purified and made sacred by the shadow of death, affected me more voluptuously than it should have done; and that repose so closely resembled slumber, that one might well have mistaken it for such. I forgot that I had come there to perform a funeral ceremony;—I fancied myself a young bridegroom entering the chamber of the bride who all modestly hides her fair face, and through coyness seeks to keep herself wholly veiled. Heartbroken with grief,—yet wild with hope.—shuddering at once with fear and pleasure, I bent over her, and grasped the corner of the sheet: I lifted it back,—holding my breath all the while through fear of waking her. My arteries throbbed with such violence that I felt them hiss through my temples: and the sweat poured from my forehead in streams, as though I had lifted a mighty slab of marble. There, indeed, lay Clarimonde, even as I had seen her at the church on the day of my ordination: she was not less charming than then;—with her, death seemed but a last coquetry.

The pallor of her cheeks, the less brilliant carnation of her lips, her long eyelashes lowered and relieving their dark fringe against that white skin, lent her an unspeakably seductive aspect of melancholy chastity and mental suffering; her long loose hair, still intertwined with some little blue flowers, made a shining pillow for her head, and veiled the nudity of her shoulders with their thick ringlets: her beautiful hands, purer, more diaphanous than the Host, were crossed on her bosom in an attitude of pious rest and silent prayer, which served to counteract all that might have proven otherwise too alluring, — even after death, — in the exquisite roundness and ivory polish of her bare arms from which the pearl bracelets had not yet been removed. I remained long in mute contemplation; and the more I gazed, the less could I persuade myself that life had really abandoned that beautiful body forever. I do not know whether it was an illusion, or a reflection of the lamplight; but it seemed to me that the blood was again commencing to circulate under that lifeless pallor, although she remained all motionless. I laid my hand lightly on her arm: it was cold, but not colder than her hand on the day when it touched mine at the portals of the church. I resumed my position, bending my face above hers, and bathing her cheeks with the warm dew of my tears. Ah! what bitter feelings of despair and helplessness,—what agonies unutterable did I endure in that long watch! Vainly did I wish that I could have gathered all my life into one mass that I might give it all to her, and breathe into her chill remains the flame which devoured me. The night advanced; and, feeling the moment of eternal separation approach, I could not deny myself the last sad sweet pleasure of imprinting a kiss upon the dead lips of her who had been my only love. . . O, miracle!—a faint breath mingled itself with my breath; and the mouth of Clarimonde responded to the passionate pressure of mine: her eyes unclosed, and lighted up with something of their former brilliancy; she uttered a long sigh, and uncrossing her arms, passed them around my neck with a look of ineffable delight. "Ah! it is thou, Romuald!"—she murmured in a voice languishingly sweet as the last vibrations of a harp: "what ailed thee, dearest? I waited so long for thee that I am dead; but we are now betrothed; I can see thee and visit thee. Adieu, Romuald! adieu!—I love thee: that is all I wished to tell thee; and I give thee back the life which thy kiss for a moment recalled; we shall soon meet again."

Her head fell back; but her arms yet encircled me, as though to retain me still. A furious whirlwind suddenly burst in the window, and entered the chamber; the last remaining leaf of the white rose for a moment palpitated at the extremity of the stalk like a butterfly's wing; — then it detached itself and flew forth through the open casement, bearing with it the soul of Clarimonde. The lamp was extinguished; and I fell insensible upon the bosom of the beautiful dead.

When I came to myself again, I was lying on the bed in my little room at the presbytery; and the old dog of the former curé was licking my hand which had been hanging down outside of the covers. Barbara, all trembling with age and anxiety, was busying herself about the room, opening and shutting drawers, and emptying powders into glasses. On seeing me open my eyes, the old woman uttered a cry of joy; the dog yelped and wagged his tail: but I was still so weak that I could not speak a single word, or make the slightest motion. Afterwards I learned that I had lain thus for three days; giving no evidence of life beyond the faintest respiration. Those three days do not reckon in my life, nor could I ever imagine whither my spirit had departed during those three days: I have no recollection of aught relating to them. Barbara told me that the same coppery-complexioned man who came to seek me on the night of my departure from the presbytery, had brought me back the next morning in a close litter, and departed immediately afterward. When I became able to collect my scattered thoughts, I reviewed within my mind all the circumstances of that fateful night. At first, I thought I had been the victim of some magical illusion; but ere long the recollection of other circumstances, real and palpable in themselves, came to forbid that supposition. I could not believe that I had been dreaming, since Barbara as well as myself, had seen the strange man with his two black horses, and described with exactness every detail of his figure and apparel. Nevertheless it appeared that none knew of any castle in the neighborhood, answering to the description of that in which I had again found Clarimonde.

One morning I found the Abbé Sérapion in my room. Barbara had advised him that I was ill; and he had come with all speed to see me. Although this haste on his part testified to an affectionate interest in me, yet his visit did not cause me the pleasure which it should have done. The Abbé Sérapion had something penetrating and inquisitorial in his gaze which made me feel very ill at ease. His presence filled me with embarrassment, and a sense of guilt. At the first glance he divined my interior trouble; and I hated him for his clairvoyance.

While he enquired after my health in hypocritically honeyed accents, he constantly kept his two great yellow lion-eyes fixed upon me, and plunged his look into my soul like a sounding lead. Then he asked me how I directed my parish,—if I was happy in it,—how I passed the leisure hours allowed me in the intervals of pastoral duty,—whether I had become acquainted with many of the inhabitants of the place,—what was my favorite reading; and a thousand other such questions. I answered these inquiries as briefly as possible; and he, without ever waiting for my answers, passed rapidly from one subject of query to another. That conversation had evidently no connection with what he actually wished to say. At last without any premonition, but as though repeating a piece of news which he had recalled on the instant, and feared might otherwise be forgotten subsequently, he suddenly said in a clear vibrant voice which rang in my ears like the trumpets of the Last Judgment:—

"The great courtesan Clarimonde died a few

days ago, at the close of an orgie which lasted eight days and eight nights. It was something infernally splendid. The abominations of the banquets of Belshazzar and Cleopatra were re-enacted there. Good God! what age are we living in? The guests were served by swarthy slaves who spoke an unknown tongue, and who seemed to me to be veritable demons:—the livery of the very least among them would have served for the gala-dress of an emperor. There have always been very strange stories told of this Clarimonde; and all her lovers came to a violent or miserable end. They used to say that she was a ghoul,—a female vampire; but I believe she was none other than Beelzebub himself."

He ceased to speak and commenced to regard me more attentively than ever,—as though to observe the effect of his words on me. I could not refrain from starting, when I heard him utter the name of Clarimonde; and this news of her death, in addition to the pain it caused me by reason of its coincidence with the nocturnal scenes I had witnessed, filled me with an agony and terror which my face betrayed, despite my utmost endeavors to appear composed. Sérapion fixed an anxious and severe look upon me; and then observed: "My son, I must warn you that you are standing with foot raised upon the brink of an abyss: take heed lest you fall therein. Satan's claws are long; and tombs are not always true to their trust. The tombstone of Clarimonde should be sealed down with a triple seal; for, if report be true, it is not the first time she has died. May God watch over you, Romuald!"

And with these words the Abbé walked slowly to the door. I did not see him again at that time; for he left for S * * almost immediately.

I became completely restored to health; and resumed my accustomed duties. The memory of Clarimonde and the words of the old Abbé were constantly in my mind: nevertheless, no extraordinary event had occurred to verify the funereal predictions of Sérapion: and I had commenced to believe that his fears and my own terrors were over-exaggerated, when one night I had a strange dream. I had hardly fallen asleep when I heard my bed-curtains drawn apart, as their rings slided back upon the curtain rod with a sharp sound: I rose up quickly upon my elbow, and beheld the shadow of a woman standing erect before me. I recognized Clarimonde immediately. She bore in her hand a little lamp, shaped like those which are placed in tombs; and its light lent her fingers a rosy transparency, which extended itself by lessening degrees even to the opaque and milky whiteness of her bare arm. Her only garment was the linen winding sheet which had shrouded her when lying upon the bed of death; — she sought to gather its folds over her bosom as though ashamed of being so scantily clad; but her little hand was not equal to the task: she was so white that the color of the drapery blended with that of her flesh under the pallid rays of the lamp. Enveloped with this subtle tissue which betrayed all the contours of her body, she seemed rather the marble statue of some fair antique bather, than a woman endowed with life. But dead or living, statue or woman, shadow or body, her beauty was still the same; — only that the green light of her eyes was less brilliant; — and her mouth, once so warmly crimson, was only tinted with a faint tender rosiness, like that of her cheeks. The little blue flowers which I had noticed entwined in her hair, were withered and dry, and had lost nearly all their leaves, but this did not prevent her from being charming, — so charming that notwithstanding the strange character of the adventure, and the unexplainable manner in which she had entered my room, I felt not even for a moment the least fear.

She placed the lamp on the table and seated herself at the foot of my bed: then bending toward me, she said in that voice at once silvery clear and yet velvety in its sweet softness,— such as I never heard from any lips save hers:

"I have kept thee long in waiting, dear Romuald; and it must have seemed to thee that I had forgotten thee. But I come from afar off, — very far off; and from a land whence no other has ever yet returned: there is neither sun nor moon in that land whence I come; all is but space and shadow:—there is neither road nor pathway: no earth for the foot, no air for the wing: and nevertheless behold me here; for Love is stronger than Death and must conquer him in the end. O what sad faces and fearful things I have seen on my way hither!—what difficulty my soul, returned to earth through the power of will alone, has had in finding its body and reinstating itself therein!—what terrible efforts I had to make ere I could lift the ponderous slab with which they had covered me! See! the palms of my poor hands are all bruised!— Kiss them, sweet love, that they may be healed!" She laid the cold palms of her hands upon my mouth, one after the other: I kissed them, indeed, many times; and she the while watched me with a smile of ineffable affection.

I confess to my shame that I had entirely forgotten the advice of the Abbé Sérapion and the sacred office wherewith I had been invested. I had fallen without resistance, and at the first assault. I had not even made the least effort to repel the tempter: the fresh coolness of Clarimonde's skin penetrated my own; and I felt voluptuous tremors pass over my whole body. Poor child! in spite of all I saw afterward, I can hardly yet believe she was a demon;—at least she had no appearance of being such, and never did Satan so skillfully conceal his claws and horns. She had drawn her feet up beneath her, and squatted down on the edge of the couch in an attitude full of negligent coquetry. From time to time she passed her little hand through my hair and twisted it into curls, as though trying how a new style of wearing it would become my face. I abandoned myself to her hands with the most guilty pleasure; while she accompanied her gentle play with the prettiest prattle. The most remarkable fact was that I felt no astonishment whatever at so extraordinary an adventure; and as in dreams one finds no difficulty in accepting the most fantastic events as simple facts, so all these circumstances seemed to me perfectly natural in themselves.

"I loved thee long ere I saw thee, dear Romuald; and sought thee everywhere. Thou wast my dream; and I first saw thee in the church at the fatal moment: I said at once,—'It is he!' I gave thee a look into which I threw all the love I ever had, all the love I now have, all the love I shall ever have for thee,—a look that would have damned a Cardinal, or brought a king to his knees at my feet in view of all his court. Thou remainedst unmoved; preferring thy God to me!

"Ah! how jealous I am of that God whom thou didst love and still lovest more than me!

"Woe is me! unhappy one that I am! I can never have thy heart all to myself,—I whom thou didst recall to life with a kiss,—dead Clarimonde who for thy sake bursts asunder the gates of the tomb, and comes to consecrate to thee a life which she has resumed only to make thee happy!"

All her words were accompanied with the most impassioned caresses, which bewildered my sense and my reason to such an extent that I did not fear to utter a frightful blasphemy for the sake of consoling her, and to declare that I loved her as much as God.

Her eyes rekindled and shone like chrysoprases. "In truth?—in very truth?—as much as God!"

she cried, flinging her beautiful arms around me. "Since it is so, thou wilt come with me; thou wilt follow me whithersoever I desire. Thou wilt cast away thy ugly black habit. Thou shalt be the proudest and most envied of cavaliers: thou shalt be my lover! To be the acknowledged lover of Clarimonde, who has refused even a Pope,—that will be something to feel proud of! Ah! the fair, unspeakably happy existence,—the beautiful golden life we shall live together! And when shall we depart, my fair sir?"

"To-morrow! to-morrow!" I cried in my delirium.

"To-morrow, then; so let it be!" she answered. "In the meanwhile I shall have opportunity to change my toilet; for this is a little too light, and in nowise suited for a voyage. I must also forthwith notify all my friends who believe me dead, and mourn for me as deeply as they are capable of doing. The money, the dresses, the carriages,—all will be ready: I shall call for thee at this same hour. Adieu, dear heart!" And she lightly touched my forehead with her lips. The lamp went out; the curtains closed again; and all became dark:—a leaden, dreamless sleep fell on me and held me unconscious until the morning following.

I awoke later than usual; and the recollection of this singular adventure troubled me during the whole day. I finally persuaded myself that it was a mere vapor of my heated imagination. Nevertheless its sensations had been so vivid that it was difficult to persuade myself that they were not real; and it was not without some presentiment of what was going to happen that I got into bed at last, after having prayed God to drive far from me all thoughts of evil, and to protect the chastity of my slumber.

I soon fell into a deep sleep, and my dream was continued. The curtains again parted; and I beheld Clarimonde, — not, as on the former occasion pale in her pale winding sheet, with the violets of death upon her cheeks; but gay, sprightly, jaunty, — in a superb traveling dress of green velvet, trimmed with gold lace, and looped up on either side, to allow a glimpse of satin petticoat. Her blonde hair escaped in thick ringlets from beneath a broad black felt hat, decorated with white feathers whimsically twisted into various shapes: in one hand she held a little riding whip terminated by a golden whistle. She tapped me lightly with it, and exclaimed, — "Well, my fine sleeper: is this the way you make your preparations? I thought I would find you up and dressed! Arise quickly: we have no time to lose "

I leaped out of bed at once.

"Come! dress yourself; and let us go," she continued, pointing to a little package she had brought with her;—"the horses are becoming impatient of delay and champing their bits at the door. We ought to have been by this time at least ten leagues distant from here."

I dressed myself hurriedly; and she handed me the articles of apparel herself, one by one,—bursting into laughter from time to time at my awkwardness, as she explained to me the use of a garment when I had made a mistake. She hurriedly arranged my hair; and, this done, held up before me a little pocket mirror of Venetian crystal, rimmed with silver filagree-work: and playfully asked,—"How dost find thyself now? Wilt engage me for thy valet-de-chambre?"

I was no longer the same person; and I could not even recognize myself. I resembled my former self no more than a finished statue resembles a block of stone. My old face seemed but a coarse daub of the one reflected in the mirror. I was handsome; and my vanity was sensibly tickled by the metamorphosis. That elegant apparel, that richly embroidered vest had made of me a totally different personage; and I marveled at the power of transformation owned by a few yards of cloth cut after a certain pattern. The spirit of my costume penetrated my very skin; and within ten minutes more I had become something of a coxcomb.

In order to feel more at ease in my new attire, I took several turns up and down the room. Clarimonde watched me with an air of maternal pleasure, and appeared well satisfied with her work. "Come! enough of this child's-play!— let us start, Romuald, dear: we have far to go, and we may not get there in time." She took my hand, and led me forth. All the doors opened before her at a touch; and we passed by the dog without awaking him.

At the gate we found Margheritone waiting,— the same swarthy groom who had once before been my escort: he held the bridles of three horses, all black like those which bore us to the castle,—one for me, one for him, one for Clarimonde. Those horses must have been Spanish genets born of mares fecundated by a zephyr; for they were fleet as the wind itself, and the moon which had just risen at our departure to light us on the way, rolled over the sky like a wheel detached from her own chariot: we beheld her on the right leaping from tree to tree, and putting herself out of breath in the effort to keep up with us. Soon we came upon a level plain where hard by a clump of trees, a carriage with four vigorous horses awaited us: we entered it; and the postillions urged their animals into a mad gallop. I had one arm around Clarimonde's waist, and one of her hands clasped in mine; her head leaned upon my shoulder, and I felt her bosom, half bare, lightly pressing against my arm. I had never known such intense happiness. In that hour I had forgotten everything; and I no more remembered having ever been a priest than I remembered what I had been doing in my mother's womb,—so great was the fascination which the evil spirit exerted upon me. From that night my nature seemed in some sort to have become halved; and there were two men within me, neither of whom knew the other. At one moment I believed myself a priest who dreamed nightly that he was a gentleman; at another that I was a gentleman who dreamed he was a priest. I could no longer distinguish the dream from the reality,—nor could I discover where the reality began, or where ended the dream. The exquisite young lord and libertine railed at the priest; the priest loathed the dissolute habits of the young lord. Two spirals entangled and confounded the one with the other, yet never touching, would afford a fair representation of this bicephalic life which I lived. Despite the strange character of my condition, I do not believe that I ever inclined,—even for a moment,—to madness. I always retained with extreme vividness all the perceptions of my two lives. Only, there was one absurd fact which I could not explain to myself;—namely, that the consciousness of the same individuality existed in two men so opposite in character. It was an anomaly for which I could not account,—whether I believed myself to be the Cure of the little village of S * *; or, *Il Signor Romualdo*, the titled lover of Clarimonde.

Be that as it may, I lived,—at least I believed that I lived,—in Venice: I have never been able to discover rightly how much of illusion and how much of reality there was in this fantastic adventure. We dwelt in a great palace on the Canaleio, filled with frescoes and statues, and containing two Titians in the noblest style of the great master, which were hung in Clarimonde's chamber: it was a palace well worthy of a king. We had each our gondola, our *barcarolli* in family livery, our music hall, and our special poet. Clarimonde always lived upon a magnificent scale: there was something of Cleopatra in her nature. As for me, I had the retinue of a prince's son; and I was regarded with as much reverential respect as though I had been of the family of one of the twelve Apostles or the four Evangelists of the Most Serene Republic: I would not have turned aside to allow even the Doge to pass; and I do not believe that since Satan fell from heaven, any creature was ever prouder or more insolent than I. I went to the Ridotto, and played with a luck which seemed absolutely infernal. I received the best of all society,—the sons of ruined families, women of the theatre, shrewd knaves, parasites, hectoring swash-bucklers. But notwithstanding the dissipation of such a life, I always remained faithful to Clarimonde. I loved her wildly. She would have excited satiety itself, and chained inconstancy. To have Clarimonde was to have twenty mistresses,—aye, to possess all women: so mobile, so varied of aspect, so fresh in new charms was she all in herself;—a very chameleon of a woman, in sooth. She made you commit with her the infidelity you would have committed with another, by donning to perfection the character, the attraction, the style of beauty of the woman who appeared to please you. She returned my love a hundred fold; and it was in vain that the young patricians and even the Ancients of the Council of Ten, made her the most magnificent proposals. A Foscari even went so far as to offer to espouse her: she rejected all his overtures. Of gold she had enough: she wished no longer for anything but love, — a love youthful, pure, evoked by herself, and which should be a first and last passion. I would have been perfectly happy but for a cursed nightmare which recurred every night, and in which I believed myself to be a poor village curé, practising mortification and penance for my excesses during the day. Reassured by my constant association with her, I never thought further of the strange manner in which I had become acquainted with Clarimonde. But the words of the Abbé Sérapion concerning her recurred often to my memory, and never ceased to cause me uneasiness.

For some time the health of Clarimonde had not been so good as usual: her complexion grew paler day by day. The physicians who were summoned could not comprehend the nature of her malady and knew not how to treat it. They all prescribed some insignificant remedies; and never called a second time. Her paleness, nevertheless, visibly increased; and she became colder and colder, until she seemed almost as white and dead as upon that memorable night in the unknown castle. I grieved with anguish unspeakable to behold her thus slowly perishing; and she, touched by my agony, smiled upon me sweetly and sadly with the fateful smile of those who feel that they must die.

One morning I was seated at her bedside, and breakfasting from a little table placed close at hand, so that I might not be obliged to leave her for a single instant. In the act of cutting some fruit, I accidentally inflicted rather a deep gash on my finger. The blood immediately gushed forth in a little purple jet; and a few drops spirted upon Clarimonde. Her eyes flashed; her face suddenly assumed an expression of savage and ferocious joy such as I had never before observed in her. She leaped out of her bed with animal agility,—the agility, as it were, of an ape or a cat,—and sprang upon my wound which she commenced to suck with an air of unutterable pleasure. She swallowed the blood in little mouthfuls, slowly and carefully, like a connoisseur tasting a wine from Xeres or Syracuse: gradually her eyelids half closed; and the pupils of her green eyes became oblong instead of round. From time to time she paused in order to kiss my hand: then she would recommence to press her lips to the lips of the wound in order to coax forth a few more ruddy drops. When she found that the blood would no longer come, she arose with eyes liquid and brilliant, rosier than a May dawn; her face full and fresh, her hand warm and moist, — in fine, more beautiful than ever, and in the most perfect health.

"I shall not die! — I shall not die!" she cried clinging to my neck, half mad with joy: "I can love thee yet for a long time. My life is thine; and all that is of me comes from thee. A few drops of thy rich and noble blood, more precious and more potent than all the elixirs of the earth, have given me back life!"

This scene long haunted my memory, and inspired me with strange doubts in regard to Clarimonde; — and the same evening when slumber had transported me to my presbytery, I beheld the Abbé Sérapion, graver and more anxious of aspect than ever. He gazed attentively at me, and sorrowfully exclaimed: "Not content with losing your soul, you now desire also to lose your body. Wretched young man, into how terrible a plight have you fallen!" The tone in which he uttered these words powerfully affected me; but in spite of its vividness even that impression was soon dissipated, and a thousand other cares erased it from my mind. At last one evening while looking into a mirror whose traitorous position she had not taken into account, I saw Clarimonde in the act of emptying a powder into the cup of spiced wine, which she had long been in the habit of preparing after our repasts. I took the cup, feigned to carry it to my lips, and then placed it on the nearest article of furniture as though intending to finish it at my leisure. Taking advantage of a moment when the fair one's back was turned, I threw the contents under the table; after which I retired to my chamber and went to bed, fully resolved not to sleep; but to watch and discover what should come of all this mystery. I did not have to wait long. Clarimonde entered in her night-dress; and having removed her apparel, crept into bed and lay down beside me. When she felt assured that I was asleep, she bared my arm and drawing a gold pin from her hair, commenced to murmur in a low voice:—

"One drop—only one drop!—one ruby at the end of my needle. . . . . . . Since thou lovest me yet, I must not die! . . . . . . Ah! poor love!—his beautiful blood, so brightly purple, I must drink it. Sleep, my only treasure! sleep, my god, my child! I will do thee no harm; I will only take of thy life what I must to keep my own from being forever extinguished. But that I love thee so much, I could well resolve to have other lovers whose veins I could drain: but since I have known thee, all other men have become hateful to me. . . . Ah, the beautiful arm!—how round it is!—how white it is!—how shall I ever dare to prick this pretty blue vein!" And while thus murmuring to herself, she wept; and I felt her tears raining on my arm as she clasped it with her hands. At last she took the resolve, slightly punctured me with her pin, and commenced to suck up the blood which oozed from the place. Although she swallowed only a few drops, the fear of weakening me soon seized her; and she carefully tied a little band around my arm, afterward rubbing the wound with an unguent which immediately cicatrized it.

Further doubts were impossible: the Abbé Sérapion was right. Notwithstanding this positive knowledge, however, I could not cease to love Clarimonde; and I would gladly of my own accord have given her all the blood she required to sustain her factitious life. Moreover, I felt but little fear of her:—the woman seemed to plead with me for the vampire; and what I had already heard and seen sufficed to reassure me completely. In those days I had plenteous veins, which would not have been so easily exhausted as at present; and I would not have thought of bargaining for my blood, drop by drop. I would rather have opened myself the veins of my arm and said to her: "Drink; and may my love infiltrate itself throughout thy body together with my blood!" I carefully avoided ever making the least reference to the narcotic drink she had prepared for me, or to the incident of the pin; and we lived in the most perfect harmony.

Yet my priestly scruples commenced to torment me more than ever; and I was at a loss to imagine what new penance I could invent in order to mortify and subdue my flesh. Although these visions were involuntary, and though I did not actually participate in anything relating to them, I could not dare to touch the body of Christ with hands so impure and a mind defiled by such debauches whether real or imaginary. In the effort to avoid falling under the influence of these wearisome hallucinations, I strove to prevent myself from being overcome by sleep: I held my eyelids open with my fingers, and stood for hours together leaning upright against the wall, fighting sleep with all my might; but the dust of drowsiness invariably gathered upon my eyes at last, and finding all resistance useless, I would have to let my arms fall in the extremity of despairing weariness, and the current of slumber would again bear me away to the perfidious shores. Sérapion addressed me with the most vehement exhortations; severely reproaching me for my softness and want of fervor. Finally one day when I was more wretched than usual, he said to me: "There is but one way by which you can obtain relief from this continual torment; and though it is an extreme measure it must be made use of:—violent diseases require violent remedies. I know where Clarimonde is buried: it is necessary that we shall disinter her remains, and that you shall behold in how pitiable a state the object of your love is;—then you will no longer be tempted to lose your soul for the sake of an unclean corpse devoured by worms, and ready to crumble into dust: that will assuredly restore you to yourself." For my part I was so tired of this double life that I at once consented: desiring to ascertain beyond a doubt whether a priest or a gentleman had been the victim of delusion. I had become fully resolved either to kill one of the two men within me for the benefit of the other, or else to kill both: for so terrible an existence could not last long and be endured. The Abbé Sérapion provided himself with a mattock, a lever, and a lantern; and at midnight we wended our way to the cemetery of * * *, the location and place of which were perfectly familiar to him. After having directed the rays of the dark lantern upon the inscriptions of several tombs, we came at last upon a great slab, half concealed by huge weeds and devoured by mosses and parasitic plants, whereupon we deciphered the opening lines of the epitaph:—

*Here lies Clarimonde
Who was famed in her life-time
As the fairest of women.
. . . . . . . . . . .
. . . .

"It is here, without a doubt!" muttered Sérapion; and placing his lantern on the ground he forced the point of the lever under the edge of the stone, and commenced to raise it. The stone yielded; and he proceeded to work with the mattock. Darker and more silent than the night itself, I stood by and watched him do it; while he, bending over his dismal toil, streamed with sweat, panted, and his hard-coming breath seemed

* Ici gît Clarimonde
Qui fut de son vivant
La plus belle du monde. . .

The broken beauty of the lines is unavoidably lost in the translation.

to have the harsh tone of a death rattle. It was a weird scene; and had any persons from without beheld us, they would assuredly have taken us rather for profane wretches and shroud-stealers than for priests of God. There was something grim and fierce in Sérapion's zeal which lent him the air of a demon rather than of an apostle or an angel; and his great aquiline face, with all its stern features brought out in strong relief by the lantern-light, had something fearsome in it which enhanced the unpleasant fancy. I felt an icy sweat come out upon my forehead in huge beads; and my hair stood up with a hideous fear:—within the depths of my own heart I felt that the act of the austere Sérapion was an abominable sacrilege; and I could have prayed that a triangle of fire would issue from the entrails of the dark clouds, heavily rolling above us, to reduce him to cinders. The owls which had been nestling in the cypress trees, startled by the gleam of the lantern, flew against it from time to time,—striking their dusty wings against its panes, and uttering plaintive cries of lamentation; wild foxes yelped in the far darkness; and a thousand sinister noises detached themselves from the silence. At last Sérapion's mattock struck the coffin itself, making its planks re-echo with a deep sonorous sound,—with that terrible sound nothingness utters when stricken: —he wrenched apart and tore up the lid; and I beheld Clarimonde, pallid as a figure of marble, with hands joined: her white winding-sheet made but one fold from her head to her feet. A little crimson drop sparkled like a speck of dew at one corner of her colorless mouth. Sérapion, at this spectacle, burst into fury:—"Ah! thou art here, demon!—impure courtesan!—drinker of blood and gold!"—and he flung holy water upon the corpse and the coffin, over which he traced the sign of the cross with his sprinkler. Poor Clarimonde had no sooner been touched by the blessed spray, than her beautiful body crumbled into dust, and became only a shapeless and frightful mass of cinders and half-calcined bones.

"Behold your mistress, my Lord Romuald!"—cried the inexorable priest as he pointed to these sad remains,—"will you be easily tempted after this to promenade on the Lido, or at Fusina with your beauty?" I covered my face with my hands: a vast ruin had taken place within me. I returned to my presbytery; and the noble Lord Romuald,—the lover of Clarimonde,—separated himself from the poor priest with whom he had kept such strange company so long. But once only,—the following night,—I saw Clarimonde:—she said to me as she had said the first time at the portals of the church: "Unhappy man, unhappy man!—what hast thou done! Wherefore have hearkened to that imbecile priest?—wert thou not happy?—and what harm had I ever done thee, that thou shouldst violate my poor tomb, and lay bare the miseries of my nothingness? All communication between our souls and our bodies is henceforth forever broken. Adieu!—thou wilt yet regret me!" She vanished in air as smoke; and I never saw her more.

Alas! she spoke truly indeed:—I have regretted her more than once; and I regret her still. My soul's peace has been very dearly bought:—the love of God was not too much to replace such a love as hers. And this, brother, is the story of my youth. Never gaze upon a woman; and walk abroad only with eyes ever fixed upon the ground,—for however chaste and watchful one may be, the error of a single moment is enough to make one lose eternity.

# ARRIA MARCELLA.

## A SOUVENIR OF POMPEII.

Three young friends, who had undertaken an Italian tour together last year, visited the Studii Museum at Naples, where the various antique objects exhumed from the ashes of Pompeii and Herculaneum have been collected.

They scattered through the halls, inspecting the mosaics, the bronzes, the frescoes detached from the walls of the dead city, each following the promptings of his own particular taste in such matters; and whenever one of the party encountered something especially curious, he summoned his comrades with cries of delight, much to the scandal of the taciturn English visitors, and the staid *bourgeois* who studiously thumbed their catalogues.

But the youngest of the three, who had paused before a glass case, appeared wholly deaf to the exclamations of his comrades, so deeply had he become absorbed in contemplation. The object that he seemed to be examining with so much interest, was a black mass of coagulated cinders, bearing a hollow imprint; one might easily have mistaken it for the fragment of some statue-mold, broken in the casting; the trained eye of an artist would have readily therein recognized the impression of a perfect bosom and a flank as faultless in its outlines as a Greek statue. It is well known,—indeed the commonest traveler's guide will tell you,—that this lava, in cooling about the body of a woman, preserved its charming contours. Thanks to the caprice of the eruption that destroyed four cities, that noble form, though crumbled to dust nearly two thousand years ago, has come down to us;—the rounded loveliness of a throat has lived through the centuries in which so many empires perished without even leaving the traces of their existence; chance-imprinted upon the volcanic scoriæ, that seal of beauty remains unobliterated.

Finding that he still remained absorbed in contemplation, Octavian's friends returned to where he stood; and Max, touching his shoulder, caused him to start like one surprised in a secret. Evidently Octavian had not been aware of the approach of Max or Fabio.

"Come, Octavian," exclaimed Max, "do not stay lingering whole hours before every cabinet, else we shall get late for the train and miss seeing Pompeii to-day."

"What is our comrade looking at?" asked Fabio, drawing near:—"Ah! the imprint found in the house of Arrius Diomedes!" And he turned a peculiar, quick glance upon Octavian.

Octavian slightly blushed, took Max's arm; and the visit terminated without further incident. On leaving the Studii Museum, the three friends entered a *corricolo*, and were driven to the railway station. The *corricolo*, with its great red wheels, its tracket seat studded with brass nails, and its thin, spirited horse harnessed like a Spanish mule, and galloping at full speed over the great slabs of lava-pavement, is too familiar to need description here;—especially as we are not recording impressions of a trip to Naples, but the simple narrative of an adventure, which although true, may seem both fantastic and incredible in the extreme.

The railroad by which Pompeii is reached, runs for almost its entire length by the sea, whose long volutes of foam advance to unroll themselves upon a beach of blackish sand resembling sifted charcoal. This beach has actually been formed by lava-streams and volcanic cinders; and its deep tone forms a strong contrast with the blue of the sky and the blue of the waters. The earth alone, in that sunny brightness, seems able to retain a shadow.

The villages bordered or traversed by the railway, — Portici, celebrated in one of Auber's operas; Resina; Torre del Græco; Torre dell' Annunziata, whose dwellings with their arcades and terraced roofs attract the traveler's gaze, — have, notwithstanding the intensity of the sunlight, and the southern love for whitewashing, something of a Plutonian and ferruginous character like Birmingham or Manchester: the very dust is black there, — an impalpable soot clings to everything, — one feels that the mighty forge of Vesuvius is panting and smoking only a few paces off.

The three friends left the station at Pompeii, laughing among themselves at the odd commingling of antique and modern ideas suggested by the sign, — "Pompeii Station," — a Græco-Roman city, and a railway depot!

They crossed the cotton-field, with its fluttering white bolls, between the railway and the disinterred city; and at the inn which has been built just without the ancient ramparts, they took a guide, or, more correctly speaking, the guide took them, — a calamity which is not easily avoided in Italy.

It was one of those delightful days, so common in Naples, when the brilliancy of the sunlight and the transparency of the air cause objects to take such hues as in the North would be deemed fabulous, and appear indeed to belong to the world of dreams rather than to that of realities. The Northern visitor who has once looked upon that glow of azure and gold is apt to carry back with him into the depths of his native fogs, an incurable nostalgia.

Having shaken off a corner of her cinder shroud, the resurrected city again rose with her thousand details under a dazzling day. The cone of Vesuvius, furrowed with striæ of blue, rosy, and violet-hued lavas, ruddily bronzed by the sun, towered sharply defined in the background. A thin haze, almost imperceptible in the sunlight, hooded the blunt crest of the mountain: — at first sight it might have been taken for one of those clouds which shadow the brows of lofty peaks on the fairest days. Upon a nearer view, slender threads of white vapor could be perceived rising from the mountain-summit, as from the orifices of a perfuming pan, to reunite above in a light cloud. The volcano, being that day in a good humor, smoked his pipe very peacefully; and but for the example of Pompeii, buried at his feet, no one would ever have suspected him of being by nature any more ferocious than

Montmartre;—on the other side fair hills, with outlines voluptuously undulating like the hips of a woman, barred the horizon; and, further yet, the sea, that in other days bore biremes and triremes under the ramparts of the city, extended its azure boundary.

Of all spectacles, the sight of Pompeii is one of the most surprising:—this sudden backward-leap of nineteen centuries astonishes even the least comprehensive and most prosaic natures;—two paces lead you from the antique life to the life of to-day, and from Christianity to paganism: thus, when the three friends beheld those streets wherein the forms of a vanished past are preserved yet intact, they were strangely and profoundly affected, however well prepared by the study of books and drawings they might have been. Octavian, above all, seemed stricken with stupefaction, and like a man walking in his sleep mechanically followed the guide, without hearing the monotonous nomenclature that the varlet had learned by heart and recited like a lesson.

He gazed wildly on those ruts hollowed out in the cyclopean pavements of the streets by the chariot wheels, and which seem to be of yesterday, so fresh do they appear:—those inscriptions in red letters skillfully traced upon the surfaces of the walls by rapid strokes of the brush (theatrical advertisements, notices of houses to let, votive formulas, signs, announcements of all descriptions — not less curious than a freshly-discovered fragment of the walls of Paris, with advertising bills and placards attached, would prove a thousand years hence for the unknown people of the future); — those houses, whose shattered roofs permit one to penetrate at a glance into all those interior mysteries, — all those domestic details which historians invariably neglect, and whereof the secrets die with dying civilizations; — those fountains that even now seem scarcely dried up; — that forum whose restoration was interrupted by the great catastrophe, and whose architraves and columns all ready cut and sculptured, still seem waiting in their purity of angle to be lifted into place; — those temples, consecrated, in that mythologic age when atheists were yet unknown, to gods that have long ceased to be; — those shops wherein the merchant only is missing; — that public tavern where may still be seen the circular stain of the drinking cups upon the marble; — that barracks with its ochre and minium-painted columns, on which the soldiers scratched grotesque caricatures of battle; — and those juxtaposed double theatres of song and drama which might even now resume their entertainments, were not the companies who performed in them turned long since to clay, and at present occupied perchance in closing the bunghole of a cask, or stopping a crevice in the wall, after the fashion of Alexander's ashes or Cæsar's dust, — according to the melancholy reflections of Hamlet?

Fabio mounted upon the thymele of the tragic theater while Max and Octavian climbed to the upper benches; and there, with extravagant gestures, he commenced to recite whatever poetical fragments came to his memory, much to the terror of the lizards who fled, vibrating their tails, and hid themselves in the joints of the ruined stonework. Although the brazen or earthern vessels, formerly used to reverberate sounds, no longer existed, Fabio's voice sounded none the less full and vibrant.

The guide then conducted them across the open fields which overlie those portions of Pompeii still buried, to the amphitheater situated at the other end of the city. They passed under those trees whose roots plunge down through the roofs of the edifices interred, — displacing tiles, cleaving ceilings asunder, and disjointing columns; — and they traversed the farms where vulgar vegetables sprout above wonders of art — material images of that oblivion wherewith time covers all things.

The amphitheater caused them little surprise: they had seen that of Verona, vaster, and equally well preserved; besides, the arrangement of such antique arenas was as familiar to them as that of those in which bullfights are held in Spain, and which they much resemble save in solidity of construction and beauty of material.

Accordingly they soon retraced their footsteps, and gained the Street of Fortune by a cross-path, listening half-distractedly to the *cicerone*, who named each house they passed by the name which had been given it immediately upon its discovery, owing to some characteristic peculiarity: The House of the Brazen Bull, the House of the Faun, the House of the Ship, the Temple of Fortune, the House of Meleager, the Tavern of Fortune, at the angle of the Consular Road [Via Consularia], the Academy of Music, the Public Market, the Pharmacy, the Surgeon's Shop, the Custom-House, the House of the Vestals, the Inn of Albinus, the Thermopolium; — and so on, until they came to that gate which leads to the Street of the Tombs.

Within the interior arch of this brick-built gate,

— once adorned with statues which have long since disappeared, — may be noticed two deep grooves designed to receive a sliding portcullis, after the style of a mediæval donjon — to which era, indeed, one might have supposed such a defense peculiar.

"Who," exclaimed Max to his friends, "could have dreamed of finding in Pompeii, the Græco-Latin city, a gate so romantically Gothic? Fancy some belated Roman knight, blowing his horn before this entrance, — summoning them to raise the portcullis — like a page of the fifteenth century!"

"There is nothing new under the sun," replied Fabio; "and the aphorism itself is not new, inasmuch as it was formulated by Solomon."

"Perhaps there may be something new under the moon," observed Octavian with a smile of melancholy irony.

"My dear Octavian," cried Max, — who during this little conversation had paused before an inscription traced in rubric upon the outer wall, — "wilt behold the combats of the gladiators? See the advertisement! — Combat and chase on the 5th day of the nones of April; — the masts of the velarium will be rigged; — twenty pairs of gladiators will fight during the nones; — if youfear for the delicacy of your complexion, be assured that the awnings will be spread; — and, as you might in any case prefer to visit the amphitheater early, these men will cut each other's throats in the morning — *matutini erunt:* nothing could be more considerate!"

Thus chatting, the three friends followed that sepulchre-fringed road which, according to our modern ideas, would be a lugubrious avenue for any city, but which had no sad significations for the ancients, whose tombs contained in lieu of hideous corpses only a pinch of dust: — abstract idea of death! Art beautified these last resting-places; and, as Gœthe says, the pagan decorated sarcophagi and funeral urns with the images of life.

It was therefore, doubtless, that Fabio and Max could visit, — with a lively curiosity and a joyous sense of being, such as they could not have felt in any Christian cemetery, — those funeral monuments, all gaily gilded by the sun, which, as they stood by the wayside, seemed still trying to cling to life, and inspired none of those chill feelings of repulsion — none of those fantastic terrors evoked by our modern dismal places of sepulture. They paused before the tomb of Mammia, the public priestess, near which a tree (either a cypress or a willow) is growing;—they seated themselves in the hemicycle of the triclinium, where the funeral feasts were held,—laughing like fortunate heirs;—they read with mock solemnity the epitaphs of Navoleia, Labeon, and the Arria family; silently followed by Octavian, who seemed more deeply touched than his careless companions by the fate of those dead of two thousand years ago.

Thus they came to the villa of Arrius Diomedes, one of the finest residences in Pompeii. It is approached by a flight of brick steps; and after entering the doorway, which is flanked by two small lateral columns, one finds himself in a court resembling the *patio* which occupies the centre of Spanish and Moorish dwellings, and which the ancients termed *impluvium* or *cavædium*:—fourteen columns of brick, overlaid with stucco, once supported on four sides a portico or covered peristyle, not unlike a convent cloister, and beneath which one could walk secure from the rain. This courtyard is paved in mosaic with brick and white marble, which presents a subdued and pleasing effect of color. In its centre a quadrilateral marble basin, which still exists, formerly caught the rain-water that dripped from the roof of the portico. It was a strange experience, — entering thus into the life of the antique world, and treading with well-blacked boots upon the marbles worn smooth by the sandals and buskins of the contemporaries of Augustus and Tiberius.

The cicerone led them through the *exedra* or summer parlor, which opened to the sea, to receive its cooling breezes. It was there that the family received company, and took their siesta during those burning hours when prevailed the mighty zephyr of Africa, laden with languors and storms. He brought them into the basilica, a long open gallery which lighted the various apartments, and in which clients and visitors erst awaited the call of the Nomenclator; — then he conducted them to the white marble terrace, whence extended a broad view of verdant gardens and blue sea; — then he showed them the *Nymphæum*, or Hall of Baths, with its yellow-painted walls, its stucco columns, its mosaic pavement, and its marble bathing-basin which had contained so many of the lovely bodies that have long since passed away like shadows; the *cubiculum* where flitted so many dreams from the Ivory Gate, and whose alcoves contrived in the wall, were once closed by a *conopeum* or curtain, of which the bronze rings still lie upon the floor;

the *tetrastyle*, or Hall of Recreation ; the Chapel of the Lares; the Cabinet of Archives; the Library; the Museum of Paintings; the *gynæceum* or women's apartment, comprising a suite of small chambers, now half fallen into ruin, but whose walls yet bear traces of paintings and arabesques,—like fair cheeks from which the rouge has been but half wiped off.

Having fully inspected all these, they descended to the lower floor;—for the ground is much lower on the garden side than it is on the side of the Street of the Tombs: they traversed eight halls painted in antique red, whereof one has its walls hollowed with architectural niches, after that style of which we have to-day a good example in the vestibule of the Hall of the Ambassadors at the Alhambra; and finally they came to a sort of cave or cellar whose purpose was clearly indicated by eight earthen amphoræ propped up against the wall, and once perfumed, doubtless, like the odes of Horace, with the wines of Crete, Faler-nia, or Massica.

One solitary bright ray of sunshine streamed through a narrow aperture above, half-choked by nettles, whose light-traversed leaves it transformed into emeralds and topazes; and this gay natural detail seemed to smile opportunely through the sadness of the place.

"It was here," observed the cicerone, in his customary indifferent tone, "that among seventeen others, was found the skeleton of the lady whose mould is exhibited at the Naples museum. She wore gold rings; and the shreds of her fine tunic still clung to the mass of cinders which have preserved her shape."

The guide's commonplace phrases deeply affected Octavian. He made the man point out to him the exact spot where the precious remains had been discovered; and had it not been for the restraining presence of his friends, he would have abandoned himself to some extravagant lyrism;—his chest heaved; his eyes glistened with a furtive moisture: though blotted out by twenty centuries of oblivion that catastrophe touched him like a recent misfortune; not even the death of a mistress or a friend could have affected him more profoundly;—and while Max and Fabio had their backs turned, a tear, two thousand years late, fell upon the spot where that woman—with whom he felt he had fallen retrospectively in love—had perished, suffocated by the hot cinders of the volcano.

"Enough of this archæology," cried Fabio:—

"we do not propose to write dissertations upon an ancient jug or a tile of the age of Julius Cæsar, in order to obtain memberships in some provincial academy: these classic souvenirs give me the stomach-ache. Let us go to dinner,—if such a thing be possible—in that picturesque hostelry; where I fear we shall be served with fossil beefsteaks and fresh eggs laid prior to the death of Pliny."

"I will not exclaim with Boileau:—

'Un sot, quelquefois, ouvre un avis important,'"

—exclaimed Max, with a laugh, "that would be ill-mannered; but your idea is a good one. Still, I think it would have been pleasant to banquet here, on some triclinium, reclining after the antique fashion, and waited upon by slaves according to the style of Lucullus or Trimalchio. It is true that I see no oysters from Lake Lucrinus; the turbots and mullets from the Adriatic are wanting; the Apuleian boar can not be had in market; and the loaves and honey-cakes on exhibition in the Naples Museum, lie, hard as stones, beside their green-gray molds;—even raw macaroni sprinkled with *caccia-cavallo*, detestable as it may be, is certainly better than nothing. What does friend Octavian think about it?"

Octavian,—who was deeply regretting that he

had not happened to be in Pompeii on the day of the eruption, so that he might have saved the lady of the gold rings, and thereby merited her love,—had not heard a syllable of this gastronomic conversation. Only the last two words uttered by Max had fallen upon his ears; and feeling no desire to broach a discussion, he gave a random nod of assent, upon which the amicable party retraced the road along the ramparts to the inn.

The table was placed under a sort of open porch which served as a vestibule to the hostelry, whose rough cast walls were decorated with various daubs that the host entitled "Salvator Rosa," "Espagnolet," "Cavalier Massimo,"—and other celebrated names of the Neapolitan school, which he deemed himself bound to extol.

"Venerable host!" cried Fabio, "do not waste your eloquence to no purpose; we are not Englishmen, and we prefer young women to old canvases. Better send us your wine list by that handsome brunette with the velvety eyes whom I just now perceived on the stairway."

Finding that his guests did not belong to the mystifiable class of Philistines and *bourgeois*, the *palforio* ceased to vaunt his gallery in order to glorify his cellar. To begin with, he had all the best vintages: —Chateau Margaux, Grand-Lafitte which had been twice to the Indies, Sillery de Moët, Hochmeyer, Scarlet wine, Port and porter, ale and ginger beer, white and red Lachryma-Christi, Caprian and Falernian.

"What! you have Falernian wine, *animal!*— and put it at the end of your list! — and you dare to subject us to an unendurable œnological litany!"— cried Max, leaping at the inn-keeper's throat with burlesque fury:—"why, you have no sentiment of local color;—you are unworthy to live in this antique neighborhood. Is it even good, this Falernian wine of yours?—was it put in amphoræ under the Consul Plancus — *consule Planco?*"

"I know nothing about the Consul Plancus; and my wine is not put up in amphoræ; but it is good, and worth ten carlins a bottle," answered the inn-keeper.

Day had faded away, and the night came, — a serene, transparent night, clearer, assuredly, than full midday in London; the earth had tints of azure, and the sky silvery reflections of inconceivable sweetness; the air was so still that the flames of the candles on the table did not even oscillate.

A young boy, playing a flute, approached the

table; and, standing there, with his eyes fixed upon the three guests, performed upon his sweet and melodious instrument, one of those popular airs in a minor key which have a penetrating charm.

Perhaps that lad was a direct descendent of the flute-player who marched before Duilius.

"Our repast is assuming quite an antique aspect: we only need some Gaditanian dancing women, and ivy-garlands," exclaimed Max, as he helped himself to a great bumper of Falernian wine.

"I feel myself in the humor for making Latin quotations like a *feuilleton* in the *Débats;*—stanzas of odes come back to my memory," added Max.

"Keep them to yourself!" cried Fabio and Octavian, justly alarmed:—"Nothing is so indigestible as Latin at dinner!"

Among young men with cigars in their mouths and elbows on the table, who find themselves contemplating a certain number of empty flagons,—especially when the wine has been capitally good,—conversation never fails to turn upon women. Each explained his own system; whereof the following is a fair summary:—

Fabio cared only for youth and beauty: voluptuous and positive, he found no pleasure in illusions, and had no preferences in love. A peasant girl would have pleased his fancy as well as a princess, provided she were beautiful; — the body, rather than its apparel, attracted him; he laughed much at certain of his friends who were enamored of so many yards of lace and silk; and he declared it were more rational to fall in love with the stock of a fashionable *marchand des nouveautés*. These opinions, which were rational enough in the main, and which he made no attempt to conceal, caused him to pass for an eccentric.

Max, less of an artist than Fabio, cared only for difficult undertakings, complicated intrigues: he sought resistances to vanquish, virtues to seduce, and played at love, as at a game of chess, with long-premeditated moves, reserved ambuscades, and stratagems worthy of Polybius. In a drawing-room he would always choose the woman who seemed least in sympathy with him, for the object of attack; — to make her pass by skillful transition from aversion to love, afforded him delicious pleasure; — to impose himself upon characters which strove to repel him, and master wills that rebelled against his influence, seemed to him the sweetest of all triumphs. Like those hunters who through rain, sunshine or snow,—through fields and woods, and over plains, pursue with excessive fatigue and unconquerable ardor, some miserable quarry which in three cases out of four they would not deign to eat,—so Max, having once captured his prey, troubled himself no further about it, and at once started off on another chase.

As for Octavian, he confessed that reality itself had little charm for him,—not because he indulged in student-dreams, all moulded of lilies and roses like one of Demoustier's madrigals, but because there were too many prosaic and repulsive details surrounding all beauty; too many doting and decorated fathers; coquettish mothers who wore natural flowers in false hair; ruddy-faced cousins, meditating proposals; ridiculous aunts in love with little dogs. An aquatinta engraving after Horace Vernet or Delaroche, hung up in a woman's room, would have been sufficient to check a growing passion within him. More poetical even than amorous, he wanted a terrace on Isola-Bella, in Lake Maggiore, under the light of a full moon, to frame a rendezvous. He would have wished to elevate his love above the midst of common life, and transport its scenes to the stars. Thus he had by turns fallen fruitlessly and madly in love with all the grand feminine types preserved by history or art. Like Faust, he had loved Helen, and would have wished that the undulations of the ages might bear to him one of those sublime personifications of human desires and dreams, whose forms, to mortal eyes invisible, live immortally beyond Space and Time. He had created for himself an ideal seraglio, with Semiramis, Aspasia, Cleopatra, Diana of Poitiers, Jane of Arragon. At times also he had fallen in love with statues; and one day, passing before the Venus of Milo in the Museum, he cried out passionately: "Oh who will restore thy arms that thou may'st crush me upon thy marble bosom!" At Rome, the sight of a matted mass of long thick human hair, exhumed from an antique tomb, had thrown him into a fantastic delirium: he had attempted, through the medium of a few of those hairs, obtained by a golden bribe from the custodian, and placed in the hands of a clairvoyant of great power, to evoke the shade and form of the dead; but the conducting fluid — the subtle odyle — had evaporated during the lapse of so many years, and the apparition could no more come forth out of the eternal night.

As Fabio had divined before the glass cabinet in the Studii Museum, the imprint discovered in the cellar at the villa of Arrius Diomedes had excited in Octavian wild impulses toward a retrospective ideal: he longed to soar beyond Life and Time and transport himself in spirit to the age of Titus.

Max and Fabio retired to their room; and being somewhat heavy-headed from the classic fumes of the Falernian, were soon sound asleep. Octavian,—who had more than once suffered the full glass to remain before him untasted, not wishing to disturb by a grosser intoxication the poetic drunkenness which boiled in his brain, felt from the agitation of his nerves that sleep would not come to him, and left the hostelry on tiptoe that he might cool his brow and calm his thoughts in the night air.

His feet bore him unawares to the entrance which leads into the dead city: he removed the wooden bar that closed it, and wandered into the ruins beyond.

The moon illuminated the pale houses with her white beams, dividing the streets into double-edged lines of silvery white and bluish shadow. This nocturnal day, with its subdued tints, disguised the degradation of the buildings. The mutilated columns, the facades streaked with fugitive lizards, the roofs crumbled in by the eruption, were less noticeable than when beheld under the clear, raw light of the sun:— the lost parts were completed by the half-tint of shadow; and here and there one brusque beam of light, like a touch of sentiment in a picture-sketch, marked where a whole edifice had crumbled away. The silent Genii of the night seemed to have repaired the fossil city for some representation of fantastic life.

At times Octavian fancied that he saw vague human forms in the shadow: but they vanished the moment they approached the edge of the lighted portion of the street. A low whispering, —an indefinite hum,—floated through the silence. Our promenader at first attributed them to a fluttering in his eyes, to a buzzing in his ears: it might even, he thought, be merely an optical delusion, coupled with the sighing of the sea-breezes, or the flight of some snake or lizard through the nettles;—for in Nature all things live,—even Death; all things make themselves heard,—even Silence. Nevertheless he felt a kind of involuntary terror,—a slight trembling, that might have been caused by the cold night-air, but which made his flesh creep. Could it be that his comrades, actuated by the same impulses as himself, were seeking him among the ruins?

Those dimly-seen forms and those indistinct sounds of footsteps! — might it not have been only Max and Fabio walking and chatting together, who had just disappeared round the corner of a crossroad? But Octavian felt to his dismay, that this very natural explanation could not be true; and the arguments which he made to himself in favor of it were the reverse of convincing. The solitude and the shadow were peopled with invisible beings whom he was disturbing: he had fallen into the midst of a mystery, and it seemed that they were awaiting his departure in order to commence again. Such were the extravagant ideas that floated through his brain, and obtained no little verisimilitude from the hour, the place, and the thousand alarming details which those can well understand who have ever found themselves alone by night in the midst of some vast ruin.

Passing before a house which he had attentively observed during the day, and which the moon shone fully upon, he beheld in perfect integrity a certain portico whereof he had vainly attempted to restore the design in fancy: four Ionic columns, — fluted for half their height and their shafts purple-robed with minium tints, — sustained a cymatium adorned with polychromatic ornaments that the artist seemed only to have completed the day before. Upon one side-wall of the entrance a Laconian molossus,—painted in encaustic, and accompanied by the warning inscription "*Cave canem*," — barked at the moon and the visitor with pictured fury. On the mosaic threshold the word HAVE, in Oscan and Latin characters, saluted the guest with its friendly syllables. The outer surfaces of the walls, tinted with ochre and rubric, were unmarred by a single crack. The house had grown a story higher; and the tiled roof, now surmounted by a bronze acroterium, projected an intact outline against the light blue of the sky, where a few stars were growing pale.

This strange restoration effected between afternoon and evening by some unknown architect, greatly puzzled Octavian, who felt certain of having the same day seen that very house in a lamentable state of ruin. The mysterious reconstructor had labored with great dispatch; for all the neighboring dwellings had the same fresh, new look; all the pillars were coiffed with their capitals; not a single stone, a brick, a pellicle of stucco or a scale of paint was wanting upon the shining surfaces of the facades; — and through the intervals of the peristyles surrounding the marble basin of the cavædium one could catch glimpses of white laurels and bayroses, myrtles and pomegranates. Surely all the historians were mistaken;—the eruption had never taken place: or else the needle of Time had moved backward twenty secular hours upon the dial of Eternity!

In the climax of his astonishment, Octavian commenced to wonder whether he might not actually be sleeping upon his feet, and walking in a dream. He even seriously asked himself whether madness might not be parading its hallucinations before his eyes; but he soon felt himself compelled to admit that he was neither asleep nor mad.

A singular change had taken place in the atmosphere: vague rose-tints were blending through brightening shades of violet with the faintly azure tints of moonlight; the sky commenced to glow brightly along its borders; daylight seemed about to dawn. Octavian took out his watch: it marked the hour of midnight. Fearing that it might have stopped, he pressed the spring of the repeating mechanism: it struck twelve times. It was midnight beyond a doubt, and yet the brightness ever increased;—the moon sank through the azure which became momentarily more and more luminous;—the sun rose!

Then Octavian, to whom all ideas of time had become hopelessly confused, was able to convince himself that he was walking, not through a dead Pompeii,— the chill corpse of a city half-shrouded, — but through a living, youthful, intact Pompeii over which the torrents of burning mud from Vesuvius had never flowed.

An inconceivable prodigy had transported him, a Frenchman of the Nineteenth Century, back to the age of Titus, not in spirit only, but in reality; — or else had called up before him from the depths of the Past a desolated city with its vanished inhabitants,— for a man clothed in the antique fashion had just passed out of a neighboring house.

This man wore his hair short; and his face was closely shaven: he was dressed in a brown tunic and a grayish mantle, the ends of which were well tucked up so as not to impede his movements; — he walked at a rapid gait, bordering upon a run, and passed by Octavian without perceiving him. He carried on his arm a basket made of Spanish broom, and proceeded towards the Forum Nundinarium. He was evidently a slave,— some Davus, going to market beyond a doubt.

The noise of wheels became audible; and an

antique wagon, drawn by white oxen and loaded with vegetables, came along the street. Beside the team walked a peasant, — with legs bare and sunburnt, and feet sandal-shod,— who was clad in a sort of canvas shirt puffed out about the waist: a conical straw hat hanging at his shoulders, and depending from his neck by the chin-band, left his face exposed to view — a type of face unknown in these days; — a forehead low and traversed by salient, knotty lines; hair black and curly; eyes tranquil as those of his oxen; and a neck like that of the rustic Hercules. As he gravely pricked his animals with the goad, his statuesque attitudes would have thrown Ingres into ecstacy.

The peasant perceived Octavian, and appeared surprised; but he proceeded on his way without being able, doubtless, to find any explanation for the appearance of this strange-looking personage; and, in his rustic simplicity, willingly leaving the solution of the enigma to those wiser than himself.

Campanian peasants also appeared on the scene, driving before them asses laden with skins of wine, and ringing their brazen bells: — their physiognomies differed from those of the modern peasants as a medallion differs from a sou.

Gradually the city became peopled, — like one

of those panoramic pictures at first desolate, but which by a sudden change of light, become animated with personages previously invisible.

Octavian's feelings had undergone a change. Only a short time before, amid the deceitful shadows of the night, he had fallen a prey to that uneasiness from which the bravest are not exempt amid such disquieting and fantastic surroundings as reason can not explain. His vague terror had ultimately yielded to a profound stupefaction: the distinctness of his perceptions forbade him to doubt the testimony of his senses; yet what he beheld seemed altogether contrary to reason. Feeling still but half convinced, he sought by the authentication of minor actual details to assure himself that he was not the victim of hallucination. Those figures which passed before his eyes could not be phantoms;—for the living sun shone upon them with unmistakable reality, and their shadows, elongated in the morning light, fell upon the pavement and the walls.

Without the faintest understanding of what had befallen him, Octavian, ravished with delight to find one of his most cherished dreams realized, no longer attempted to resist the fate of his adventure: he abandoned himself to the mystery of these marvels, without any further attempt to explain them; — he averred to himself that since he had been permitted, by virtue of some mysterious power, to live for a few hours in a vanished age, he would not waste time in efforts to solve an incomprehensible problem; and he proceeded fearlessly, gazing to right and left upon this scene at once so old and yet so new to him. But to what epoch of Pompeiian life had he been transported? An ædile inscription engraved upon a wall showed him by the names of public personages there recorded, that it was about the commencement of the reign of Titus, or in the year 79 of our own era. A sudden thought flashed across Octavian's mind; — the woman whose mold he had seen in the museum at Naples must be living, inasmuch as the eruption of Vesuvius by which she had perished took place on the 24th of August in this very year: he might therefore discover her, behold her, speak to her! . . . . . The mad longing which had seized him at the sight of that mass of cinders molded upon a divinely perfect form, was perhaps about to be fully satisfied; for surely naught could be impossible to a love which had had the strength to make Time itself recoil, and the same hour to pass twice through the sand-glass of Eternity!

While Octavian was abandoning himself to

these reflections, beautiful young girls were passing by on their way to the fountains, all balancing urns upon their heads with their white finger-tips; and patricians clad in white togas bordered with purple bands, were proceeding toward the Forum, each followed by an escort of clients. The buyers commenced to throng about the booths, which were all designated by sculptured or pictured signs, and recalled by reason of their shape and small dimensions, the moresque booths of Algiers: — over most of them a glorious phallus of baked and painted clay, together with the inscription, *Hic habitat Felicitas*, testified to superstitious precautions against the evil eye. Octavian also noticed an amulet shop, whose shelves were stocked with horns, bifurcated branches of coral, and little figures of Priapus in gold, — like those worn in Naples even at this day as a safeguard against the *jettatura*; — and he thought to himself that a superstition often outlives a religion.

Following the sidewalk which borders each street in Pompeii (and deprives the English of all claim to this invention), Octavian suddenly found himself face to face with a beautiful young man of about his own age, clad in a saffron colored tunic, and a mantle of snowy linen as supple as cashmere. The sight of Octavian in his frightful modern hat, girthed about with a scanty black frock-coat; his legs confined in pantaloons. and his feet cramped in well-polished boots, seemed to surprise the young Pompeiian in much the same way as one of us would feel astonished to meet on the Boulevard de Gand some Iowa Indian or native of Butocudo, bedecked with his feathers, necklace of bear's-claws, or whimsical tattooing. Nevertheless, being a well-bred young man, he did not burst out laughing in Octavian's face; and pitying the poor barbarian who had lost his way, no doubt, in that Græco-Roman city, he said to him in a soft, clear voice:—

"*Advena, salve!*"

Nothing could be more natural than that an inhabitant of Pompeii, in the reign of the divine, most powerful, and most august Emperor Titus, should speak Latin;—yet Octavian started at hearing this dead tongue in a living mouth. It was then, indeed, that he congratulated himself on having been proficient in his college studies, and taken the honors at the annual examinations. The Latin taught him by the University served him in good stead on that unique occasion; and calling back to mind some souvenirs of his college course, he returned the salutation of the Pompeiian after the style of *De Viris Illustribus* and *Selectæ E Profanis*, in a tolerably intelligible manner, but with a Parisian accent which forced the young man to smile, despite himself.

"Perhaps it will be easier for you to converse in Greek," said the Pompeiian: "I am also acquainted with that language; for I studied at Athens."

"I am even less familiar with Greek than with Latin," replied Octavian; "I am from the land of Gaul,—from Paris,—from Lutetia."

"I know that country. My grandfather served under the great Julius Cæsar in the Gallic wars. But what a strange dress you wear!—the Gauls whom I saw at Rome were not thus attired."

Octavian attempted to explain to the young Pompeiian that twenty centuries had rolled by since the conquest of Gaul by Julius Cæsar, and that the fashions had changed: but he forgot his Latin; and indeed, to tell the truth, he had but little to forget.

"My name is Rufus Holconius; and my house is at your service," said the young man,—"unless, indeed, you prefer the freedom of the tavern: it is hard by the public-house of Albinus, near the gate of the suburb of Augustus Felix and the Inn of Sarinus, son of Publius, just at the second turn;—but if you wish, I will be your guide through this city, in which you do not seem to be acquainted. Young barbarian, I like you,—although you endeavored to impose upon my credulity by pretending that the Emperor Titus, who now reigns, died two thousand years ago, and that the Nazarean (whose infamous followers were plastered with pitch and burned to illuminate Nero's gardens) rules sole master of the deserted heavens whence the great gods have fallen! .... By Pollux!"—he continued as his eyes fell upon a rubric inscription at a street-corner,—"you have just come in good time;—the *Casina* of Plautus, which has quite recently been put upon the stage, will be played to-day: it is a curious and laughable comedy which will amuse you, even if you only comprehend the pantomime of it. Come with me!—it is nearly time for the play already: I will find you a place in the seat set apart for guests and strangers." And Rufus Holconius led the way toward the little comic theatre which the three friends had visited during the day.

The Frenchman and the citizen of Pompeii proceeded along the Street of the Fountains of Abundance, and the Street of the Theatres, passing by the College, the Temple of Isis and the Studio of the Sculptor; and entered the Odeon or Comic Theatre by a lateral vomitory. Through the recommendations of Holconius, Octavian obtained a seat near the proscenium in a part of the theatre corresponding to our private boxes which front upon the stage. All eyes were immediately turned upon him with good-natured curiosity; and a low whispering arose all through the amphitheatre.

The play had not yet commenced; and Octavian profited by the interval to examine the building. The semicircular seats, terminated at either end by a magnificent lion's paw sculptured in Vesuvian lava, receded, broadening as they rose, from an empty space corresponding to our *parterre*, but much narrower and paved in mosaic with Greek marble: the rows of seats widened above one another in regular gradation according to distance; and four stairways, corresponding with the vomitories, and sloping from the base to the summit of the amphitheatre, divided it into five *cunei* or wedge-shaped compartments, with the broad end uppermost. The spectators, — all furnished with tickets consisting of little slips of ivory, upon which were indicated in numerical order the row, division and seat, together with the name of the play and its author,—took their places without confusion. The magistrates, nobility, married men, young folks, and the soldiers—who attracted attention by the gleaming of their bronze helmets,—all occupied different rows of seats.

It was an admirable spectacle:—those beautiful togas and great white mantles displayed in the first row of seats, contrasting with the varicolored garments of the women seated in the circle above, and the gray capes of the populace who were assigned to the upper benches near the columns which supported the roof, and between which were visible glimpses of a sky intensely blue as the azure back-ground of the Panathenæa.

A fine spray aromatized with saffron, fell from the friezes above in imperceptible mist, at once cooling and purifying the air. Octavian thought of the fetid emanations which vitiate the atmosphere of our modern theatres,—theatres so uncomfortable that they may justly be considered places of torture rather than places of amusement; and he found that modern civilization had not, after all, made much progress.

The curtain, sustained by a transverse beam, sank into the depths of the orchestra; the musicians took their seats; and the Prologue appeared in grotesque attire, his face concealed by a frightful mask which fitted the head like a helmet.

Having saluted the audience and demanded applause, the Prologue commenced a merry argumentation. Old plays, he said, were like old wine which improves with age; and *Casina*, so dear to the old, should not be less so to the young: all could take pleasure in it, — some because they were familiar with it; others, because they were not. Moreover the play had been carefully remounted, and should be heard with a cheerful mind,—without thinking about one's debts or one's creditors; for people were not liable to be arrested at the theatre: — it was a happy day; the weather was fair; and the halcyons hovered over the forum.

Then he gave an analysis of the comedy about to be performed by the actors, with that minuteness of detail which shows how little the element of surprise entered into the theatrical pleasures of the ancients: — he told how the aged Stalino, being enamored of his beautiful slave Casina, desired to marry her to his farmer Olympio — a complaisant spouse whose place he himself would fill on the nuptial night; — and how Lycostrata, wife of Stalino, in order to thwart the luxury of her vicious husband, sought to unite Casina in marriage to the groom Chalinus with the further idea of favoring the amours of her son;—in fine, how the deceived Stalino mistook a young slave in disguise for Casina, who, being discovered to be free, and of free birth, espouses the young master whom she loves and by whom she is beloved.

As in a reverie, the young Frenchman watched the actors with their bronze-mouthed masks, exerting themselves upon the stage; the slaves ran hither and thither, feigning great haste; the old man wagged his head and extended his trembling hands; the matron with high words and scornful mien strutted in her importance and quarreled with her husband, to the great delight of the audience. All these personages made their entrances and exits through three doors contrived in the foundation-wall and communicating with the green-room of the actors. The house of Stalino occupied one corner of the stage; and that of his old friend Alcesimus faced it on the opposite side. These decorations, although very well painted, represented the idea of a place rather than the place itself,—like most of the vague scenery of the classic theatres.

When the nuptial procession, pompously escorting the false Casina, entered upon the stage, a mighty burst of laughter, such as Homer attributes to the gods, rang through all the amphitheatre; and thunders of applause evoked the vibrating echoes of the enclosure; — but Octavian heard no more and saw no more of the play.

In the circle of seats occupied by the women, he had just beheld a creature of marvelous beauty. From that moment all the other charming faces which had attracted his attention became eclipsed as the stars before the face of Phœbus: all vanished, all disappeared as in a dream; a mist clouded the circles of seats with their swarming multitudes; and the high-pitched voices of the actors seemed lost in infinite distance.

His heart received a sudden shock as of electricity; and it seemed to him that sparks flew from his breast, when the eyes of that woman turned upon him.

She was dark and pale; her locks, crisp-flowing and black as the tresses of Night, streamed backward over her temples after the fashion of the Greeks; and in her pallid face beamed soft, melancholy eyes, heavy with an indefinable expression of voluptuous sadness and passionate *ennui:* her mouth, with its disdainful curves, protested by the living warmth of its burning crimson against the tranquil pallor of her cheeks; and the curves of her neck presented those pure and beautiful outlines now to be found only in statues. Her arms were naked to the shoulder; and from the peaks of her splendid bosom, which betrayed its superb curves beneath a mauve-rose tunic, fell two graceful folds of drapery that seemed to have been sculptured in marble by Phidias or Cleomenes.

The sight of that bosom, so faultless in contour, so pure in its outlines, magnetically affected Octavian: it seemed to him that those rich curves corresponded perfectly to that hollow mould in the museum at Naples which had thrown him into so ardent a reverie; and from the depths of his heart a voice cried out to him that this woman was indeed the same who had been suffocated in the villa of Arrius Diomedes by the cinders of Vesuvius. What prodigy, then, enabled him to behold her living, and witnessing the performance of the *Casina* of Plautus? But he forbore to seek an explanation of the problem:—for that matter, how did he himself happen to be there? He accepted the fact of his presence as in dreams we never question the intervention of persons actually long dead, but who seem to act nevertheless like living people: besides, his emotion forbade him to reason. For him the Wheel of Time had left its track; and his all-conquering love had chosen its place among the ages passed away. He found himself face to face with his chimera, one of the most unattainable of all,—a retrospective chimera. The cup of his whole life had in a single instant been filled to overflowing.

While gazing upon that face, at once so calm and passionate,—so cold and yet so replete with warmth,—so dead, yet so radiant with life,—he felt that he beheld before him his first and last love,—his cup of supreme intoxication: he felt all the memories of all the women whom he ever believed that he had loved, vanish like impalpable shadows; and his heart became once more virginally pure of all anterior passion. The past was dead within him.

Meanwhile the fair Pompeiian, resting her chin upon the palm of her hand, turned upon Octavian,—though feigning the while to be absorbed in the performance,—the velvet gaze of her nocturnal eyes; and that look fell upon him heavy and burning as a jet of molten lead. Then she turned to whisper some words in the ear of a maid seated at her side.

The performance closed; the crowd poured out of the theatre through the vomitories; and Octavian, disdaining the kindly offices of his friend Holconius, rushed to the nearest doorway. He had scarcely reached the entrance when a hand was lightly laid upon his arm; and a feminine voice exclaimed in tones at once low yet so distinct that not a syllable escaped him: —

"I am Tyche Novaleia, entrusted with the pleasures of Arria Marcella, daughter of Arrius Diomedes: My mistress loves you: follow me."

Arria Marcella had just entered her litter — borne by four strong Syrian slaves, naked to the waist, whose bronze torsos shone under the sunlight. The curtain of the litter was drawn aside; and a pale hand, starred with brilliant rings, waved a friendly signal to Octavian, as though in confirmation of the attendant's words. Then the purple folds of the curtain fell again; and the litter was borne away to the rhythmical sound of the footsteps of the slaves.

Tyche conducted Octavian along winding byways, tripping lightly across the streets over the stepping-stones which connected the foot-paths, and between which the wheels of the chariots rolled; — wending her way through the labyrinth with that certainty which bears witness to thorough familiarity with a city. Octavian noticed that he was traversing portions of Pompeii which had never been excavated, and which were in consequence totally unknown to him. Among so many other equally strange circumstances, this caused him no astonishment. He had made up his mind to be astonished at nothing. Amid all this archaic phantasmagory, which would have driven an antiquarian mad with joy, he no longer saw anything save the dark, deep eyes of Arria Marcella, and that superb bosom which had vanquished even Time, and which Destruction itself had sought to preserve.

They arrived at last before a private gate which opened to admit them, and closed again as soon as they had entered; and Octavian found himself in a court surrounded by Ionic columns of Greek marble, painted bright yellow for half their height, and crowned with capitals relieved with blue and red ornaments. A wreath of aristolochia suspended its great green heart-shaped leaves from the projections of the architecture like a natural arabesque; and near a marble basin framed in plants, one flaming rose towered on a single stalk, — a plume-flower in the midst of natural flowers. The walls were adorned with paneled fresco-work, representing fanciful architecture, or imaginary landscape views.

Octavian obtained only a hurried glance at all these details; for Tyche immediately placed him in the hands of the slaves who had charge of the bath, and who subjected him, notwithstanding his impatience, to all the refinements of the antique *thermæ*. After having submitted to the several necessary degrees of vapor-heat, endured the scraper of the *strigillarius*, and felt cosmetics and perfumed oils poured over him in streams, he was reclothed with a white tunic, and again met Tyche at the opposite door, who took him by the hand, and conducted him into another apartment, gorgeously decorated.

Upon the ceiling were painted,—with a purity of design, brilliancy of color, and freedom of touch which bespoke the hand of a great master rather than of the mere ordinary decorator,—Mars, Venus, and Love: a frieze composed of deer, hares, and birds, disporting themselves amid rich foliage, ran around the apartment above a wainscoting of cipollino marble; the mosaic pavement,—a marvelous work from the hand, perhaps, of Sosimus of Pergamos,—represented banquet-scenes in relief, with a perfection of art which deluded the eye.

At the further end of the hall, upon a biclinium, or double couch, reclined Arria Marcella in an attitude which recalled the reclining woman of Phidias, upon the pediment of the Parthenon: her pearl-embroidered shoes lay at the foot of the couch; and her beautiful bare foot, purer and whiter than marble, extended from beneath the light covering of byssus which had been thrown over her.

Two earrings, fashioned in the form of balance-scales, and bearing pearls in either scale, trembled in the light against her pale cheeks: a necklace of golden balls, with pear-shaped pendants attached, hung down upon her bosom, which the negligent folds of a straw-colored peplum, with a Greek border in black lines, had left half uncovered; a gold-and-black fillet passed and glittered here and there through her ebon tresses,—for she had changed her dress upon returning from the theatre;—and around her arm, like the asp about the arm of Cleopatra, a golden serpent with jeweled eyes entwined itself in many folds, and sought to bite its own tail.

Close by the double couch had been placed a little table, supported upon griffins' paws, inlaid with mother-of-pearl, and freighted with different viands served upon dishes of silver and gold, or of earthenware, enameled with costly paintings. A Phasian bird, cooked in its plumage, was visible; and also various fruits which are seldom seen together in any one season.

Everything seemed to indicate that a guest was expected; the floor had been strewn with fresh flowers; and the amphoræ of wine were plunged into urns filled with snow.

Arria Marcella made a sign to Octavian to lie down upon the biclinium beside her and share her repast. Half-maddened with astonishment and love, the young man took at random a few mouthfuls from the plates extended to him by little curly-haired Asiatic slaves, who wore short tunics. Arria did not eat; but she frequently raised to her lips an opal-tinted myrrhine vase filled with a wine darkly purple like thickened blood;—as she drank, an imperceptible rosy vapor mounted to her cheeks from her heart,—the heart that had never throbbed for so many centuries: nevertheless, her bare arm, which Octavian lightly touched in the act of raising his cup, was cold as the skin of a serpent or the marble of a tomb.

"Ah! when you paused in the Studii Museum, to contemplate the mass of hardened clay which still preserves my form,"—exclaimed Arria Marcella, turning her long, liquid eyes upon Octavian,—"and your thoughts were ardently directed to me, my spirit felt it in that world where I float, invisible to vulgar eyes: faith makes God; and love makes woman. One is truly dead only when one is no longer loved; your desire has restored life to me; — the mighty invocation of your heart overcame the dim distances that separated us."

The idea of amorous invocation which the young woman spoke of, entered into the philosophic beliefs of Octavian, beliefs which we ourselves are not far from sharing.

In effect, nothing dies; all things are eternal: no power can annihilate that which once had being. Every action, every word, every thought which has fallen into the universal Ocean of being, therein creates circles which travel, and increase in traveling, even to the confines of Eternity. To vulgar eyes only do natural forms disappear; and the spectres which have thence detached themselves people Infinity: — Paris, in some unknown region of Space, continues to carry off Helen; — the galley of Cleopatra still floats down with swelling sails of silk upon the azure current of an ideal Cydnus; — a few passionate and powerful minds have been able to recall before them ages apparently long passed away, and to restore to life personages dead to all the world beside. Faust has had for his mistress the daughter of Tyndarus, and conducted her to his gothic castle in the depths of the mysterious abysses of Hades. Octavian had been able to live a day under the reign of Titus, and to make himself beloved of Arria Marcella, daughter of Arrius Diomedes,—she who was at that moment lying upon an antique couch beside him in a city destroyed for all the rest of the world.

"From my disgust with other women," replied Octavian, — "from the unconquerable reverie which attracted me toward its radiant shapes as to stars that lure on, I knew that I could never love save beyond the confines of Time and Space. It was you that I awaited; and that frail vestige of your being, preserved by the curiosity of men, has by its secret magnetism placed me in communication with your spirit. I know not if you be a dream or a reality, a phantom or a woman; —if, like Ixion, I press but a cloud to my cheated breast;—if I am only the victim of some vile spell of sorcery: but what I do truly know is that you will be my first and my last love."

"May Eros, son of Aphrodite, hear your promise," returned Arria Marcella, dropping her head upon the shoulder of her lover, who lifted her in a passionate embrace:—"Oh, press me to your young breast!—envelop me with your warm breath: I am cold through having remained so long without love." And against his heart Octavian felt that beautiful bosom rise and fall, whose mould he had that very morning admired through the glass of a cabinet in the museum:—the coolness of that beautiful flesh penetrated him through his tunic and made him burn. The gold-and-black fillet had become detached from Arria's head, passionately thrown back; and her hair streamed like a black river over the purple pillow.

The slaves had removed the table. A confused sound of sighs and kisses was alone audible. The pet quails, indifferent to this amorous scene, plundered the crumbs of the banquet upon the mosaic pavement; uttering sharp little cries.

Suddenly the brazen rings of the curtain which closed the entrance to the apartment slided back upon the curtain-rod; and an aged man of stern demeanor, and wrapped in a great brown mantle, appeared upon the threshold. His grey beard was divided into two points after the manner of the Nazareans: his face seemed furrowed by the suffering of ascetic mortifications; and a little cross of black wood was suspended from his neck, leaving no doubt as to his faith:—he belonged to the sect, then new, of the Disciples of Christ.

On perceiving him, Arria Marcella, overwhelmed with confusion, hid her face in the folds of her mantle, like a bird which puts its head under its wing at the approach of an enemy from whom it cannot escape, to save itself at least from the horror of seeing him; — while Octavian, rising on his elbow, stared fixedly at the provoking being who had thus abruptly interrupted his happiness.

"Arria, Arria!" exclaimed the austere personage in a voice of reproach, — "did not your lifetime suffice for your misconduct; and must your infamous amours encroach upon centuries to which they do not belong? Can you not leave the living in their sphere? Have not your ashes cooled since the day when you perished unrepentant beneath the rain of volcanic fire? So, then, even two thousand years have not sufficed to calm your passion; and your voracious arms still draw to your heartless breast of marble the poor madmen whom your philters have intoxicated!"

"Arrius, father! mercy!—do not crush me, in the name of that morose religion which was never mine!—I believed in our ancient gods, who loved life and youth and beauty and pleasure:—do not hurl me back into pale nothingness!—let me enjoy this life that love has given back to me!"

"Silence! impious woman!—speak not to me of your gods, which are demons. Let this man, whom you have fettered with your impure seductions, depart hence: draw him no more beyond the circle of that life which God measured out for him;—return to the Limbo of Paganism with your Asiatic, Roman, or Greek lovers. Young Christian, forsake that Larva, who would seem to you more hideous than Empousa or Phorkyas, could you but see her as she is!"

Pale and frozen with horror, Octavian tried to speak; but his voice clung to his throat, according to the expression of Virgil.

"Will you obey me, Arria?" imperiously cried the tall old man.

"No! never!" responded Arria, with flashing eyes, dilated nostrils, and passion-trembling lips. —as she suddenly encircled the body of Octavian with her beautiful statuesque arms, cold, hard. and rigid as marble. Her furious beauty, enhanced by the struggle, shone forth at that supreme moment, with supernatural brightness, as though to leave its imperishable souvenir with her young lover.

"Then, unhappy woman," exclaimed the old man, "I must needs employ extreme measures, and render your nothingness palpable and visible to this fascinated child." And in a voice of command, he pronounced a formula of exorcism that banished from Arria's cheeks the purple tints with which the black wine from the myrrhine vase had suffused them.

At the same moment, the distant bell of one of those hamlets which border the sea-coast, or lie hidden in the mountain hollows, rang out the first peal of the Angelus.

A sob of agony burst from the broken heart of the young woman at that sound. Octavian felt her encircling arms untwine; the draperies which covered her sank fold on fold, as though the contours which sustained them had suddenly given way; and the wretched night-walker beheld on the banquet-couch beside him only a handful of cinders mingled with a few fragments of calcined bones, among which gold bracelets and jewelry glittered,—together with such other shapeless remains as were found in excavating the villa of Arrius Diomedes.

He uttered one fearful cry, and became insensible.

The old man had disappeared; the sun rose; and the hall, so brilliantly decorated but a short time before, became only a dismantled ruin.

---

After a heavy slumber, inspired by the libations of the previous evening, Max and Fabio started from their sleep, and at once called their comrade,—whose room adjoined their own,—with one of those burlesque rallying cries which are so commonly made use of by travelers:—Octavian, for the best of reasons, returned no answer. Fabio and Max, hearing no response, entered their friend's chamber and perceived that the bed had not been disturbed.

"He must have fallen asleep in some chair," said Fabio, "without being able to get to bed; for our good Octavian can not bear much liquor: and most likely he is taking an early walk to dissipate the fumes of the wine in the fresh morning air."

"But he did not drink much," returned Max, in a thoughtful manner. "All this seems very strange to me: let us go and find him!"

Accompanied by the cicerone, the two friends searched all the streets, squares, crossroads, and alleys of Pompeii,—entering every curious building where they thought Octavian might be occupied in copying a painting or taking down an inscription, and finally discovered him lying insensible upon the disjointed mosaic pavement of a small ruined chamber. They had much difficulty in restoring him to consciousness; and, on reviving, his only explanation of the circumstance was that he had taken a fancy to see Pompeii by moonlight, and had been seized with a sudden faintness, which would doubtless result in nothing serious.

The little party returned by rail to Naples, as they had come; and the same evening, from their private box at the San Carlo, Max and Fabio watched through their opera glasses a troupe of nymphs dancing in a ballet, under the leadership of Amalia Ferraris, the *danseuse* then in vogue, —all wearing under their gauzy skirts frightful green drawers, which made them look like so many frogs stung by a tarantula. Pale, with woful eyes, and the general air of one crushed by suffering, Octavian seemed to doubt the reality of what transpired upon the stage,—so difficult did he find it to resume the sentiments of real life after the marvelous adventures of the night.

From the time of that visit to Pompeii, Octavian fell into a dismal melancholy, which the good-humored pleasantry of his companions rather aggravated than soothed:—the image of Arria Marcella haunted him incessantly; and the sad termination of his fantastic good-fortune had never destroyed its charm.

Unable to contain his misery, he returned secretly to Pompeii, and once again wandered among the ruins by moonlight as before,—his heart palpitating with maddening hope; but the hallucination never returned:—he saw only the lizards fleeing over the stones; he heard only the screams of the startled night-birds: he met his friend Rufus Holconius no more; — Tyche came not to lay her supple hand upon his arm; — Arria Marcella obstinately slumbered in her dust.

Abandoning all hope, Octavian finally married a charming young English girl, who is madly in love with him. He is perfectly well behaved to his wife; yet Ellen, with that subtle instinct of the heart which nothing can deceive, feels that her husband is enamored of another; but of whom? That is a mystery which the most unflagging watchfulness can not enable her to unravel. Octavian never entertains actresses;—in society he addresses to women only the most common place gallantries: he even returned with the greatest coldness, the marked advances of a certain Russian princess, celebrated for her beauty and her coquetry. A secret drawer, opened during her husband's absence, afforded no confirmation of infidelity to Ellen's suspicions. But how could she permit herself to be jealous of Arria Marcella, daughter of Arrius Diomedes, the freedman of Tiberius?

# THE MUMMY'S FOOT.

I had entered, in an idle mood, the shop of one of those curiosity-venders, who are called *marchands de bric-a-brac* in that Parisian *argot* which is so perfectly unintelligible elsewhere in France.

You have doubtless glanced occasionally through the windows of some of these shops, which have become so numerous now that it is fashionable to buy antiquated furniture, and that every petty stockbroker thinks he must have his *chambre au moyen âge.*

There is one thing there which clings alike to the shop of the dealer in old iron, the wareroom of the tapestry maker, the laboratory of the chemist, and the studio of the painter:—in all those gloomy dens where a furtive daylight filters in through the window-shutters the most manifestly ancient thing is dust;—the cobwebs are more authentic than the guimp laces; and the old pear-tree furniture on exhibition is actually younger than the mahogany which arrived but yesterday from America.

The warehouse of my bric-a-brac dealer was

a veritable Capharnaum; all ages and all nations seemed to have made their rendezvous there; an Etruscan lamp of red clay stood upon a Boule cabinet, with ebony panels, brightly striped by lines of inlaid brass; a duchess of the court of Louis XV nonchalantly extended her fawn-like feet under a massive table of the time of Louis XIII, with heavy spiral supports of oak, and carven designs of chimeras and foliage intermingled.

Upon the denticulated shelves of several sideboards glittered immense Japanese dishes with red and blue designs relieved by gilded hatching; side by side with enameled works by Bernard Palissy, representing serpents, frogs, and lizards in relief.

From disemboweled cabinets escaped cascades of silver-lustrous Chinese silks and waves of tinsel, which an oblique sunbeam shot through with luminous beads; while portraits of every era, in frames more or less tarnished, smiled through their yellow varnish.

The striped breastplate of a damascened suit of Milanese armor glittered in one corner; Loves and Nymphs of porcelain; Chinese Grotesques, vases of *céladon* and crackle-ware; Saxon and old Sevres cups, encumbered the shelves and nooks of the apartment.

The dealer followed me closely through the tortuous way contrived between the piles of furniture; warding off with his hand the hazardous sweep of my coat-skirts; watching my elbows with the uneasy attention of an antiquarian and a usurer.

It was a singular face, that of the merchant:—an immense skull, polished like a knee, and surrounded by a thin aureole of white hair, which brought out the clear salmon tint of his complexion all the more strikingly, lent him a false aspect of patriarchal *bonhomie*, counteracted, however, by the scintillation of two little yellow eyes which trembled in their orbits like two louis-d'or upon quicksilver. The curve of his nose presented an aquiline silhouette, which suggested the Oriental or Jewish type. His hands,—thin, slender, full of nerves which projected like strings upon the finger-board of a violin, and armed with claws like those on the terminations of bats' wings,—shook with senile trembling; but those convulsively agitated hands became firmer than steel pincers or lobsters' claws when they lifted any precious article,—an onyx cup, a Venetian glass, or a dish of Bohemian crystal. This strange old man had an aspect so thoroughly rabbinical and cabalistic that he would have been burnt on the mere testimony of his face three centuries ago.

"Will you not buy something from me to-day, sir? Here is a Malay kreese with a blade undulating like flame: look at those grooves contrived for the blood to run along, those teeth set backward so as to tear out the entrails in withdrawing the weapon,—it is a fine character of ferocious arm, and will look well in your collection: this two-handed sword is very beautiful,—it is the work of Josepe de la Hera; and this *colichemarde*, with its fenestrated guard,—what a superb specimen of handicraft!"

"No; I have quite enough weapons and instruments of carnage;—I want a small figure, something which will suit me as a paper-weight; for I cannot endure those trumpery bronzes which the stationers sell, and which may be found on everybody's desk."

The old gnome foraged among his ancient wares, and finally arranged before me some antique bronzes,—so-called, at least; fragments of malachite; little Hindoo or Chinese idols,—a kind of poussah-toys in jade-stone, representing the incarnations of Brahma or Vishnoo, and wonderfully appropriate to the very undivine office of holding papers and letters in place.

I was hesitating between a porcelain dragon, all constellated with warts,—its mouth formidable with bristling tusks and ranges of teeth,—and an abominable little Mexican fetish, representing the god Vitziliputzili *au naturel;* when I caught sight of a charming foot, which I at first took for a fragment of some antique Venus.

It had those beautiful ruddy and tawny tints that lend to Florentine bronze that warm living look so much preferable to the gray-green aspect of common bronzes, which might easily be mistaken for statues in a state of putrefaction: satiny gleams played over its rounded forms, doubtless polished by the amorous kisses of twenty centuries; for it seemed a Corinthian bronze, a work of the best era of art,—perhaps moulded by Lysippus himself.

"That foot will be my choice," I said to the merchant, who regarded me with an ironical and saturnine air, and held out the object desired that I might examine it more fully.

I was surprised at its lightness; it was not a foot of metal, but in sooth a foot of flesh, —an embalmed foot,—a mummy's foot: on examining it still more closely the very grain of the skin, and the almost imperceptible lines impressed upon it by the texture of the bandages, became perceptible. The toes were slender and delicate, and terminated by perfectly formed nails, pure and transparent as agates; the great toe, slightly separated from the rest, afforded a happy contrast, in the antique style, to the position of the other toes, and lent it an aeriel lightness,—the grace of a bird's foot;—the sole, scarcely streaked by a few almost imperceptible cross lines, afforded evidence that it had never touched the bare ground, and had only come in contact with the finest matting of Nile rushes, and the softest carpets of panther skin.

"Ha, ha!—you want the foot of the Princess Hermonthis,"—exclaimed the merchant, with a strange giggle, fixing his owlish eyes upon me—"ha, ha, ha!—for a paper-weight!—an original idea!—artistic idea! Old Pharaoh would certainly have been surprised had some one told him that the foot of his adored daughter would be used for a paper-weight after he had had a mountain of granite hollowed out as a receptacle for the triple coffin, painted and gilded,—covered with hieroglyphics and beautiful paintings of the Judgment of Souls,"—continued the queer little merchant, half audibly, as though talking to himself!

"How much will you charge me for this mummy fragment?"

"Ah, the highest price I can get; for it is a superb piece: if I had the match of it you could not have it for less than five hundred francs;—the daughter of a Pharaoh! nothing is more rare."

"Assuredly that is not a common article; but, still, how much do you want? In the first place let me warn you that all my wealth consists of just five louis: I can buy anything that costs five louis, but nothing dearer;—you might search my vest pockets and most secret drawers without even finding one poor five-franc piece more."

"Five louis for the foot of the Princess Hermonthis! that is very little, very little indeed; 'tis an authentic foot," muttered the merchant, shaking his head, and imparting a peculiar rotary motion to his eyes. "Well, take it, and I will give you the bandages into the bargain," he added, wrapping the foot in an ancient damask rag—"very fine! real damask—Indian damask which has never been redyed; it is strong, and yet it is soft," he mumbled, stroking the frayed tissue with his fingers, through the trade-acquired habit which moved him to praise even an object of so little value that he himself deemed it only worth the giving away.

He poured the gold coins into a sort of mediæval alms-purse hanging at his belt, repeating:—

"The foot of the Princess Hermonthis, to be used for a paper-weight!"

Then turning his phosphorescent eyes upon me, he exclaimed in a voice strident as the crying of a cat which has swallowed a fish-bone:

"Old Pharaoh will not be well pleased: he loved his daughter,— the dear man!"

"You speak as if you were a contemporary of his: you are old enough, goodness knows! but you do not date back to the Pyramids of Egypt," I answered, laughingly, from the threshold.

I went home, delighted with my acquisition.

With the idea of putting it to profitable use as soon as possible, I placed the foot of the divine Princess Hermonthis upon a heap of papers scribbled over with verses, in themselves an undecipherable mosaic work of erasures; articles freshly began; letters forgotten, and posted in the table drawer instead of the letter-box,—an error to which absent-minded people are peculiarly liable. The effect was charming, *bizarre* and romantic.

Well satisfied with this embellishment, I went out with the gravity and pride becoming one who feels that he has the ineffable advantage over all the passers-by whom he elbows, of possessing a piece of the Princess Hermonthis, daughter of Pharaoh.

I looked upon all who did not possess, like myself, a paper weight so authentically Egyptian, as very ridiculous people; and it seemed to me that the proper occupation of every sensible man should consist in the mere fact of having a mummy's foot upon his desk.

Happily I met some friends, whose presence distracted me in my infatuation with this new acquisition: I went to dinner with them; for I could not very well have dined with myself.

When I came back that evening, with my brain slightly confused by a few glasses of wine, a vague whiff of Oriental perfume delicately titillated my olfactory nerves: the heat of the room had warmed the natron, bitumen, and myrrh in which the *paraschistes*, who cut open the bodies of the dead, had bathed the corpse of the princess;—it was a perfume at once sweet and penetrating,—a perfume that four thousand years had not been able to dissipate.

The Dream of Egypt was Eternity: her odors have the solidity of granite, and endure as long.

I soon drank deeply from the black cup of sleep: for a few hours all remained opaque to me; Oblivion and Nothingness inundated me with their somber waves.

Yet light gradually dawned upon the darkness of my mind: dreams commenced to touch me softly in their silent flight.

The eyes of my soul were opened; and I beheld my chamber as it actually was: I might have believed myself awake, but for a vague consciousness which assured me that I slept, and that something fantastic was about to take place.

The odor of the myrrh had augmented in intensity: and I felt a slight headache, which I very naturally attributed to several glasses of champagne that we had drank to the unknown gods and our future fortunes.

I peered through my room with a feeling of expectation which I saw nothing to justify: every article of furniture was in its proper place; the lamp, softly shaded by its globe of ground crystal, burned upon its bracket; the water-color sketches shone under their Bohemian glass; the curtains hung down languidly; everything wore an aspect of tranquil slumber.

After a few moments, however, all this calm interior appeared to become disturbed; the woodwork cracked stealthily; the ash-covered log suddenly emitted a jet of blue flame; and the disks of the pateras seemed like great metallic eyes, watching, like myself, for the things which were about to happen.

My eyes accidentally fell upon the desk where I had placed the foot of the Princess Hermonthis.

Instead of remaining quiet—as behooved a foot which had been embalmed for four thousand years,—it commenced to act in a nervous manner; contracted itself, and leaped over the papers like a startled frog; — one would have imagined that it had suddenly been brought into contact with a galvanic battery: I could distinctly hear the dry sound made by its little heel, hard as the hoof of a gazelle.

I became rather discontented with my acquisition, inasmuch as I wished my paper-weights to be of a sedentary disposition, and thought it very unnatural that feet should walk about without legs; and I commenced to experience a feeling closely akin to fear.

Suddenly I saw the folds of my bed-curtain stir; and heard a bumping sound, like that caused by some person hopping on one foot across the floor. I must confess I became alternately hot and cold; that I felt a strange wind chill my back; and that my suddenly-rising hair caused my night-cap to execute a leap of several yards.

The bed-curtains opened and I beheld the strangest figure imaginable before me.

It was a young girl of a very deep coffee-brown complexion, like the bayadere Amani, and possessing the purest Egyptian type of perfect beauty: her eyes were almond-shaped and oblique, with eyebrows so black that they seemed blue; her nose was exquisitely chiseled, almost Greek in its delicacy of outline; and she might indeed have been taken for a Corinthian statue of bronze, but for the prominence of her cheek-bones and the slightly African fullness of her lips, which compelled one to recognize her as belonging beyond all doubt to the hieroglyphic race which dwelt upon the banks of the Nile.

Her arms, slender and spindle-shaped, like those of very young girls, were encircled by a peculiar kind of metal bands, and bracelets of glass beads; her hair was all twisted into little cords; and she wore upon her bosom a little idol-figure of green paste, bearing a whip with seven lashes, which proved it to be an image of Isis: her brow was adorned with a shining plate of gold; and a few traces of paint relieved the coppery tint of her cheeks.

As for her costume, it was very odd indeed.

Fancy a *pagne* or skirt all formed of little strips of material bedizened with red and black hieroglyphics, stiffened with bitumen, and apparently belonging to a freshly unbandaged mummy.

In one of those sudden flights of thought so common in dreams I heard the hoarse falsetto of the *bric-a-brac* dealer, repeating like a monotonous refrain, the phrase he had uttered in his shop with so enigmatical an intonation:

"Old Pharaoh will not be well pleased: he loved his daughter, the dear man!"

One strange circumstance, which was not at all calculated to restore my equanimity, was that the apparition had but one foot; the other was broken off at the ankle!

She approached the table where the foot was starting and fidgetting about more than ever; and there supported herself upon the edge of the desk. I saw her eyes fill with pearly-gleaming tears.

Although she had not as yet spoken, I fully comprehended the thoughts which agitated her: she looked at her foot—for it was indeed her own—with an exquisitely graceful expression of coquettish sadness; but the foot leaped and ran hither and thither, as though impelled on steel springs.

Twice or thrice she extended her hand to seize it, but could not succeed.

Then commenced between the Princess Hermonthis and her foot—which appeared to be endowed with a special life of its own—a very fantastic dialogue in a most ancient Coptic tongue, such as might have been spoken thirty centuries ago in the syrinxes of the land of Ser: luckily I understood Coptic perfectly well that night.

The Princess Hermonthis cried, in a voice sweet and vibrant as the tones of a crystal bell:

"Well, my dear little foot, you always flee from me; yet I always took good care of you. I bathed you with perfumed water in a bowl of alabaster; I smoothed your heel with pumice-stone mixed with palm oil; your nails were cut with golden scissors and polished with a hippopotamus tooth; I was careful to select *tatbebs* for you, painted and embroidered and turned up at the toes, which were the envy of all the young girls in Egypt: you wore on your great toe rings bearing the device of the sacred Scarabæus; and you supported one of the lightest bodies that a lazy foot could sustain."

The foot replied in a pouting and chagrined tone:—

"You know well that I do not belong to myself any longer:—I have been bought and paid for: the old merchant knew what he was about: he bore you a grudge for having refused to espouse him:—this is an ill turn which he has done you. The Arab who violated your royal coffin in the subterranean pits of the necropolis of Thebes was sent thither by him: he desired to prevent you from being present at the reunion of the shadowy nations in the cities below. Have you five pieces of gold for my ransom?"

"Alas, no!"—my jewels, my rings, my purses of gold and silver, were all stolen from me," answered the Princess Hermonthis, with a sob.

"Princess," I then exclaimed, "I never retained anybody's foot unjustly;—even though you have not got the five louis which it cost me, I present it to you gladly: I should feel unutterably wretched to think that I were the cause of so amiable a person as the Princess Hermonthis being lame."

I delivered this discourse in a royally gallant, troubadour tone which must have astonished the beautiful Egyptian girl.

She turned a look of deepest gratitude upon me; and her eyes shone with bluish gleams of light.

She took her foot,—which surrendered itself willingly this time,—like a woman about to put on her little shoe; and adjusted it to her leg with much skill.

This operation over, she took a few steps about the room; as though to assure herself that she was really no longer iame.

"Ah, how pleased my father will be!—he who was so unhappy because of my mutilation; and who from the moment of my birth, set a whole nation at work to hollow me out a tomb so deep that he might preserve me intact until that last day, when souls must be weighed in the balance of Amenthi! Come with me to my father; — he will receive you kindly; for you have given me back my foot."

I thought this proposition natural enough. I arrayed myself in a dressing-gown of large-flowered pattern, which lent me a very Pharaonic aspect; hurriedly put on a pair of Turkish slippers; and informed the Princess Hermonthis that I was ready to follow her.

Before starting, Hermonthis took from her neck the little idol of green paste, and laid it on the scattered sheets of paper which covered the table.

"It is only fair," she observed, smilingly, "that I should replace your paper-weight."

She gave me her hand, which felt soft and cold, like the skin of a serpent; and we departed.

We passed for some time with the velocity of an arrow through a fluid and greyish expanse, in which half-formed silhouettes flitted swiftly by us, to right and left.

For an instant we saw only sky and sea.

A few moments later obelisks commenced to tower in the distance: pylons and vast flights of steps guarded by sphinxes became clearly outlined against the horizon.

We had reached our destination

The princess conducted me to a mountain of rose-colored granite, in the face of which appeared an opening so narrow and low that it would have been difficult to distinguish it from the fissures in the rock, had not its location been marked by two stelæ wrought with sculptures.

Hermonthis kindled a torch, and led the way before me.

We traversed corridors hewn through the living rock: their walls, covered with hieroglyphics and paintings of allegorical processions, might well have occupied thousands of arms for thousands of years in their formation;—these corridors, of interminable length, opened into square chambers, in the midst of which pits had been contrived, through which we descended by cramp-irons or spiral stairways;—these pits again conducted us into other chambers, opening into other corridors, likewise decorated with painted sparrow-hawks, serpents coiled in circles, the symbols of the *tau* and *pedum*,—prodigious works of art which no living eye can ever examine,—interminable legends of granite which only the dead have time to read through all eternity.

At last we found ourselves in a hall so vast, so enormous, so immeasurable, that the eye could not reach its limits; files of monstrous columns stretched far out of sight on every side, between which twinkled livid stars of yellowish flame;—points of light which revealed further depths incalculable in the darkness beyond.

The Princess Hermonthis still held my hand, and graciously saluted the mummies of her acquaintance.

My eyes became accustomed to the dim twilight; and objects became discernible.

I beheld the kings of the subterranean races seated upon thrones,—grand old men, though dry, withered, wrinkled like parchment, and blackened with naphtha and bitumen,—all wearing *pshents* of gold, and breast-plates and gorgets glittering with precious stones; their eyes immovably fixed like the eyes of sphinxes, and their long beards whitened by the snow of centuries. Behind them stood their peoples, in the stiff and constrained posture enjoined by Egyptian art, all eternally preserving the attitude prescribed by the hieratic code. Behind these nations, the cats, ibixes, and crocodiles cotemporary with them,—rendered monstrous of aspect by their swathing bands,—mewed, flapped their wings, or extended their jaws in a saurian giggle.

All the Pharaohs were there—Cheops, Chephrenes, Psammetichus, Sesostris, Amenotaph—all the dark rulers of the pyramids and syrinxes: — on yet higher thrones sat Chronos and Xixouthros, — who was contemporary with the deluge; and Tubal Cain, who reigned before it.

The beard of King Xixouthros had grown seven times around the granite table, upon which he leaned, lost in deep reverie,— and buried in dreams.

Further back, through a dusty cloud, I beheld dimly the seventy-two Preadamite Kings, with their seventy-two peoples—forever passed away.

After permitting me to gaze upon this bewildering spectacle a few moments, the Princess Hermonthis presented me to her father Pharaoh, who favored me with a most gracious nod.

"I have found my foot again! — I have found my foot!" cried the princess, clapping her little hands together with every sign of frantic joy: "it was this gentleman who restored it to me."

The races of Kemi, the races of Nahasi, — all the black, bronzed, and copper-colored nations repeated in chorus:

"The Princess Hermonthis has found her foot again!"

Even Xixouthros himself was visibly affected.

He raised his heavy eyelids, stroked his moustache with his fingers, and turned upon me a glance weighty with centuries.

"By Oms, the dog of Hell, and Tmei, daughter of the Sun and of Truth! this is a brave and worthy lad!" exclaimed Pharaoh, pointing to me with his scepter which was terminated with a lotus-flower.

"What recompense do you desire?"

Filled with that daring inspired by dreams in which nothing seems impossible, I asked him for the hand of the Princess Hermonthis; — the hand seemed to me a very proper antithetic recompense for the foot.

Pharaoh opened wide his great eyes of glass in astonishment at my witty request.

"What country do you come from? and what is your age?"

"I am a Frenchman; and I am twenty-seven years old, venerable Pharaoh."

"—— Twenty-seven years old! and he wishes to espouse the Princess Hermonthis, who is thirty centuries old!"—cried out at once all the Thrones and all the Circles of Nations.

Only Hermonthis herself did not seem to think my request unreasonable.

"If you were even only two thousand years old," replied the ancient King, "I would willingly give you the Princess; but the disproportion is too great; and, besides, we must give our daughters husbands who will last well: you do not know how to preserve yourselves any longer; even those who died only fifteen centuries ago are already no more than a handful of dust; — behold! my flesh is solid as basalt; my bones are bars of steel!

"I will be present on the last day of the world, with the same body and the same features which I had during my life-time: my daughter Hermonthis will last longer than a statue of bronze.

"Then the last particles of your dust will have been scattered abroad by the winds; and even Isis herself, who was able to find the atoms of Osiris, would scarce be able to recompose your being.

"See how vigorous I yet remain, and how mighty is my grasp," he added, shaking my hand in the English fashion with a strength that buried my rings in the flesh of my fingers.

He squeezed me so hard that I awoke, and found my friend Alfred shaking me by the arm to make me get up.

"O you everlasting sleeper! — must I have you carried out into the middle of the street, and fireworks exploded in your ears? It is after noon; don't you recollect your promise to take me with you to see M. Aguado's Spanish pictures?"

"God! I forgot all, all about it," I answered, dressing myself hurriedly; "we will go there at once; I have the permit lying there on my desk."

I started to find it;—but fancy my astonishment when I beheld, instead of the mummy's foot I had purchased the evening before, the little green paste idol left in its place by the princess Hermonthis!

# OMPHALE: A ROCOCO STORY.

---

My uncle, the Chevalier de . . ., resided in a small mansion which looked out upon the dismal Rue de Tournelles on one side, and the equally dismal Boulevard St. Antoine upon the other. Between the Boulevard and the house itself a few ancient elm-trees, eaten alive by mosses and insects, piteously extended their skeleton arms from the depth of a species of sink surrounded by high black walls. Some emaciated flowers hung their heads languidly, like young girls in consumption; waiting for a ray of sunshine to dry their half-rotten leaves. Weeds had invaded the walks, which were almost undistinguishable owing to the length of time that had elapsed since they were last raked. One or two goldfish floated rather than swam in a basin covered with duckweed and half-choked by water plants.

My uncle called that his garden!

Besides all the fine things above described in my uncle's garden, there was also a rather unpleasant pavilion, which he had entitled the

*Délices*,—doubtless by antiphrasis. It was in a state of extreme dilapidation. The walls were bulging outwardly; great masses of detached plaster still lay among the nettles and wild oats where they had fallen; the lower portions of the wall-surfaces were green with putrid mold; the woodwork of the window-shutters and doors had been badly sprung, and they closed only partially or not at all. A species of decoration, strongly suggestive of an immense kitchen-pot with various effluvia radiating from it, ornamented the main entrance; for in the time of Louis XV, when it was the custom to build *Délices*, there were always two entrances to such pleasure houses for precaution's sake. The cornice, overburthened with ovulos, foliated arabesques, and volutes, had been badly dismantled by the infiltration of rain-water. In short, the *Délices* of my uncle, the Chevalier de . . ., presented a rather lamentable aspect.

This poor ruin,—dating only from yesterday, although wearing the dilapidated look of a thousand years' decay,—a ruin of plaster, not of stone,—all cracked and warped; covered with a leprosy of lichen growths, moss-eaten and moldy—seemed to resemble one of those precociously old men worn out by filthy debauches: it inspired no feeling of respect; for there is nothing in the world so ugly and so wretched as either an old gauze robe or an old plaster-wall,—two things which ought not to endure, yet which do.

It was in this pavilion that my uncle had lodged me.

The interior was not less rococo than the exterior, although remaining in a somewhat better state of preservation. The bed was hung with yellow lampas, spotted over with large white flowers. An ornamental shell-work clock ticked away upon a pedestal inlaid with ivory and mother-of-pearl. A wreath of ornamental roses coquettishly twined around a Venetian glass: above the door the Four Seasons were painted in cameo. A fair lady with thickly-powdered hair, a sky-blue corset, and an array of ribbons of the same hue; who had a bow in her right hand, a partridge in her left, a crescent upon her forehead, and a leverette at her feet,—strutted and smiled with ineffable graciousness from within a large oval frame. This was one of my uncle's mistresses of old, whom he had had painted as Diana. It will scarcely be necessary to observe that the furniture itself was not of the most modern style: there was, in fact, nothing to prevent one from fancying himself living at the time of the Regency; and the mythological tapestry with which the walls were hung rendered the illusion complete.

The tapestry represented Hercules spinning at the feet of Omphale. The design was tormented after the fashion of Vanloo, and in the most *Pompadour* style possible to imagine. Hercules had a spindle decorated with rose-colored favors; he elevated his little finger with a peculiar and special grace,— like a marquis in the act of taking a pinch of snuff,— while turning a white flake of flax between his thumb and index finger; his muscular neck was burthened with bows of ribbons, rosettes, strings of pearls, and a thousand other feminine gew-gaws; and a large *gorge-de-pigeon* colored petticoat, with two very large panniers, lent quite a gallant air to the monster-conquering hero.

Omphale's white shoulders were half-covered by the skin of the Nemean lion; her slender hand leaned upon her lover's knotty club; her lovely blonde hair, powdered to ash-color, fell loosely over her neck — a neck as supple and undulating in its outlines as the neck of a dove; her little feet — true realizations of the typical Andalusian or Chinese foot, and which would have been lost in Cinderella's glass slippers—were shod with half-antique buskins of a tender lilac color, sprinkled with pearls. In truth, she was a charming creature. Her head was thrown back with an adorable little mock swagger; her dimpled mouth wore a delicious little pout; her nostrils were slightly expanded; her cheeks had a delicate glow —an *assassin** cunningly placed there relieved their beauty in a wonderful way; she only needed a little moustache to make her a first-class mousquetaire.

There were many other personages also represented in the tapestry,—the kindly female attendant, the indispensable little Cupid; but they did not leave a sufficiently distinct outline in my memory to enable me to describe them.

In those days I was quite young,—not that I wish to be understood as saying that I am now very old; but I was fresh from college, and was to remain in my uncle's care until I could choose a profession. If the good man had been able to foresee that I should embrace that of a fantastic story-writer, he would certainly have turned me out of doors forthwith and irrevocably disinherited me; for he always entertained the most aristocratic contempt for literature in general and authors in particular. Like the fine gentleman that he was, it would have pleased him to have had all those petty scribblers who busy themselves in disfiguring paper, and speaking irreverentially about people of quality,—hung or beaten to death

* Beauty-spot.

by his attendants. Lord have mercy on my poor uncle!—he really esteemed nothing in the world except the epistle to Zetulba.

Well, then, I had only just left college. I was full of dreams and illusions; I was as naive as a *rosière* of Salency,—perhaps more so. Delighted at having no more pensums to make, everything seemed to me for the best in the best of all possible worlds. I believed in an infinity of things: I believed in M. de Florian's Shepherdess, with her combed and powdered sheep; I never for a moment doubted the reality of Madame Deshoulière's flock. I believed that there were actually nine muses, as stated in Father Jouvency's *Appendix de Diis et Heroïbus.* My recollections of Berquin and of Gessner had created a little world for me in which everything was rose-colored, sky-blue, and apple-green. O holy innocence!—*sancta simplicitas!* as Mephistopheles says.

When I found myself alone in this fine room,—my own room, all to myself!—I felt superlatively overjoyed. I made a careful inventory of every thing, even the smallest article of furniture; I rummaged every corner, and explored the chamber in the fullest sense of the word. I was in the fourth heaven, as happy as a king, or rather as two kings. After supper (for we used to sup at my uncle's—a charming custom, now obsolete, together with many other equally charming customs which I mourn for with all the heart I have left), I took my candle and retired forthwith, so impatient did I feel to enjoy my new dwelling-place.

While I was undressing, I fancied that Omphale's eyes had moved: I looked more attentively in that direction, not without a slight sensation of fear; for the room was very large, and the feeble luminous penumbra which floated about the candle only served to render the darkness still more visible. I thought I saw her turning her head towards me. I became frightened in earnest, and blew out the light. I turned my face to the wall, pulled the bed-clothes over my head, drew my night-cap down to my chin, and finally went to sleep.

I did not dare to look at the accursed tapestry again for several days.

It may be well here,—for the sake of imparting something of verisimilitude to the very unlikely story I am about to relate,—to inform my fair readers that in those days I was really a very pretty boy. I had the handsomest eyes in the world,—at least they used to tell me so; a much fairer complexion than I have now,—a true carnation tint; curly-brown hair, which I still have, and seventeen years, which I have no longer. I needed only a pretty stepmother to be a very tolerable Cherub; — unfortunately mine was fifty-seven years of age, and had only three teeth, which was too much of one thing, and too little of the other.

One evening, however, I finally plucked up courage enough to take a peep at the fair mistress of Hercules: — she was looking at me with the saddest and most languishing expression possible. This time I pulled my nightcap down to my very shoulders, and buried my head in the coverlets.

I had a strange dream that night, — if indeed it was a dream.

I heard the rings of my bed-curtains sliding with a sharp squeak upon their curtain-rods, as if the curtains had been suddenly pulled back. I awoke, — at least in my dream it seemed to me that I awoke. I saw no one.

The moon shone full upon the window-panes, and projected her wan bluish light into the room. Vast shadows, fantastic forms, were defined upon the floor and the walls. The clock chimed a quarter, and the vibration of the sound took a long time to die away: it seemed like a sigh. The plainly audible strokes of the pendulum seemed like the pulsations of a young heart, throbbing with passion.

I felt anything but comfortable; and a very bewilderment of fear took possession of me.

A furious gust of wind banged the shutters and made the window-sashes tremble. The woodwork cracked; the tapestry undulated. I ventured to glance in the direction of Omphale, with a vague suspicion that she was instrumental in all this unpleasantness, for some secret purpose of her own. I was not mistaken.

The tapestry became violently agitated. Omphale detached herself from the wall and leaped lightly to the carpet: she came straight towards my bed, after having first turned herself carefully in my direction. I fancy it will hardly be necessary to describe my stupefaction. The most intrepid old soldier would not have felt very comfortable under similar circumstances; and I was neither old nor a soldier. I awaited the end of the adventure in terrified silence.

A flute-toned, pearly little voice sounded softly in my ears, with that pretty lisp affected during the Regency by Marchionesses and people of high degree:—

"Do I really frighten you, my child? It is

true that you are only a child: but it is not nice to be afraid of ladies, especially when they are young ladies and only wish you well;—it is uncivil and unworthy of a French gentleman: you must be cured of such silly fears. Come, little savage, leave off these foolish airs, and cease hiding your head under the bedclothes. Your education is by no means complete yet, my pretty page; and you have not learned so very much: in my time Cherubs were more courageous."

"But, lady, it is because . . .

"Because it seems strange to you to find me here instead of there," she said, biting her ruddy lip with her white teeth, and pointing toward the wall with her long taper finger. "Well, in fact the thing does not look very natural; but were I to explain it all to you you would be none the wiser: let it be sufficient for you to know that you are not in any danger."

"I am afraid you may be the—the . . .

"The Devil—out with the word!—is it not? that is what you wanted to say. Well, at least you will grant that I am not black enough for a devil; and that, if hell were peopled with devils shaped as I am, one might have quite as pleasant a time there as in Paradise."

And, to prove that she was not flattering herself, Omphale threw back her lion's skin and allowed me to behold her exquisitely molded shoulders and bosom, dazzling in their white beauty.

"Well, what do you think of me?" she exclaimed with a pretty little air of satisfied coquetry.

"I think that, even were you the devil himself, I should not feel afraid of you any more, Madame Omphale."

"Ah, now you talk sensibly; but do not call me Madame, or Omphale. I do not wish you to look upon me as a Madame; and I am no more Omphale than I am the devil."

"Then who are you?"

"I am the Marchioness de T . . . A short time after I was married the Marquis had this tapestry made for my apartments, and had me represented on it in the character of Omphale: he himself figures there as Hercules. That was a queer notion he took; for God knows there never was anybody in the world who bore less resemblance to Hercules than the poor Marquis! It has been a long time since this chamber was occupied: I naturally love company, and I almost died of ennui in consequence. It gave me the headache. To be only with one's husband is the same thing as being alone. When you came, I was overjoyed, this dead room became reanimated; I had found some one to feel interested in. I watched you come in and go out; I heard you murmuring in your sleep; I watched you reading, and my eyes followed the pages. I found you were nicely behaved, and had a fresh, innocent way about you that pleased me; — in short, I fell in love with you. I tried to make you understand; I sighed, — you thought it was only the sighing of the wind; I made signs to you; I looked at you with languishing eyes, and only succeeded in frightening you terribly. So at last in despair I resolved upon this rather improper course which I have taken, — to tell you frankly what you could not take a hint about. Now that you know I love you, I hope that . ."

The conversation was interrupted at this juncture by the grating of a key in the lock of the chamber door.

Omphale started and blushed to the very whites of her eyes.

"Adieu," she whispered, — "till to-morrow." And she returned to her place on the wall; walking backward, for fear that I should see her reverse side, doubtless.

It was Baptiste, who came to brush my clothes.

"You ought not to sleep with your bed-curtains open, sir," he remarked: "You might catch a bad cold;—this room is so chilly."

The curtains were actually open; and as I had been under the impression that I was only dreaming I felt very much astonished; for I was certain that they had been closed when I went to bed.

As soon as Baptiste left the room, I ran to the tapestry, I felt it all over; it was indeed a real woolen tapestry, rough to the touch like any other tapestry. Omphale resembled the charming phantom of the night only as a dead body resembles a living one. I lifted the hangings: the wall was solid throughout; there were no masked panels or secret doors. I only noticed that a few threads were broken in the groundwork of the tapestry where the feet of Omphale rested. This afforded me food for reflection.

All that day I remained buried in the deepest brown study imaginable: I longed for evening with a mingled feeling of anxiety and impatience. I retired early, resolved on learning how this mystery was going to end. I got into bed: the Marchioness did not keep me waiting long;—she leaped down from the tapestry in front of the pier-glass, and dropped right by my bed: she seated herself by my pillow, and the conversation commenced.

I asked her questions as I had done the evening before, and demanded explanations. She eluded the former, and replied in an evasive manner to the latter; yet always after so witty a fashion that within a quarter of an hour I felt no scruples whatever in regard to my liaison with her.

While conversing, she passed her fingers through my hair, tapped me gently on the cheeks, and softly kissed my forehead.

She chatted and chatted in a pretty mocking way—in a style at once elegantly polished and yet familiar and altogether like a great lady—such as I have never since heard from the lips of any human being.

She was then seated upon the easy chair beside the bed: in a little while she slipped one of her arms around my neck; and I felt her heart beating passionately against me. It was indeed a charming and handsome real woman,—a veritable marchioness whom I found beside me. Poor student of seventeen! There was more than enough to make one lose his head, so I lost mine. I did not know very well what was going to happen: but I felt a vague presentiment that it would displease the Marquis.

"And Monsieur le Marquis, on the wall up there,—what will he say?"

The lion's skin had fallen to the floor; and the soft lilac-colored buskins, filagreed with silver, were lying beside my shoes.

"He will not say anything," replied the Marchioness, laughing heartily. "Do you suppose he ever sees anything. Besides, even should he see, he is the most philosophical and inoffensive husband in the world. He is used to such things.—Do you love me, little one?"

"Indeed I do,—ever so much!—ever so much?"

. . . . . . . . . .

Morning dawned: my mistress stole away.

The day seemed to me frightfully long. At last evening came. The same things happened as on the evening before; and the second night left no regrets for the first. The Marchioness became more and more adorable; and this state of affairs continued for a long time. As I never slept at night, I wore a somnolent expression in the daytime, which did not augur well for me with my uncle. He suspected something: he probably listened at the door and heard everything; for one fine morning he entered my room so brusquely that Antoinette had scarcely time to get back to her place on the tapestry.

He was followed by a tapestry-hanger, with pincers and a ladder.

He looked at me with a shrewd and severe expression which convinced me that he knew all.

"This Marchioness de T . . is certainly crazy: what the devil could have put it into her head to fall in love with a brat like that?"—muttered my uncle between his teeth,—"she promised to behave herself!

"Jean, take that tapestry down; roll it up, and put it in the garret."

Every word my uncle spoke went through my heart like a poniard-thrust.

Jean rolled up my sweetheart Omphale—otherwise the Marchioness Antoinette de T . . ; together with Hercules, or the Marquis de T . ., —and carried the whole thing off to the garret. I could not restrain my tears.

Next day my uncle sent me back, in the B—— diligence, to my respectable parents—to whom, you may feel assured, I never breathed a word of my adventure.

My uncle died: his house and furniture were sold; probably the tapestry was sold with the rest.

But a long time afterward, while foraging the shop of a bric-a-brac merchant in search of oddities, I stumbled over a great dusty roll of something covered with cobwebs.

"What is that?" I said to the Auvergnat.

"That is a rococo tapestry representing the amours of Madame Omphale and Monsieur Hercule; it is genuine Beauvais, worked in silk, and in an excellent state of preservation. Buy this from me for your study: I will not charge you dear for it, since it is you."

At the name of Omphale, all my blood rushed to my heart.

"Unroll that tapestry," I said to the merchant in a hurried, gasping voice, like one in a fever.

It was indeed she! I fancied that her mouth smiled graciously at me, and that her eye lighted up on meeting mine.

"How much do you ask?"

"Well, I could not possibly let you have it for any less than five hundred francs."

"I have not that much with me now, I will get it, and be back in an hour."

I returned with the money; but the tapestry was no longer there. An Englishman had bargained for it during my absence, offered six hundred francs for it, and taken it away with him.

After all, perhaps it was best that it should have been thus; and that I should preserve this delicious souvenir intact. They say one should never return to a first love, or look at the rose which one admired the evening before.

And then I am no longer so young or so pretty that tapestries should come down from their walls to honor me.

# KING CANDAULES.

## CHAPTER I.

Five hundred years before the Trojan war, and seventeen hundred and fifteen years before our own era, there was a grand festival at Sardes. King Candaules was going to marry. The people were affected with that sort of pleasurable interest and aimless emotion wherewith any royal event inspires the masses, even though it in no wise concerns them, and transpires in superior spheres of life which they can never hope to reach.

As soon as Phœbus-Apollo, standing in his quadriga, had gilded to saffron the summits of fertile Mount Tmolus with his rays, the good people of Sardes were all astir — going and coming, mounting or descending the marble stairways leading from the city to the waters of the Pactolus, that opulent river whose sands Midas filled with tiny sparks of gold, when he bathed in its stream. One would have supposed that each one of these good citizens was himself about to marry; so solemn and important was the demeanor of all.

Men were gathering in groups in the Agora, upon the steps of the temples and along the porticoes. At every street corner one might have encountered women leading by the hand little children, whose uneven walk ill suited the maternal anxiety and impatience. Maidens were hastening to the fountains—all with urns gracefully balanced upon their heads, or sustained by their white arms as with natural handles—so as to procure early the necessary water provision for the household, and thus obtain leisure at the hour when the nuptial procession should pass. Washerwomen hastily folded the still damp tunics and chlamidæ, and piled them upon mule-wagons. Slaves turned the mill without any need of the overseer's whip to tickle their naked and scar-seamed shoulders. Sardes was hurrying itself to finish with those necessary every-day cares which no festival can wholly disregard.

The road along which the procession was to pass had been strewn with fine yellow sand. Brazen tripods, disposed along the way at regular intervals, sent up to heaven the odorous smoke of cinnamon and spikenard. These vapors, moreover, alone clouded the purity of the azure above; the clouds of a hymeneal day ought, indeed, to be formed only by the burning of perfumes. Myrtle and rose-laurel branches were strewn upon the ground; and from the walls of the palaces were suspended by little rings of bronze rich tapestries, whereon the needles of industrious captives—intermingling wool, silver, and gold—had represented various scenes in the history of the gods and heroes: Ixion embracing the Cloud; Diana surprised in the bath by Actæon; the shepherd Paris as judge in the contest of beauty held upon Mount Ida between Hera, the Snowy-armed, Athena of the sea-green eyes, and Aphrodite, girded with her magic cestus; the old men of Troy rising to honor Helena as she passed through the Skaian gate, a subject taken from one of the poems of the blind man of Meles. Others exhibited in preference scenes taken from the life of Heracles the Theban, through flattery to Candaules, himself a Heracleid, being descended from the hero through Alcæus. Others contented themselves by decorating the entrances of their dwellings with garlands and wreaths in token of rejoicing.

Among the multitudes marshaled along the way, from the royal house even as far as the gates of the city through which the young queen would pass on her arrival, conversation naturally turned upon the beauty of the bride, whereof the re nown had spread throughout all Asia; and upon the character of the bridegroom, who, although not altogether an eccentric, seemed nevertheless one not readily appreciated from the common standpoint of observation.

Nyssia, daughter of the Satrap Megabazus, was gifted with marvelous purity of feature and perfection of form — at least such was the rumor spread abroad by the female slaves who attended her, and a few female friends who had accompanied her to the bath; for no man could boast of knowing aught of Nyssia, save the color of her veil and the elegant folds that she involuntarily impressed upon the soft materials which robed her statuesque body.

The barbarians did not share the ideas of the Greeks in regard to modesty: while the youths of Achaia made no scruple of allowing their oil-anointed torsos to shine under the sun in the stadium, and while the Spartan virgins danced ungarmented before the altar of Diana; those of Persepolis, Ebactana, and Bactria, attaching more importance to chastity of the body than to chastity of mind, considered those liberties allowed to the pleasure of the eyes by Greek manners as impure and highly reprehensible; and held no woman virtuous who permitted men to obtain a glimpse of more than the tip of her foot in walking, as it slightly deranged the discreet folds of a long tunic.

Despite all this mystery, or rather, perhaps, by very reason of this mystery, the fame of Nyssia had not been slow to spread throughout all Lydia, and become popular there to such a degree that it had reached even. Candaules, although kings are ordinarily the most illy-informed people in their kingdoms, and live like the gods in a kind of cloud which conceals from them the knowledge of terrestrial things.

The Eupatridæ of Sardes, who hoped that the young king might, perchance, choose a wife from their family; the hetairæ of Athens, of Samos, of Miletus and of Cyprus; the beautiful slaves from the banks of the Indus; the blonde girls brought at a vast expense from the depths of the Cimmerian fogs, were heedful never to utter in the presence of Candaules, whether within hearing or beyond hearing, a single word which bore any relation to Nyssia. The bravest, in a question of beauty, recoil before the prospect of a contest in which they can anticipate being outrivaled.

And nevertheless no person in Sardes, or even in Lydia, had beheld this redoubtable adversary, no person save one solitary being, who from the time of that encounter had kept his lips as firmly closed upon the subject as though Harpocrates, the god of silence, had sealed them with his finger; and that was Gyges, chief of the guards of Candaules. One day Gyges, his mind filled with various projects and vague ambitions, had been wandering among the Bactrian hills, whither his master had sent him upon an important and secret mission: he was dreaming of the intoxication of omnipotence, of treading upon purple with sandals of gold, of placing the diadem upon the brows of the fairest of women;—these thoughts made his blood boil in his veins, and, as though to pursue the flight of his dreams, he smote his sinewy heel upon the foam-whitened flanks of his Numidian horse.

The weather, at first calm, had changed and waxed tempestuous like the warrior's soul; and Boreas, his locks bristling with Thracian frosts, his cheeks puffed out, his arms folded upon his breast, smote the rain-freighted clouds with the mighty beatings of his wings.

A bevy of young girls who had been gathering flowers in the meadow, fearing the coming storm, were returning to the city in all haste, each carrying her perfumed harvest in the lap of her tunic. Seeing a stranger on horseback approaching in the distance, they had hidden their faces in their mantles, after the custom of the Barbarians; but at the very moment that Gyges was passing by the one whose proud carriage and richer habiliments seemed to designate her the mistress of the little band, an unusually violent gust of wind carried away the veil of the fair unknown, and, whirling it through the air like a feather, chased it to such a distance that it could not be recovered. It was Nyssia, daughter of Megabazus, who found herself thus with face unveiled in the presence of Gyges, an humble captain of King Candaules' guard. Was it only the breath of Boreas which had brought about this accident? or had Eros, who delights to vex the hearts of men, amused himself by severing the string which had fastened the protecting tissue? However they may have been, Gyges was stricken motionless at the sight of that Medusa of beauty; and not till long after the folds of Nyssia's robe had disappeared beyond the gates of the city could he think of proceeding on his way. Although there was nothing to justify such a conjecture, he cherished the belief that he had seen the satrap's daughter; and that meeting, which affected him almost like an apparition, accorded so fully with the thoughts which were occupying him at the moment of its occurrence, that he could not help perceiving therein some thing fateful and ordained of the gods. In truth it was upon that brow that he would have wished to place the diadem. What other could be more worthy of it? But what probability was there that Gyges would ever have a throne to share? He had not sought to follow up this adventure, and assure himself whether it was indeed the daughter of Megabazus whose mysterious face had been revealed to him by Chance, the great filcher. Nyssia had fled so swiftly that it would have been impossible for him then to overtake her; and moreover, he had been dazzled, fascinated, thunder-stricken, as it were, rather than charmed by that superhuman apparition — by that monster of beauty!

Nevertheless, that image, although seen only in the glimpse of a moment, had engraved itself upon his heart in lines deep as those which the sculptors trace on ivory with tools reddened in the fire. He had endeavored, although vainly, to efface it; for the love which he felt for Nyssia inspired him with a secret terror. Perfection in such a degree is ever awe-inspiring; and women so like unto goddesses could only work evil to feeble mortals; they are formed for divine adulteries; and even the most courageous men never risk themselves in such amours without trembling. Therefore no hope had blossomed in the soul of Gyges, overwhelmed and discouraged in advance by the sentiment of the impossible. Ere opening his lips to Nyssia, he would have wished to despoil the heaven of its robe of stars,—to take from Phœbus his crown of rays, forgetting that women only give themselves to those unworthy of them, and that to win their love one must act as though he desired to earn their hate.

From that day the roses of joy no longer bloomed upon his cheeks; by day he was sad and mournful, and seemed to wander abroad in solitary dreaming, like a mortal who has beheld a divinity; at night he was haunted by dreams in which he beheld Nyssia seated by his side upon cushions of purple between the golden griffins of the royal throne.

Therefore Gyges, the only one who could speak of his own knowledge concerning Nyssia, having never spoken of her, the Sardians were left to their own conjectures in her regard; and their conjectures, it must be confessed, were fantastic and altogether fabulous. The beauty of Nyssia, thanks to the veils which shrouded her, became a sort of myth, a canvas, a poem to which each one added ornamentation as the fancy took him.

"If report be not false," lisped a young debauchee from Athens, who stood with one hand upon the shoulder of an Asiatic boy, "neither Plangon, nor Archianassa, nor Thais can be compared with this marvelous barbarian; yet I can scarce believe that she equals Theano of Colophon, from whom I once bought a single night at the price of as much gold as she could bear away, after having plunged both her white arms up to the shoulder in my cedar-wood coffer."

"Beside her," added a Eupatrid, who pretended to be better informed than any other person upon all manner of subjects, "beside her the daughter of Cœlus and the Sea would seem but a mere Ethiopian servant."

"Your words are blasphemy; and although Aphrodite be a kind and indulgent goddess, beware of drawing down her anger upon you."

"By Hercules!—and that ought to be an oath of some weight in a city ruled by one of his descendants—I can not retract a word of it."

"You have seen her, then?"

"No; but I have a slave in my service who once belonged to Nyssia, and who has told me a hundred stories about her."

"Is it true," demanded in infantile tones an equivocal looking woman whose pale-rose tunic, painted cheeks, and locks shining with essences betrayed wretched pretensions to a youth long passed away, "is it true that Nyssia has two pupils in each eye? It seems to me that must be very ugly; and I can not understand how Candaules could fall in love with such a monstrosity, while there is no lack, at Sardes and in Lydia, of women whose eyes are irreproachable."

And uttering these words, with all sorts of affected airs and simperings, Lamia took a little significant peep in a small mirror of cast metal which she drew from her bosom, and which enabled her to lead back to duty certain wandering curls disarranged by the impertinence of the wind.

"As to the double pupil, that seems to me nothing more than an old nurse's tale," observed the well-informed patrician; "but it is a fact that Nyssia's eyes are so piercing that she can see through walls; lynxes are myopic compared with her."

"How can a sensible man coolly argue about such an absurdity?" interrupted a citizen, whose bald skull, and the flood of snowy beard into which he plunged his fingers while speaking, lent him an air of preponderance and philosophical sagacity. "The truth is that the daughter of Megabazus can not naturally see through a wall any better than you or I, but the Egyptian priest Thoutmosis, who knows so many wondrous secrets, has given her the mysterious stone which is found in the heads of dragons, and whose property, as every one knows, renders all shadows and the most opaque bodies transparent to the eyes of those who possess it. Nyssia always carries this stone in her girdle, or else set into her bracelet; and in that may be found the secret of her clairvoyance."

The citizen's explanation seemed the most natural one to those of the group whose conversation we are endeavoring to reproduce; and the opinions of Lamia and the patrician were abandoned as improbable.

"At all events," returned the lover of Theano, "we are going to have an opportunity of judging for ourselves; for it seems to me that I hear the clarions sounding in the distance; and, though Nyssia is still invisible, I can see the herald yonder approaching with palm-branches in his hands, to announce the arrival of the nuptial cortége, and make the crowd fall back."

At this news, which spread rapidly through the crowd, the strong men elbowed their way toward the front ranks; the agile boys, embracing the shafts of the columns, sought to climb up to the capitals and there seat themselves; others, not without having skinned their knees against the bark, succeeded in perching themselves comfortably enough in the Y of some tree-branch; the women lifted their little children upon their shoulders, warning them to hold tightly to their necks. Those who had the good fortune to dwell on the street along which Candaules and Nyssia were about to pass leaned over from the summit of their roofs, or, rising on their elbows, abandoned for a time the cushions upon which they had been reclining.

A murmur of satisfaction and gratified expectation ran through the crowd, which had already been waiting many long hours; for the arrows of the midday sun were commencing to sting.

The heavy-armed warriors, with cuirasses of bull's-hide covered with overlapping plates of metal,— helmets adorned with plumes of horse-hair dyed red, — *knemides* or greaves faced with tin, — baldrics studded with nails, — emblazoned bucklers, and swords of brass, rode behind a line of trumpeters who blew with might and main upon their long tubes, which gleamed under the sunlight. The horses of these warriors were all white as the feet of Thetis, and might have served, by reason of their noble paces and purity of breeds, as models for those which Phidias at a later day sculptured upon the metopes of the Parthenon.

At the head of this troop rode Gyges, the well-named, for his name in the Lydian tongue signifies beautiful. His features, of the most exquisite regularity, seemed chiseled in marble, owing to his intense pallor, for he had just discovered in Nyssia, although she was veiled with the veil of a young bride, the same woman whose face had been betrayed to his gaze by the treachery of Boreas under the walls of Bactria.

"Handsome Gyges looks very sad," said the young maidens. "What proud beauty could have secured his love, or what forsaken one has caused some Thessalian witch to cast a spell on him? Has that cabalistic ring (which he is said to have found hidden within the flanks of a brazen horse in the midst of some forest) lost its virtue; and, suddenly ceasing to render its owner invisible, have betrayed him to the astonished eyes of some innocent husband, who had deemed himself alone in his conjugal chamber?"

"Perhaps he has been wasting his talents and his drachmas at the game of Palamedes; or else it may be that he is disappointed at not having won the prize at the Olympian games — he had great faith in his horse Hyperion."

No one of these conjectures was true. A fact is never guessed.

After the battalion commanded by Gyges, there

came young boys crowned with myrtle-wreaths, and singing epithalamic hymns after the Lydian manner, accompanying themselves upon lyres of ivory, which they played with bows: all were clad in rose-colored tunics ornamented with a silver Greek border; and their long hair flowed down over their shoulders in thick curls.

They preceded the gift-bearers, strong slaves whose half-nude bodies exposed to view such interlacements of muscle as the stoutest athletes might have envied.

Upon brancards, supported by two or four men or more, according to the weight of the objects borne, were placed enormous brazen cratera, chiseled by the most famous artists;—vases of gold and silver whose sides were adorned with bas-reliefs and whose handles were elegantly worked into chimeras, foliage and nude women;—magnificent ewers to be used in washing the feet of illustrious guests;—flagons incrusted with precious stones and containing the rarest perfumes; myrrh from Arabia, cinnamon from the Indies, spikenard from Persia, essence of roses from Smyrna;—kamklins or perfuming pans, with perforated covers;—cedar-wood or ivory coffers of marvelous workmanship, which opened with a secret spring that none, save the inventor, could find, and which contained bracelets wrought from the gold of Ophir, necklaces of the most lustrous pearls, mantle-brooches constellated with rubies and carbuncles;—toilet boxes containing blonde sponges, curling-irons, sea-wolves teeth to polish the nails, the green rouge of Egypt, which turns to a most beautiful pink on touching the skin, powders to darken the eyelashes and eyebrows, and all the refinements that feminine coquetry could invent. Other litters were freighted with purple robes of the finest linen and of all possible shades from the incarnadine hue of the rose to the deep crimson of the blood of the grape,—*calasires* of the linen of Canopus, which is thrown all white into the vat of the dyer, and comes forth again, owing to the various astringents in which it had been steeped, diapered with the most brilliant colors,—tunics brought from the fabulous land of Seres, made from the spun slime of a worm which feeds upon leaves, and so fine that they might be drawn through a finger-ring.

Ethiopians, whose bodies shone like jet, and whose temples were tightly bound with cords, lest they should burst the veins of their foreheads in the effort to uphold their burthen, carried in great pomp a statue of Hercules, the ancestor of Candaules, of colossal size, wrought of ivory and gold, with the club, the skin of the Nemean lion, the three apples from the garden of the Hesperides, and all the traditional attributes of the hero.

Statues of Venus Urania, and of Venus Genitrix, sculptured by the best pupils of the Sicyon school in that marble of Paros, whose gleaming transparency seemed expressly created for the representation of the ever-youthful flesh of the Immortals, were borne after the statue of Hercules, which admirably relieved the harmony and elegance of their proportions by contrast with its massive outlines and rugged forms.

A painting by Bularchus, which Candaules had purchased for its weight in gold, executed upon the wood of the female larch tree, and representing the defeat of the Magnesians, evoked universal admiration by the beauty of its design, the truthfulness of the attitude of its figures, and the harmony of its coloring, although the artist had only employed in its production the four primitive colors: Attic ochre, white, Pontic *sinopis*, and *atramentum*. The young king loved painting and sculpture, even more, perhaps, than well became a monarch; and he had not unfrequently bought a picture at a price equal to the annual revenue of a whole city.

Camels and dromedaries, splendidly caparisoned,

with musicians seated on their necks, performing upon drums and cymbals, carried the gilded stakes, the cords, and the material of the tent designed for the use of the queen during voyages and hunting parties.

These spectacles of magnificence would upon any other occasion have ravished the people of Sardes with delight; but their curiosity had been enlisted in another direction, and it was not without a certain feeling of impatience that they watched this portion of the procession file by. The young maidens and the handsome boys, bearing flaming torches, and strewing handfuls of crocus flowers along the way, hardly attracted any attention. The idea of beholding Nyssia had preoccupied all minds.

At last Candaules appeared, riding in a chariot drawn by four horses, as beautiful and spirited as those of the Sun; all rolling their golden bits in foam, shaking their purple-decked manes, and restrained with great difficulty by the driver, who stood erect at the side of Candaules, and was leaning back to gain more power on the reins.

Candaules was a young man full of vigor, and well worthy of his Herculean origin. His head was joined to his shoulders by a neck massive as a bull's, and almost without a curve; his hair, black and lustrous, twisted itself into rebellious little curls, here and there concealing the circlet of his diadem; his ears, small and upright, were of a ruddy hue; his forehead was broad and full, though a little low, like all antique foreheads; his eyes full of gentle melancholy, his oval cheeks, his chin with its gentle and regular curves, his mouth with its slightly parted lips—all bespoke the nature of the poet rather than that of the warrior. In fact, although he was brave, skilled in all bodily exercises, could subdue a wild horse as well as any of the Lapithæ, or swim across the current of rivers when they descended, swollen with melted snow, from the mountains—although he might have bent the bow of Odysseus or borne the shield of Achilles, he seemed little occupied with dreams of conquest; and war, usually so fascinating to young kings, had little attraction for him. He contented himself with repelling the attacks of his ambitious neighbors, and sought not to extend his own dominions. He preferred building palaces, after plans suggested by himself to the architects, who always found the king's hints of no small value; or to form collections of statues and paintings by artists of the elder and later schools. He had the works of Telephanes of Sicyon, Cleanthes, Ardices of Corinth, Hygiemon, Deinias,

Charmides, Eumarus, and Cimon, some being simple drawings, and others paintings in various colors or mono-chromes. It was even said that Candaules had not disdained to wield with his own royal hands — a thing hardly becoming a prince — the chisel of the sculptor and the sponge of the encaustic painter.

But why should we dwell upon Candaules? The reader undoubtedly feels like the people of Sardes: and it is of Nyssia that he desires to hear.

The daughter of Megabazus was mounted upon an elephant, with wrinkled skin and immense ears which seemed like flags, who advanced with a heavy but rapid gait, like a vessel in the midst of the waves. His tusks and his trunk were encircled with silver rings; and around the pillars of his limbs were entwined necklaces of enormous pearls. Upon his back, which was covered with a magnificent Persian carpet of striped pattern, stood a sort of estrade overlaid with gold finely chased, and constellated with onyx stones, carnelians, chrysolites, lapis-lazuli, and girasols; upon this estrade sat the young queen, so covered with precious stones as to dazzle the eyes of the beholders. A mitre, shaped like a helmet, on which pearls formed flower designs and letters after the Oriental manner, was placed upon her head; her ears, both the lobes and rims of which had been pierced, were adorned with ornaments in the form of little cups, crescents, and balls; necklaces of gold and silver beads which had been hollowed out and carved, thrice encircled her neck and descended with a metallic tinkling upon her bosom; emerald serpents with topaz or ruby eyes coiled themselves in many folds about her arms, and clasped themselves by biting their own tails. These bracelets were connected by chains of precious stones; and so great was their weight that two attendants were required to kneel beside Nyssia, and support her elbows. She was clad in a robe embroidered by Syrian workmen with shining designs of golden foliage and diamond fruits; and over this she wore the short tunic of Persepolis, which hardly descended to the knee, and of which the sleeves were slit and fastened by sapphire clasps; her waist was encircled from hip to loins by a girdle wrought of narrow material, variegated with stripes and flowered designs, which formed themselves into symmetrical patterns as they were brought together by a certain arrangement of the folds which Indian girls alone know how to make. Her trowsers of byssus, which the Phœnicians called *syndon*, were confined at the ankles by anklets adorned with gold and silver bells; and completed this toilet so fantastically rich and wholly opposed to Greek taste. But, alas! a saffron-colored *flammeum* pitilessly masked the face of Nyssia, who seemed embarrassed, veiled though she was, at finding so many eyes fixed upon her, and frequently signed to a slave behind her to lower the parasol of ostrich plumes and thus conceal her yet more from the curious gaze of the crowd.

Candaules had vainly begged of her to lay aside her veil, even for that solemn occasion. The young barbarian had refused to pay the welcome of her beauty to his people. Great was the disappointment: Lamia declared that Nyssia dared not uncover her face for fear of showing her double pupil; the young libertine remained convinced that Theano of Colophon was more beautiful than the queen of Sardes; and Gyges sighed when he beheld Nyssia, after having made her elephant kneel down, descend upon the inclined heads of Damascus slaves as upon a living ladder, to the threshold of the royal dwelling, where the elegance of Greek architecture was blended with the fantasies and enormities of Asiatic taste.

## CHAPTER II.

In our character of poet, we have the right to lift the saffron-colored *flammeum* which concealed the young bride; being more fortunate in this wise than the Sardians, who after a whole day's waiting were obliged to return to their houses and were left, as before, to their own conjectures.

Nyssia was really far superior to her reputation, great as it was. It seemed as though Nature in creating her had resolved to exhaust her utmost powers, and thus make atonement for all former experimental attempts and fruitless essays. One would have said that, moved by jealousy of the future marvels of the Greek sculptors, she also had resolved to model a statue herself, and to prove that she was still sovereign mistress in the plastic art.

The grain of snow, the micaceous brilliancy of Parian marble, the sparkling pulp of balsamine flowers, would render but a feeble idea of the ideal substance whereof Nyssia had been formed. That flesh, so fine, so delicate, permitted day-light to penetrate it, and modeled itself in transparent contours, in lines as sweetly harmonious as music itself. According to different surroundings it took the color of the sunlight or of purple, like the aromal body of a divinity; and seemed to radiate light and life. The world of perfections inclosed within the nobly-lengthened oval of her chaste face could have been rendered by no earthly art—neither by the chisel of the sculptor nor the brush of the painter, nor the style of any poet—though it were Praxiteles, Apelles, or Mimnernus; and on her smooth brow, bathed by waves of hair amber-bright as molten electrum and sprinkled with gold filings, according to the Babylonian custom, sat as upon a jasper throne the unalterable serenity of perfect loveliness.

As for her eyes, though they did not justify what popular credulity said of them, they were at least wonderfully strange eyes; brown eyebrows, with extremities ending in points elegant as those of the arrows of Eros, and which were joined to each other by a streak of henna after the Asiatic fashion, and long fringes of silkily-shadowed eyelashes contrasted strikingly with the twin sapphire stars rolling in the heaven of dark silver which formed those eyes. The irises of those eyes, whose pupils were blacker than atrament, varied singularly in shades of shifting color: from sapphire they changed to turquoise, from turquoise to beryl, from beryl to yellow amber; and sometimes, like a limpid lake whose bottom is strewn with jewels, they offered, through their incalculable depths, glimpses of golden and diamond sands upon which green fibrils vibrated and twisted themselves into emerald serpents. In those orbs of phosphoric lightning the rays of suns extinguished, the splendors of vanished worlds, the glories of Olympus eclipsed — all seemed to have concentrated their reflections. When contemplating them one thought of Eternity, and felt himself seized with a mighty giddiness, as though he were leaning over the verge of the Infinite.

The expression of those extraordinary eyes was not less variable than their tint. At times their lids opened like the portals of celestial dwellings, they invited you into Elysiums of light, of azure, of ineffable felicity; they promised you the realization, ten-fold, a hundred-fold, of all your dreams of happiness—as though they had divined your soul's most secret thoughts; again, impenetrable as seven-fold plated shields of the hardest metals, they flung back your gaze like blunted and broken arrows. With a simple inflexion of the brow, a mere flash of the pupil, more terrible than the thunder of Zeus, they precipitated you from the heights of your most ambitious escalades into depths of nothingness so profound that it was impossible to rise again. Typhon himself who writhes under Ætna, could not have lifted the mountains of disdain with which they overwhelmed you; one felt that though he should live for a thousand Olympiads endowed with the beauty of the fair son of Latona—the genius of Orpheus—the unbounded might of Assyrian kings—the treasures of the Cabeirei, the Telchines, and the Dactyli, gods of subterranean wealth, he could never change their expression to mildness.

At other times their languishment was so liquidly persuasive, their brilliancy and irradiation so penetrating, that the icy coldness of Nestor and Priam would have melted under their gaze, like the wax of the wings of Icarus when he approached the flaming zones. For one such glance a man would have gladly steeped his hands in the blood of his host, scattered the ashes of his father to the four winds, overthrown the holy images of the gods, and stolen the fire of heaven itself, like the sublime thief, Prometheus.

Nevertheless, their most ordinary expression, it must be confessed, was of a chastity to make one desperate—a sublime coldness—an ignorance of all possibilities of human passion, such as would have made the moon-bright eyes of Phœbe or the sea-green eyes of Athena appear by comparison more liquidly tempting than those of a young girl of Babylon sacrificing to the goddess Mylitta within the cord-circled enclosure of Succoth-Benohl. Their invincible virginity seemed to bid love defiance.

The cheeks of Nyssia, which no human gaze had ever profaned, save that of Gyges on the day when the veil was blown away, possessed a youthful bloom, a tender pallor, a delicacy of grain and a downiness whereof the faces of our women, perpetually exposed to sunlight and air, cannot convey the most distant idea; modesty created fleeting rosy clouds upon them like those which a drop of crimson essence would form in a cup of milk; and when uncolored by any emotion they took a silvery sheen, a warm light, like an alabaster vessel illumined by a lamp within. That lamp was her charming soul, which exposed to view the transparency of her flesh.

A bee would have been deceived by her mouth, whose form was so perfect, whose corners were so purely dimpled, whose crimson was so rich and warm that the gods would have descended from their Olympian dwellings in order to touch it with lips humid with immortality, but that the jealousy of the goddesses restrained their impetuosity. Happy the wind which passed through that purple and pearl—which dilated those pretty nostrils, so finely cut and shaded with rosy tints like the mother-of-pearl of the shells thrown by the sea on the shore of Cyprus at the feet of Venus Anadyomene! But are there not a multitude of favors thus granted to things which can not understand them? What lover would not wish to be the tunic of his well beloved or the water of her bath?

Such was Nyssia, if we dare make use of the expression after so vague a description of her face. If our foggy Northern idioms had the warm liberty, the burning enthusiasm of the Sir-Hasirim, we might, perhaps, by comparisons—awakening in the mind of the reader memories of flowers and perfumes, of music and sunlight—evoking, by the magic of words, all the graceful and charming images that the universe can contain, have been able to give some idea of Nyssia's features; but it is permitted to Solomon alone to compare the nose of a beautiful woman to the tower of Lebanon which looketh toward Damascus. And yet what is there in the world of more importance than the nose of a beautiful woman? Had Helen, the white Tyndarid, been flat-nosed, would the Trojan war have taken place? And if the profile of Semiramis had not been perfectly regular, would she have bewitched the old monarch of Nineveh and encircled her brow with the mitre of pearls, the symbol of supreme power?

Although Candaules had brought to his palace the most beautiful slaves from the people of the Sorae, of Askalon, of Sogdiana, of the Sacæ, of Rhapta, — the most celebrated courtesans from Ephesus, from Pergamus, from Smyrna, and from Cyprus, he was completely fascinated by the charms of Nyssia. Up to that time he had not even suspected the existence of such perfection.

Privileged as a husband to enjoy fully the contemplation of this beauty, he found himself dazzled, giddy, like one who leans over the edge of an abyss, or fixes his eyes upon the sun; he felt himself seized, as it were, with the delirium of possession, like a priest drunk with the god who fills and moves him. All other thoughts disappeared from his soul; and the universe seemed to him only as a vague mist in the midst of which beamed the shining phantom of Nyssia. His happiness transformed itself into ecstacy; and his love into madness. At times his very felicity terrified him. To be only a wretched king — only a remote descendant of a hero who had become a god by mighty labors — only a common man formed of flesh and bone; and, without having in aught rendered himself worthy of it — without having even, like his ancestor, strangled some hydra, or torn some lion asunder — to enjoy a happiness whereof Zeus of the ambrosial hair would scarce be worthy, though lord of all Olympus! He felt as it were a shame to thus hoard up for himself alone so rich a treasure, — to steal this marvel from the world, — to be the dragon with scales and claws who guarded the living type of the ideal of lovers, sculptors, and poets. All they had ever dreamed of in their hope, their melancholy, and their despair, he possessed, — he, Candaules, poor tyrant of Sardes, who had only a few wretched coffers filled with pearls, a few cisterns filled with gold pieces, and thirty or forty thousand slaves, purchased or taken in war.

Candaules' felicity was too great for him; and the strength which he would doubtless have found at his command in time of misfortune was wanting to him in time of happiness. His joy overflowed from his soul like water from a vase placed upon the fire; and in the exasperation of his enthusiasm for Nyssia he had reached the point of desiring that she were less timid and less modest; for it cost him no little effort to retain in his own breast the secret of such wondrous beauty.

"Ah!" he would murmur to himself during

the deep reveries which absorbed him at all hours that he did not spend at the queen's side; "how strange a lot is mine!!—I am wretched because of that which would make any other husband happy. Nyssia will not leave the shadow of the gynæceum, and refuses, with barbarian modesty, to lift her veil in the presence of any other than myself. Yet with what an intoxication of pride would my love behold her, radiantly sublime, gaze down upon my kneeling people from the summit of the royal steps, and, like the rising dawn, extinguish all those pale stars who, during the night, thought themselves suns! Proud Lydian women, who believe yourselves beautiful, but for Nyssia's reserve you would appear, even to your lovers, as ugly as the oblique-eyed and thick-lipped slaves of Nahasi and Kush. Were she but once to pass along the streets of Sardes with face unveiled, you might in vain pull your adorers by the lappet of their tunics, for none of them would turn his head, or, if he did, it would be to demand your name, so utterly would he have forgotten you! They would rush to precipitate themselves beneath the silver wheels of her chariot, that they might have even the pleasure of being crushed by her, like those devotees of the Indus who pave the pathway of their idol with their bodies.

"And you, O goddesses, whom Paris-Alexander judged, had Nyssia appeared among you, not one of you would have borne away the golden apple — not even Aphrodite, despite her cestus and her promise to the shepherd-arbiter that she would make him beloved by the most beautiful woman in the world! . . . . . .

"Alas! to think that such beauty is not immortal, and that years will alter those divine outlines —that admirable hymn of forms—that poem whose strophes are contours, and which no one in the world has ever read or may ever read save myself; to be the sole depositary of so splendid a treasure! If I knew even, by imitating the play of light and shadow with the aid of lines and colors, how to fix upon wood a reflection of that celestial face; — if marble were not rebellious to my chisel, — how well would I fashion in the purest vein of Paros or Pentelicus an image of that charming body, which would make the proud effigies of the goddesses fall from their altars! And long after, when deep below the slime of deluges, and beneath the dust of ruined cities, the men of future ages should find a fragment of that petrified shadow of Nyssia, they would cry: 'Behold, how the women of this vanished world were formed!' And they would erect a temple wherein to enshrine the divine fragment. But I have naught save a senseless admiration, and a love that is madness! Sole adorer of an unknown divinity, I possess no power to spread her worship through the world!"

Thus in Candaules had the enthusiasm of the artist extinguished the jealousy of the lover; — admiration was mightier than love. If in place of Nyssia, daughter of the Satrap Megabazus, all imbued with Oriental ideas, he had espoused some Greek girl from Athens or Corinth, he would certainly have invited to his court the most skillful painters and sculptors, and have given them the queen for their model, as did afterward Alexander his favorite Campaspe, who posed naked before Apelles. Such a whim would have encountered no opposition from a woman of the land where even the most chaste made a boast of having contributed — some for the back, some for the bosom — to the perfection of a famous statue. But hardly would the bashful Nyssia consent to unveil herself in the discreet shadow of the thalamus; and the earnest prayers of the king really shocked her rather than gave her pleasure. The sentiment of duty and obedience alone induced her to yield at times to what she styled the whims of Candaules.

Sometimes he besought her to allow the flood of her hair to flow over her shoulders in a river of gold richer than the Pactolus, — to encircle her brow with a crown of ivy and linden leaves like a bacchante of Mount Mænalus,—to lie, hardly veiled by a cloud of tissue finer than woven wind, upon a tiger-skin with silver claws and ruby eyes, — or to stand erect in a great shell of mother-of-pearl, with a dew of pearls falling from her tresses in lieu of drops of sea-water.

When he had placed himself in the best position for observation, he became absorbed in silent contemplation; his hand, tracing vague contours in the air, seemed to be sketching the outlines for some picture; and he would have remained thus for whole hours, if Nyssia, soon becoming weary of her role of model, had not reminded him in chill and disdainful tones that such amusements were unworthy of royal majesty and contrary to the holy laws of matrimony. "It is thus," she would exclaim, as she withdrew, draped to her very eyes, into the most mysterious recesses of her apartment, "that one treats a mistress—not a virtuous woman of noble blood!"

These wise remonstrances did not cure Candaules, whose passion augmented in inverse ratio to the coldness shown him by the queen. And it had at last brought him to that point that he could no longer keep the secrets of the nuptial couch. A confidant became as necessary to him as to the prince of a modern tragedy. He did not proceed, you may feel assured, to fix his choice upon some crabbed philosopher of frowning mien, with a flood of grey-and-white beard rolling down over a mantle in proud tatters; nor a warrior who could talk of nothing save balista, catapults, and scythed chariots; nor a sententious Eupatrid full of counsels and politic maxims,—but Gyges, whose reputation for gallantry caused him to be regarded as a connoisseur in regard to women.

One evening he laid his hand upon his shoulder in a more than ordinarily familiar and cordial manner; and after giving him a look of peculiar significance he suddenly strode away from the group of courtiers, saying in a loud voice:—

"Gyges, come and give me your opinion in regard to my effigy, which the Sicyon sculptors have just finished chiseling on the genealogical bas-relief where the deeds of my ancestors are celebrated."

"O King, your knowledge is greater than that of your humble subject; and I know not how to express my gratitude for the honor you do me in deigning to consult me," replied Gyges, with a sign of assent.

Candaules and his favorite traversed several halls ornamented in the Hellenic style, where the

Corinthian acanthus and the Ionic volute bloomed or curled in the capitals of the columns,—where the friezes were peopled with little figures in polychromatic plastique representing processions and sacrifices;—and they finally arrived at a remote portion of the ancient palace whose walls were built with stones of irregular form put together without cement in the Cyclopean manner. This ancient architecture was colossally proportioned and weirdly grim. The immeasurable genius of the elder civilizations of the Orient was there legibly written, and recalled the granite and brick debauches of Egypt and Assyria. Something of the spirit of the ancient architects of the tower of Lylax survived in those thick-set pillars with their deep-fluted trunks, whose capitals were formed by four heads of bulls, placed forehead to forehead, and bound together by knots of serpents that seemed striving to devour them,—an obscure cosmogonic symbol whereof the meaning was no longer intelligible, and had descended into the tomb with the hierophants of preceding ages. The gates were neither of a square nor rounded form; they described a sort of ogive much resembling the miter of the Magi, and by their fantastic character gave still more intensity to the character of the building.

This portion of the palace formed a sort of court surrounded by a portico whose architecture was ornamented with the genealogical bas-relief to which Candaules had alluded.

In the midst thereof sat Heracles upon a throne, with the upper part of his body uncovered, and his feet resting upon a stool, according to the rite for the representation of divine personages. His colossal proportions would otherwise have left no doubt as to his apotheosis; and the archaic rudeness and hugeness of the work, wrought by the chisel of some primitive artist, imparted to his figure an air of barbaric majesty, a savage grandeur more appropriate, perhaps, to the character of this monster-slaying hero than would have been the work of a sculptor consummate in his art.

On the right of the throne were Alcæus, son of the hero and of Omphale, Ninus, Belus, Argon, the earlier kings of the dynasty of the Heracleidæ;—then all the line of intermediate kings, terminating with Ardys, Alyattes, Meles or Myrsus, father of Candaules, and finally Candaules himself.

All these personages, with their hair braided into little strings, their beards spirally twisted, their oblique eyes, angular attitudes, cramped and stiff gestures, seemed to own a sort of factitious life, due to the rays of the setting sun, and the ruddy hue which time lends to marble in warm climates. The inscriptions in antique characters, graven beside them after the manner of legends, enhanced still more the mysterious weirdness of the long procession of figures in strange barbarian garb.

By a singular chance, which Gyges could not help observing, the statue of Candaules occupied the last available place at the right hand of Heracles;—the dynastic cycle was closed, and in order to find a place for the descendants of Candaules it would be absolutely necessary to build a new portico and commence the formation of a new bas-relief.

Candaules, whose arm still rested on the shoulder of Gyges, walked slowly round the portico in silence; he seemed to hesitate to enter into the subject, and had altogether forgotten the pretext under which he had led the captain of his guards into that solitary place.

"What would you do, Gyges," said Candaules, at last breaking the silence which had been growing painful to both, "if you were a diver, and should bring up from the green bosom of the ocean a pearl of incomparable purity and luster, and of worth so vast as to exhaust the richest treasures of the earth?"

"I would inclose it," answered Gyges, a little surprised at this brusque question, "in a cedar-box overlaid with plates of brass, and I would bury it under a detached rock in some desert place; and from time to time, when I should feel assured that none could see me, I would go thither to contemplate my precious jewel and admire the colors of the sky mingling with its nacreous tints."

"And I," replied Candaules, his eye illuminated with enthusiasm, "if I possessed so rich a gem, I would enshrine it in my diadem, that I might exhibit it freely to the eyes of all men, in the pure light of the sun,—that I might adorn myself with its splendor and smile with pride when I should hear it said: 'Never did king of Assyria or Babylon,—never did Greek or Trinacrian tyrant possess so lustrous a pearl as Candaules, son of Myrsus and descendant of Heracles, King of Sardes and of Lydia! Compared with Candaules, Midas, who changed all things to gold, were only a mendicant as poor as Irus.'"

Gyges listened with astonishment to this discourse of Candaules, and sought to penetrate the hidden sense of these lyric divagations. The king appeared to be in a state of extraordinary excitement: his eyes sparkled with enthusiasm; a feverish rosiness tinted his cheeks; his dilated nostrils inhaled the air with unusual effort.

"Well, Gyges," continued Candaules without appearing to notice the uneasiness of his favorite, —"I am that diver. Amid this dark ocean of humanity, wherein confusedly move so many defective or misshapen beings, — so many forms incomplete or degraded, — so many types of bestial ugliness, — wretched outlines of nature's experimental essays, — I have found beauty, pure, radiant, without spot, without flaw, — the ideal made real, the dream accomplished, — a form which no painter or sculptor has ever been able to translate upon canvas or into marble: — I have found Nyssia!"

"Although the queen has the timid modesty of the women of the Orient, and that no man save her husband has ever beheld her features, Fame, hundred-tongued and hundred-eared, has celebrated her praise throughout the world," answered Gyges, respectfully inclining his head as he spoke.

"Mere vague, insignificant rumors. They say of her, as of all women not actually ugly, that she is more beautiful than Aphrodite or Helen; but no person could form even the most remote idea of such perfection. In vain have I besought Nyssia to appear unveiled at some public festival, some solemn sacrifice; or to show herself for an instant leaning over the royal terrace, — bestowing upon her people the immense favor of one look, the prodigality of one profile-view,—more generous than the goddesses who permit their worshipers to behold only pale simulacra of ivory or alabaster. She would never consent to that. Now there is one strange thing, which I blush to acknowledge even to you, dear Gyges: formerly I was jealous; I wished to conceal my amours from all eyes,—no shadow was thick enough,—no mystery sufficiently impenetrable. Now I can no longer recognize myself: I have the feelings neither of a lover nor a husband;—my love has melted in adoration like thin wax in a fiery brazier. All petty feelings of jealousy or possession have vanished. No: the most finished work that heaven has ever given to earth, since the day that Prometheus held the flame under the right breast of the statue of clay, can not thus be kept hidden in the chill shadow of the gynæceum. Were I to die, then the secret of this beauty would forever remain shrouded beneath the somber draperies of widowhood! I feel myself culpable in its concealment, as though I had the sun in my house, and prevented it from illuminating the world. And when I think of those harmonious lines, those divine contours which I dare scarcely touch with a timid kiss, I feel my heart ready to burst, I wish that some friendly eye could share my happiness and,—like a severe judge to whom a picture is shown,—recognize after careful examination that it is irreproachable, and that the possessor has not been deceived by his enthusiasm. Yes: often do I feel myself tempted to tear off with rash hand those odious tissues; but Nyssia, in her fierce chastity, would never forgive me. And still I cannot alone endure such felicity: I must have a confidant for my ecstacies, an echo which will answer my cries of admiration,—and it shall be none other than you!"

Having uttered these words, Candaules brusquely turned and disappeared through a secret passage. Gyges, left thus alone, could not avoid noticing the peculiar concourse of events which seemed to place him always in Nyssia's path. A chance had enabled him to behold her beauty, though walled up from all other eyes;—among many princes and satraps she had chosen to espouse Candaules, the very king he served;—and, through some strange caprice, which he could only regard as fateful, this king had just made him, Gyges, his confidant in regard to the mysterious creature whom none else had approached, and absolutely sought to complete the work of Boreas on the plain of Bactria! Was not the hand of the gods visible in all these circumstances? That specter of beauty, whose veil seemed to be lifted slowly, a little at a time, as though to enkindle a flame within him,—was it not leading him, without his having suspected it, toward the accomplishment of some mighty destiny? Such were the questions which Gyges asked himself; but, being unable to penetrate the obscurity of the future, he resolved to await the course of events, and left the Court of Images, where the twilight darkness was commencing to pile itself up in all the angles, and to render the effigies of the ancestors of Candaules yet more and more weirdly menacing.

Was it a mere effort of light? or was it rather an illusion produced by that vague uneasiness with which the boldest hearts are filled by the approach of night amid ancient monuments? As he stepped across the threshold, Gyges fancied that he heard deep groans issue from the stone lips of the bas-reliefs; and it seemed to him that Heracles was making enormous efforts to loosen his granite club.

## CHAPTER III.

On the following day Candaules again took Gyges aside and continued the conversation begun under the portico of the Heracleidæ. Having freed himself from the embarrassment of broaching the subject, he freely unbosomed himself to his confidant; and had Nyssia been able to overhear him she might perhaps have been willing to pardon his conjugal indiscretions for the sake of his passionate eulogies of her charms.

Gyges listened to all these bursts of praise with the slightly constrained air of one who is yet uncertain whether his interlocutor is not feigning an enthusiasm more ardent than he actually feels, in order to provoke a confidence naturally cautious to utter itself. Candaules at last said to him in a tone of disappointment: "I see, Gyges, that you do not believe me; you think I am boasting, or have allowed myself to be fascinated like some clumsy laborer by a robust country girl on whose cheeks Hygeia has crushed the gross hues of health! No! by all the gods! I have collected within my home, like a living bouquet, the fairest flowers of Asia and of Greece. I know all that the art of sculptors and painters has produced since the time of Dædalus, whose statues walked and spoke. Linus, Orpheus, Homer, have taught me harmony and rhythm: I do not look about me with Love's bandage blindfolding my eyes. I judge of all things coolly. The passions of youth never influence my admiration; and when I am as withered, decrepit, wrinkled, as Tithonus in his swaddling bands, my opinion will be still the same. But I forgive your incredulity and want of sympathy. In order to understand me fully, it is necessary that you should see Nyssia in the radiant brilliancy of her shining whiteness,—free from jealous drapery,—even as nature with her own hands moulded her in a lost moment of inspiration which never can return. This evening I will hide you in a corner of the bridal chamber . . . . you shall see her!"

"Sire! what do you ask of me!" returned the young warrior with respectful firmness. "How shall I, from the depths of my dust,—from the abyss of my nothingness,—dare to raise my eyes to this sun of perfections, at the risk of remaining blind for the rest of my life, or being able to see naught but a dazzling specter in the midst of darkness? Have pity on your humble slave, and do not compel him to an action so contrary to the maxims of virtue:—no man should look upon what does not belong to him. We know that the Immortals always punish those who through imprudence or audacity, surprise them in their divine nudity. Nyssia is the loveliest of all women; you are the happiest of lovers and husbands:—Heracles your ancestor never found in the course of his many conquests aught to compare with your queen. If you, the prince of whom even the most skillful artists seek judgment and counsel,—if you find her incomparable, of what consequence can the opinion of an obscure soldier like me be to you? Abandon, therefore, this fantasy, which I presume to say is unworthy of your royal majesty; and of which you would repent so soon as it had been satisfied."

"Listen, Gyges," returned Candaules; "I perceive that you suspect me; you think that I seek to put you to some proof; but, by the ashes of that funeral pyre whence my ancestor arose a god! I swear to you that I speak frankly and without any after-purpose."

"O Candaules, I doubt not of your good faith; your passion is sincere;—but, perchance, after I should have obeyed you, you would conceive a deep aversion to me, and learn to hate me for not having more firmly resisted your will. You would seek to take back from these eyes, indiscreet through compulsion, the image which you allowed them to glance upon in a moment of delirium; and who knows but that you would condemn them to the eternal night of the tomb to punish them for remaining open at a moment when they ought to have been closed."

"Fear nothing; I pledge my royal word that no evil shall befall you!"

"Pardon your slave, if he still dares to offer some objection, even after such a promise. Have you reflected that what you propose to me is a violation of the sanctity of marriage,—a species of visual adultery? A woman often lays aside her modesty with her garments; and once violated by a look, without having actually ceased to be virtuous, she might deem that she had lost her flower of purity. You promise, indeed, to feel no resentment against me; but who can insure me against the wrath of Nyssia,—she who is so reserved and chaste, so apprehensive, fierce and virginal in her modesty that she might be deemed still ignorant of the laws of Hymen? Should she ever learn of the sacrilege which I am about to render myself guilty of in deferring to my master's wishes, what punishment would she condemn me to suffer in expiation of such a crime?

Who could place me beyond the reach of her avenging anger?"

"I did not know you were so wise and prudent," said Candaules, with a slightly ironical smile; "but such dangers are all imaginary; and I shall hide you in such a way that Nyssia will never know she has been seen by any one except her royal husband."

Being unable to offer any further defense, Gyges made a sign of assent in token of complete submission to the king's will. He had made all the resistance in his power; and thenceforward his conscience could feel at ease in regard to whatever might happen: besides, by any further opposition to the will of Candaules, he would have feared to oppose destiny itself, which seemed striving to bring him still nearer to Nyssia for some grim ulterior purpose into which it was not given to him to see further.

Without actually being able to foresee any result, he beheld a thousand vague and shadowy images passing before his eyes. That subterranean love, so long crouched at the foot of his soul's stairway, had climbed a few steps higher, guided by some fitful glimmer of hope: the weight of the Impossible no longer pressed so heavily upon his breast,—now that he believed himself aided by the gods. In truth, who would have dreamed that the much-boasted charms of the daughter of Megabazus would ere long cease to own any mystery for Gyges!

"Come, Gyges," said Candaules, taking him by the hand, "let us make profit of the time. Nyssia is walking in the garden with her women; let us look at the place, and plan our stratagems for this evening."

The King took his confidant by the hand and led him along the winding ways which conducted to the nuptial apartment. The doors of the sleeping-room were made of cedar planks so perfectly put together that it was impossible to discover the joints. By dint of rubbing them with wool steeped in oil, the slaves had rendered the wood as polished as marble: the brazen nails, with heads cut in facets, which studded them, had all the brilliancy of the purest gold. A complicated system of straps and metallic rings, whereof Candaules and his wife alone knew the combination, served to secure them; for in those heroic ages the locksmith's art was yet in its infancy.

Candaules unloosed the knots, made the rings slide back upon the thongs, raised with a handle which fitted into a mortise, the bar that fastened the door from within; and bidding Gyges place himself against the wall, turned back one of the folding doors upon him in such a way as to hide him completely;—yet the door did not fit so perfectly to its frame of oaken beams, all carefully polished and put up according to line by a skillful workman, that the young warrior could not obtain a distinct view of the chamber interior through the interstices contrived to give room for the free play of the hinges.

Facing the entrance, the royal bed stood upon an estrade of several steps, covered with purple drapery: columns of chased silver supported the entablature, all ornamented with foliage wrought in relief, amid which Loves were sporting with dolphins; and heavy curtains embroidered with gold surrounded it like the folds of a tent.

Upon the altar of the household gods were placed vases of precious metal, pateræ enameled with flowers, double-handled cups, and all things needful for libations.

Along the walls, which were faced with planks of cedar-wood, marvelously worked, at regular intervals stood tall statues of black basalt in the constrained attitudes of Egyptian art, each sustaining in its hand a bronze torch into which a splinter of resinous wood had been fitted.

An onyx lamp, suspended by a chain of silver,

hung from that beam of the ceiling which is called the black beam, because more exposed than the others to the embrowning smoke. Every evening a slave carefully filled this lamp with odoriferous oil.

Near the head of the bed, on a little column, hung a trophy of arms, consisting of a visored helmet, a two-fold buckler made of four bulls' hides and covered with plates of brass and tin, a two-edged sword, and several ashen javelins with brazen heads.

The tunics and mantles of Candaules were hung upon wooden pegs: they comprised garments both simple and double, that is, capable of going twice around the body;—a mantle of thrice-dyed purple, ornamented with embroidery representing a hunting scene wherein Laconian hounds were pursuing and tearing deer;—and a tunic whereof the material, fine and delicate as the skin which envelopes an onion, had all the sheen of woven sun-beams, were especially noticeable. Opposite to the trophy stood an arm-chair inlaid with silver and ivory upon which Nyssia hung her garments: its seat was covered with a leopard skin more eye-spotted than the body of Argus; and its foot-support was richly adorned with open-work carving.

"I am generally the first to retire," observed

Candaules to Gyges; "and I always leave this door open as it is now: Nyssia, who has invariably some tapestry flower to finish, or some order to give her women, usually delays a little in joining me; but at last she comes, and slowly takes off—one by one, as though the effort cost her dearly—and lays upon that ivory chair all those draperies and tunics which by day envelope her like mummy-bandages. From your hiding place you will be able to follow all her graceful movements, admire her unrivalled charms, and judge for yourself whether Candaules be a young fool prone to vain boasting, or whether he does not really possess the richest pearl of beauty that ever adorned a diadem."

"O King, I can well believe your words without such a proof as this," replied Gyges, stepping forth from his hiding place.

"When she has laid aside her garments," continued Candaules, without heeding the exclamation of his confidant, "she will come to lie down with me:—you must take advantage of the moment to steal away; for in passing from the chair to the bed she turns her back to the door. Step lightly as though you were treading upon ears of ripe wheat; take heed that no grain of sand squeaks under your sandals; hold your breath, and retire as stealthily as possible. The vestibule is all in darkness; and the feeble rays of the only lamp which remains burning do not penetrate beyond the threshold of the chamber. It is therefore certain that Nyssia can not possibly see you: and to-morrow there will be some one in the world who can comprehend my ecstacies, and will feel no longer astonished at my bursts of admiration. But see, the day is almost spent; the Sun will soon water his steeds in the Hesperian waves at the further end of the world, and beyond the Pillars erected by my ancestors;—return to your hiding place, Gyges; and though the hours of waiting may seem long, I can swear by Eros of the Golden Arrows that you will not regret having waited!"

After this assurance, Candaules left Gyges again hidden behind the door. The compulsory quiet which the king's young confidant found himself obliged to maintain left him ample leisure for thought. His situation was certainly a most extraordinary one. He had loved Nyssia as one loves a star: convinced of the hopelessness of the undertaking, he had made no effort to approach her. And nevertheless, by a succession of extraordinary events he was about to obtain a knowledge of treasures reserved for lovers and husbands only: not a word, not a glance had been exchanged between himself and Nyssia, who probably ignored the very existence of the one being for whom her beauty would so soon cease to be a mystery. Unknown to her whose modesty would have naught to sacrifice for you, how strange a situation!—to love a woman in secret and find oneself led by her husband to the threshold of the nuptial chamber,—to have for guide to that treasure the very dragon who should defend all approach to it,—was there not in all this ample food for astonishment and wonder at the combination of events wrought by destiny?

In the midst of these reflections, he suddenly heard the sound of footsteps on the pavement. It was only the slaves coming to replenish the oil in the lamp, throw fresh perfumes upon the coals of the *klamklins*, and arrange the purple and saffron-tinted sheepskins which formed the royal bed.

The hour approached, and Gyges felt his heart beat faster, and the pulsation of his arteries quicken. He even felt a strong impulse to steal away before the arrival of the queen, and, after averring subsequently to Candaules that he had remained, abandon himself confidently to the most extravagant eulogiums. He felt a strong repugnance—(for despite his somewhat free life, Gyges was not without delicacy)—to take by stealth a favor for the free granting of which he would gladly have paid with his life. The husband's complicity rendered this theft more odious in a certain sense; and he would have preferred to owe to any other circumstance the happiness of beholding the marvel of Asia in her nocturnal toilet. Perhaps, indeed, the approach of danger—let us acknowledge, as veracious historians—had no little to do with his virtuous scruples. Undoubtedly Gyges did not lack courage: mounted upon his war-chariot, with quiver rattling upon his shoulder, and bow in hand, he would have defied the most valiant warriors; in the chase he would have attacked without fear the Calydon boar or the Nemean lion; but—explain the enigma as you will—he trembled at the idea of looking at a beautiful woman through a chink in a door. No one possesses every kind of courage. He felt likewise that he could not behold Nyssia with impunity. It would be a decisive epoch in his life: through having obtained but a momentary glimpse of her he had lost all peace of mind;—what then would be the result of that which was about to take place? Could life itself continue for him when to that divine head which fired his dreams should be added a charming body—formed for the kisses of the Immortals? What would become of him should he find himself unable thereafter to contain his passion in darkness and silence as he had done till that time? Would he exhibit to the court of Lydia the ridiculous spectacle of an insane love?—or would he strive by some extravagant action to bring down upon himself the disdainful pity of the queen? Such a result was strongly probable, since the reason of Candaules himself, the legitimate possessor of Nyssia, had been unable to resist the vertigo caused by that superhuman beauty,—he, the thoughtless young king who till then had laughed at love, and preferred pictures and statues before all things. These arguments were very rational but wholly useless;—for at the same moment Candaules entered the chamber, and exclaimed in a low but distinct voice as he passed the door:—

"Patience, my poor Gyges, Nyssia will soon come!"

When he saw that he could no longer retreat, Gyges, who was but a young man after all, forgot every other consideration; and no longer thought of aught save the happiness of feasting his eyes upon the charming spectacle which Candaules was about to offer him. One can not demand from a captain of twenty-five the austerity of a hoary philosopher.

At last a low whispering of raiment sweeping and trailing over marble,—distinctly audible in the deep silence of the night,—announced the approach of the queen. In effect it was she: with a step as cadenced and rhythmic as an ode, she crossed the threshhold of the thalamus; and the wind of her veil with its floating folds almost touched the burning cheek of Gyges, who felt well nigh on the point of fainting, and found himself compelled to seek the support of the wall: but soon recovering from the violence of his emotions, he approached the chink of the door, and took the most favorable position for enabling him to lose nothing of the scene whereof he was about to be an invisible witness.

Nyssia advanced to the ivory chair and commenced to detach the pins, terminated by hollow balls of gold, which fastened her veil upon her head; and Gyges from the depths of the shadow-filled angle where he stood concealed, could examine at his ease the proud and charming face of which he had before obtained only a hurried glimpse;—that rounded neck, at once delicate and powerful, whereon Aphrodite had traced with the nail of her little finger, those three faint lines which are still at this very day known as the "Necklace of Venus;"—that white nape on whose alabaster surface little wild rebellious curls were disporting and entwining themselves ;—those silver shoulders, half-rising from the opening of the chlamys, like the moon's disk emerging from an opaque cloud. Candaules, half-reclining upon his cushions, gazed with fondness upon his wife, and thought to himself: "Now Gyges, who is so cold, so difficult to please, and so skeptical, must be already half convinced."

Opening a little coffer which stood on a table supported by one leg terminating in carven lion's paws, the queen freed her beautiful arms from the weight of the bracelets and jewelry wherewith they had been overburthened during the day,—arms whose form and whiteness might well have enabled them to compare with those of Hera, sister and wife of Zeus, the lord of Olympus. Precious as were her jewels, they were assuredly not worth the spots which they concealed, and had Nyssia been a coquette, one might have well supposed that she only donned them in order that she should be entreated to take them off: the rings and chased work had left upon her skin,—fine and tender as the interior pulp of a lily,—light rosy imprints, which she soon dissipated by rubbing them with her little taper-fingered hand, all rounded and slender at its extremities.

Then with the movement of a dove trembling in the snow of its feathers, she shook her hair, which being no longer held by the golden pins, rolled down in languid spirals like hyacinth flowers over her back and bosom:—thus she remained for a few moments ere reassembling the scattered curls and finally reuniting them into one mass. It was marvelous to watch the blonde ringlets streaming like jets of liquid gold between the silver of her fingers; and her arms undulating like swans' necks as they were arched above her head in the act of twisting and confining the natural bullion. If you have ever by chance examined one of those beautiful Etruscan vases with red figures on a black ground, and decorated with one of those subjects which are designated under the title of "Greek Toilette,"—then you will have some idea of the grace of Nyssia in that attitude which, from the age of antiquity to our own era, has furnished such a multitude of happy designs for painters and statuaries.

Having thus arranged her coiffure, she seated herself upon the edge of the ivory footstool and commenced to untie the little bands which fastened her buskins. We moderns, owing to our horrible system of footgear,—which is hardly less absurd than the Chinese shoe,—no longer know what a foot is. That of Nyssia was of a perfection rare even in Greece and antique Asia. The great toe, a little apart like the thumb of a bird,—the other toes, slightly long, and all ranged in charming symmetry,—the nails well shaped and brilliant as agates,—the ankles well rounded and supple,—the heel slightly tinted with a rosy hue,—nothing was wanting to the perfection of the little member. The leg attached to this foot, and which gleamed like polished marble under the lamp light, was irreproachable in the purity of its outlines and the grace of its curves.

Gyges, lost in contemplation, though all the while fully comprehending the madness of Candaules, said to himself that had the gods bestowed such a treasure upon him he would have known how to keep it to himself.

"Well, Nyssia, are you not coming to sleep with me?" exclaimed Candaules, seeing that the queen was not hurrying herself in the least, and feeling desirous to abridge the watch of Gyges.

"Yes, my dear lord; I will soon be ready," answered Nyssia.

And she detached the cameo which fastened the peplum upon her shoulder:—there remained only the tunic to let fall. Gyges, behind the door, felt his veins hiss through his temples; his heart beat so violently that he feared it must make itself heard in the chamber, and to repress its fierce pulsations he pressed his hand upon his bosom:—and when Nyssia, with a movement of careless grace, unfastened the girdle of her tunic, he thought his knees would give way beneath him.

Nyssia—was it an instinctive presentiment? or was her skin, virginally pure from profane looks, so delicately magnetic in its susceptibility that it could feel the rays of a passionate eye though that eye was invisible?—Nyssia hesitated to strip herself of that tunic, the last rampart of her modesty. Twice or thrice her shoulders, her bosom, and bare arms, shuddered with a nervous chill, as though they had been suddenly grazed by the wings of a nocturnal butterfly, or as though an insolent lip had dared to touch them in the darkness.

At last, seeming to nerve herself for a sudden resolve, she doffed the tunic in its turn; and the white poem of her divine body suddenly appeared in all its splendor—like the statue of a goddess unveiled on the day of a temple's inauguration. Shuddering with pleasure the light glided and gloated over those exquisite forms, and covered them with timid kisses, profiting by an occasion, alas, rare indeed!—the rays scattered through the chamber, disdaining to illuminate golden arms, jeweled clasps, or brazen tripods, all concentrated themselves upon Nyssia, and left all other objects in obscurity. Were we Greeks of the age of Pericles, we might at our ease eulogize those beautiful serpentine lines,—those polished flanks, those elegant curves, those breasts which might have served as molds for the cup of Hebe; but modern prudery forbids such descriptions, for the pen can not find pardon for what is permitted to the chisel; and besides, there are some things which can be written of only in marble.

Candaules smiled in proud satisfaction. With a rapid step,—as though ashamed of being so beautiful, for she was only the daughter of a man and a woman,—Nyssia approached the bed, her arms folded upon her bosom;—but with a sudden movement she turned round ere taking her place upon the couch beside her royal spouse, and beheld through the aperture of the door a gleaming eye flaming like the carbuncle of Oriental legend; —for if it were false that she had a double pupil and that she possessed the stone which is found in the heads of dragons, it was at least true that her green glance penetrated darkness like the glaucous eye of the cat and tiger.

A cry, like that of a fawn who receives an arrow in her flank while tranquilly dreaming among the leafy shadows, was on the point of bursting from her lips; yet she found strength to control herself, and lay down beside Candaules, cold as a serpent, with the violets of death upon her cheeks and lips: not a muscle of her limbs quivered; not a fiber of her body palpitated; and soon her slow, regular breathing seemed to indicate that Morpheus had distilled his poppy juice upon her eyelids.

She had divined and comprehended all.

## CHAPTER IV.

Gyges, trembling and distracted with passion, had retired, following exactly the instructions of Candaules; and if Nyssia, through some unfortunate chance, had not turned her head ere taking her place upon the couch, and perceived him in the act of taking flight, doubtless she would have remained forever unconscious of the outrage done to her charms by a husband more passionate than scrupulous.

Accustomed to the winding corridors of the palace, the young warrior had no difficulty in finding his way out. He passed through the city at a reckless pace like a madman escaped from Anticyra, and by making himself known to the sentinels who guarded the ramparts, he had the gates opened for him and gained the fields beyond. His brain burned; his cheeks flamed as with the fires of fever; his breath came hotly panting through his lips:—he flung himself down upon the meadow-sod humid with the tears of the night;—and at last hearing in the darkness, through the thick grass and water-plants the silvery respiration of a Naiad, he dragged himself to the spring, plunged his hands and arms into the crystal flood, bathed his face, and drank several mouthfuls of the water in the hope to cool the ardor which was devouring him. Any one who could have seen him thus hopelessly bending over the spring in the feeble starlight would have taken him for Narcissus pursuing his own shadow; but it was not of himself assuredly that Gyges was enamored.

The rapid apparition of Nyssia had dazzled his eyes like the keen zigzag of a lightning-flash: he beheld her floating before him in a luminous whirlwind, and felt that never through all his life could he banish that image from his vision. His love had grown to vastness; its flower had suddenly burst, like those plants which open their blossoms with a clap of thunder. To master his passion were henceforth a thing impossible:—as well counsel the empurpled waves which Poseidon lifts with his trident to lie tranquilly in their bed of sand and cease to foam upon the rocks of the shore. Gyges was no longer master of himself; and he felt a miserable despair, as of a man riding in a chariot, who finds his terrified and uncontrollable horses rushing with all the speed of a furious gallop toward some rock-bristling precipice. A hundred thousand projects, each wilder than the last, whirled confusedly through his brain: he blasphemed Destiny; he cursed his mother for having given him life, and the gods that they had not caused him to be born to a throne; for then he might have been able to espouse the daughter of the satrap.

A frightful agony gnawed at his heart;—he was jealous of the king. From the moment of the tunic's fall at the feet of Nyssia, like the flight of a white dove alighting upon a meadow, it had seemed to him that she belonged to him,—he deemed himself despoiled of his wealth by Candaules. In all his amorous reveries he had never until then thought of the husband;—he had thought of the queen only as of a pure abstraction, without representing to himself in fancy all those intimate details of conjugal familiarity, so poignant, so bitter for those who love a woman in the power of another. Now he had beheld Nyssia's blonde head bending like a blossom beside the dark head of Candaules;—the very thought of it had inflamed his anger to the highest degree, although a moment's reflection should have convinced him that things could not have come to pass otherwise; and he felt growing within him a most unjust hatred against his master. The act of having compelled his presence at the queen's dishabille seemed to him a barbarous irony, an odious refinement of cruelty; for he did not remember that his love for her could not have been known by the king, who had sought in him only a confidant of easy morals and a connoisseur in beauty. That which he ought to have regarded as a great favor affected him like a mortal injury for which he was meditating vengeance. While thinking that to-morrow the same scene of which he had been a mute and invisible witness would infallibly renew itself, his tongue clove to his palate, his forehead became imbeaded with drops of cold sweat; and his hand convulsively grasped the hilt of his great double-edged sword.

Nevertheless, thanks to the freshness of the night, that excellent counselor, he became a little calmer, and returned to Sardes before the morning light had become bright enough to enable a few early rising citizens and slaves to notice the pallor of his brow and the disorder of his apparel: he betook himself to his regular post at the palace, well suspecting that Candaules would shortly send for him; and, however violent the agitation of his feelings, he felt he was not powerful enough to brave the anger of the king, and could in no way escape submitting again to this *rôle* of confidant, which could thenceforth only inspire him with horror. Having arrived at the palace, he seated himself upon the steps of the cypress-paneled vestibule, leaned his back against a column, and, under the pretext of being fatigued by the long vigil under arms, he covered his head with his mantle and feigned sleep to avoid answering the questions of the other guards.

If the night had been terrible to Gyges, it had not been less so to Nyssia; as she never for an instant doubted that he had been purposely hidden there by Candaules. The king's persistency in begging her not to veil so austerely a face which the gods had made for the admiration of men; his evident vexation upon her refusal to appear in Greek costume at the sacrifices and public solemnities; his unsparing raillery at what he termed her Barbarian shyness,—all tended to convince her that the young Heracleid had sought to admit some one into those mysteries which should remain secret to all: for without his encouragement, no man could have dared to risk himself in an undertaking the discovery of which would have resulted in the punishment of a speedy death.

How slowly did the black hours seem to her to pass!—how anxiously did she await the coming of dawn to mingle its bluish tints with the yellow gleams of the almost exhausted lamp! It seemed to her that Apollo would never mount his chariot again; and that some invisible hand was sustaining the sand of the hour-glass in air. Though brief as any other, that night seemed to her like the Cimmerian nights,—six long months of darkness.

While it lasted she lay motionless and rigid at full length on the very edge of her couch in dread of being touched by Candaules. If she had not up to that night felt a very strong love for the son of Myrsus, she had, at least, ever exhibited toward him that grave and serene tenderness which every virtuous woman entertains for her husband, although the altogether Greek freedom of his morals frequently displeased her, and though he entertained ideas at variance with her own in regard to modesty: but after such an affront she could only feel the chilliest hatred and most icy contempt for him;—she would have preferred even death to one of his caresses. Such an outrage it was impossible to forgive; for among the Barbarians, and above all among the Persians and Bactrians, it was held a great disgrace, not for women only, but even for men, to be seen without their garments.

At length Candaules arose; and Nyssia, awaking from her simulated sleep, hurried from that chamber now profaned in her eyes as though it had served for the nocturnal orgies of Bacchantes and courtesans. It was agony for her to breathe that impure air any longer; and that she might freely give herself up to her grief she took refuge in the upper apartments reserved for the women; summoned her slaves by clapping her hands; and poured ewers of water over her shoulders, her bosom, and her whole body, as though hoping by this species of lustral ablution to efface the soil imprinted by the eyes of Gyges. She would have voluntarily torn, as it were, from her body that skin upon which the rays shot from a burning pupil seemed to have left their traces. Taking from the hands of her waiting women the thick downy materials which served to drink up the last pearls of the bath, she wiped herself with such violence that a slight purple cloud rose to the spots she had rubbed.

"In vain," she exclaimed, letting the damp tissues fall, and dismissing her attendants,—"in vain would I pour over myself all the waters of all the springs and the rivers;—the ocean, with all its bitter gulfs, could not purify me. Such a stain may be washed out only with blood. Oh! that look, that look!—it has incrusted itself upon me; it clasps me, covers me, burns me like the tunic dipped in the blood of Nessus; I feel it beneath my draperies, like an envenomed tissue which nothing can detach from my body! Now, indeed, would I vainly pile garments upon garments, select materials the least transparent, and the thickest of mantles: I would none the less bear upon my naked flesh this infamous robe woven by one adulterous and lascivious glance. Vainly, since the hour when I issued from the chaste womb of my mother, have I been brought up in private, enveloped like Isis, the Egyptian goddess, with a veil of which none might have lifted the hem without paying for his audacity with his life;—in vain have I remained guarded from all evil desires, from all profane imaginings, unknown of men, virgin as the snow on which the eagle himself could not imprint the seal of his talons, so loftily does the mountain which it covers lift its head in the pure and icy air: the depraved caprice of a Lydian Greek has sufficed to make me lose in a single instant, without any guilt of mine, all the fruit of long years of precaution and reserve. Innocent and dishonored, hidden from all yet made public to all . . . this is the lot to which Candaules has condemned me. Who can assure me, that, at this very moment, Gyges is not in the act of discoursing upon my charms with some soldiers at the very threshold of the palace? O shame! O infamy!—two men have beheld me naked and yet at this instant enjoy the sweet light of the sun! In what does Nyssia now differ from the most shameless hetaira,—from the vilest of courtesans? This body which I have striven to render worthy of being the habitation of a pure and noble soul, serves for a theme of conversation; —it is talked of like some lascivious idol brought from Sicyon or from Corinth;—it is commended or found fault with: the shoulder is perfect, the arm is charming, perhaps a little thin,—what know I? All the blood of my heart leaps to my cheeks at such a thought. O beauty, fatal gift of the gods! why am I not the wife of some poor mountain goatherd of innocent and simple habits?—he would not have suborned a goatherd like himself at the threshold of his cabin to profane his humble happiness! My lean figure, my unkempt hair, my complexion faded by the burning sun, would then have saved me from so gross an insult; and my honest homeliness would not have been compelled to blush. How shall I dare, after the scene of this night, to pass before those men, proudly erect under the folds of a tunic which has no longer aught to hide from either of them:—I should drop dead with shame upon the pavement! Candaules,

Candaules! I was at least entitled to more respect from you; and there was nothing in my conduct which could have provoked such an outrage. Was I one of those ones whose arms forever cling like ivy to their husbands' necks, and who seem more like slaves bought with money for a master's pleasure than free-born women of noble blood?—have I ever after a repast sung amorous hymns accompanying myself upon the lyre, with wine-moist lips, naked shoulders, and a wreath of roses about my hair; or given you cause, by any immodest action, to treat me like a mistress whom one shows after a banquet to his companions in debauch?"

While Nyssia was thus buried in her grief, great tears overflowed from her eyes like rain-drops from the azure chalice of a lotus-flower after some storm, and rolling down her pale cheeks fell upon her fair forlorn hands, languishingly open, like roses whose leaves are half-shed; for no order came from the brain to give them activity. The attitude of Niobe, beholding her fourteenth child succumb beneath the arrows of Apollo and Diana, was not more sadly despairing; but soon starting from this state of prostration, she rolled herself upon the floor, rent her garments, covered her beautiful disheveled hair with ashes, tore her bosom and cheeks with her nails amid convulsive sobs, and abandoned herself to all the excesses of Oriental grief, —the more violently that she had been forced so long to contain her indignation, shame, pangs of wounded dignity and all the agony that convulsed her soul; for the pride of her whole life had been broken, and the idea that she had nothing wherewith to reproach herself afforded her no consolation. As a poet has said, only the innocent know remorse. She was repenting of the crime which another had committed.

Nevertheless she made an effort to recover herself, ordered the baskets filled with wools of different colors, and the spindles wrapped with flax to be brought to her; and distributed the work to her women as she had been accustomed to do: but she thought she noticed that the slaves looked at her in a very peculiar way, and had ceased to entertain the same timid respect for her as before. Her voice no longer rang with the same assurance; there was something humble and furtive in her demeanor: she felt herself interiorly fallen.

Doubtless her scruples were exaggerated; and her virtue had received no stain from the folly of Candaules; but ideas imbibed with a mother's milk obtain irresistible sway; and the modesty of the body is carried by Oriental nations to an extent almost incomprehensible to Occidental races. When a man desired to speak to Nyssia in the palace of Megabazus at Bactria, he was obliged to do so keeping his eyes fixed upon the ground; and two eunuchs stood beside him, poniard in hand, ready to plunge their keen blades through his heart should he dare lift his head to look at the princess, notwithstanding that her face was veiled. You may readily conceive, therefore, how deadly an injury the action of Candaules would seem to a woman thus brought up, while any other would doubtless have considered it only a culpable frivolity. Thus the idea of vengeance had instantly presented itself to Nyssia, and had given her sufficient self-control to strangle the cry of her offended modesty ere it reached her lips, at the moment when, turning her head, she beheld the burning eyes of Gyges flaming through the darkness. She must have possessed the courage of the warrior in ambush, who, wounded by a random dart, utters no syllable of pain through fear of betraying himself behind his shelter of foliage or river-reeds; and in silence permits his blood to stripe his flesh with long red lines. Had she not withheld that first impulse to cry aloud, Candaules, alarmed and forewarned, would have kept upon his guard, which must have rendered it more difficult, if not impossible, to carry out her purpose.

Nevertheless, as yet she had conceived no definite plan; but she had resolved that the insult done to her honor should be fully expiated. At first she had thought of killing Candaules herself while he slept, with the sword hung at the bedside. But she recoiled from the thought of dipping her beautiful hands in blood; she feared lest she might miss her blow; and, with all her bitter anger, she hesitated at so violent and unwomanly an act.

Suddenly she appeared to have decided upon some project: She summoned Statira, one of the waiting women who had come with her from Bactria, and in whom she placed much confidence; and whispered a few words close to her ear in a very low voice, although there were no other persons in the room, as if she feared that even the walls might hear her.

Statira bowed low, and immediately left the apartment.

Like all persons who are actually menaced by some great peril, Candaules presumed himself perfectly secure. He was certain that Gyges had stolen away unperceived; and he thought only upon the delight of conversing with him about the unrivaled attractions of his wife.

So he caused him to be summoned, and conducted him to the Court of the Heracleidæ.

"Well, Gyges!" he said to him with laughing mien, "I did not deceive you when I assured you that you would not regret having passed a few hours behind that blessed door? Am I right? Do you know of any living woman more beautiful than the queen? If you know of any superior to her, tell me so frankly; and go bear her in my name this string of pearls, the symbol of power."

"Sire," replied Gyges in a voice trembling with emotion, "no human creature is worthy to compare with Nyssia: it is not the pearl fillet of queens which should adorn her brows, but only the starry crown of the Immortals."

"I well knew that your ice must melt at last in the fires of that sun!—Now you can comprehend my passion, my delirium, my mad desires?—Is it not true, Gyges, that the heart of a man is not great enough to contain such a love?—It must overflow and diffuse itself."

A hot blush overspread the cheeks of Gyges, who now but too well comprehended the admiration of Candaules.

The king noticed it, and said, with a manner half smiling, half serious:

"My poor friend, do not commit the folly of becoming enamored of Nyssia; you would lose your pains: it is a statue which I have enabled you to see,—not a woman. I have allowed you to read some stanzas of a beautiful poem, whereof I alone possess the manuscript, merely for the purpose of having your opinion: that is all!"

"You have no need, Sire, to remind me of my nothingness. Sometimes the humblest slave is visited in his slumbers by some radiant and lovely vision, with ideal forms, nacreous flesh, ambrosial hair. I,—I have dreamed with open eyes;—you are the god who sent me that dream."

"Now," continued the king, "it will scarcely be necessary for me to enjoin silence upon you: if you do not keep a seal upon your lips you might learn to your cost that Nyssia is not as good as she is beautiful."

The king waved his hand in token of farewell to his confidant, and retired for the purpose of inspecting an antique bed sculptured by Ikmalius, a celebrated artisan, which had been offered him for purchase.

Candaules had scarcely disappeared when a woman, wrapped in a long mantle so as to leave but one of her eyes exposed, after the fashion of the Barbarians, came forth from the shadow of a column behind which she had kept herself hidden during the conversation of the king and his favorite; walked straight to Gyges; placed her finger upon his shoulder, and made a sign to him to follow her.

## CHAPTER V.

Statira, followed by Gyges, paused before a little door, of which she raised the latch by pulling a silver ring attached to a leathern strap, and commenced to ascend a stairway with rather high steps contrived in the thickness of the wall. At the head of the stairway was a second door, which she opened with a key wrought of ivory and brass. As soon as Gyges entered, she disappeared without any further explanation in regard to what was expected of him.

The curiosity of Gyges was mingled with uneasiness: he could form no idea as to the significance of this mysterious message. He had a vague fancy that he could recognize in the silent Iris one of Nyssia's women; and the way by which she had made him follow her led to the queen's apartments. He asked himself in terror whether he had been perceived in his hiding-place or betrayed by Candaules; for both suppositions seemed probable.

At the idea that Nyssia knew all, he felt his face bedewed with a sweat alternately burning and icy: he sought to fly; but the door had been fastened upon him by Statira, and all escape was cut off; then he advanced into the chamber, which was shadowed by heavy purple hangings,—and found himself face to face with Nyssia. He thought he beheld a statue rise before him, such was her pallor. The hues of life had abandoned her face; a feeble rose-tint alone animated her lips; on her tender temples a few almost imperceptible veins intercrossed their azure net-work; tears had swollen her eyelids, and left shining furrows upon the down of her cheeks; the chrysoprase tints of her eyes had lost their intensity. She was even more beautiful and touching thus. Sorrow had given soul to her marmorean beauty.

Her disordered robe, scarcely fastened to her shoulders, left visible her beautiful bare arms, her throat, and the commencement of her death-white bosom. Like a warrior vanquished in his first conflict, her beauty had laid down its arms. Of what use to her would have been the draperies which conceal form,—the tunics with their carefully fastened folds? Did not Gyges know her? Wherefore defend what has been lost in advance?

She walked straight to Gyges; and fixing upon him an imperial look, clear and commanding, said to him, in a quick, abrupt voice:

"Do not lie; seek no vain subterfuges; have at

least the dignity and courage of your crime: I know all;—I saw you!—Not a word of excuse: I would not listen to it.—Candaules himself concealed you behind the door. Is it not so the thing happened? And you fancy, doubtless, that it is all over? Unhappily I am not a Greek woman, pliant to the whims of artists and voluptuaries. Nyssia will not serve for anyone's toy. There are now two men, one of whom is a man too much upon the earth:—he must disappear from it! Unless he dies, I can not live. It will be either you or Candaules: I leave you master of the choice. Kill him, avenge me, and win by that murder both my hand and the throne of Lydia; or else shall a prompt death henceforth prevent you from beholding, through a cowardly complaisance, what you have not the right to look upon. He who commanded is more culpable than he who has only obeyed; and moreover, should you become my husband, no one will have ever seen me without having the right to do so. But make your decision at once; for two of those four eyes in which my nudity has reflected itself must before this very evening be forever extinguished."

This strange alternative, proposed with a terrible coolness, with an immutable resolution, so utterly surprised Gyges, who was expecting reproaches, menaces, and a violent scene, that he remained for several minutes without color and without voice, livid as a Shade on the shores of the black rivers of hell.

"I!—to dip my hands in the blood of my master! Is it indeed you, O Queen, who demand of me so great a penalty? I comprehend all your anger; I feel it to be just; and it was not my fault that this outrage took place: but you know that Kings are mighty; they descend from a divine race. Our destinies repose on their august knees; and it is not we, feeble mortals, who may hesitate at their commands. Their will overthrows our refusal, as a dyke is swept away by a torrent. By your feet that I kiss, by the hem of your robe which I touch as a suppliant, be clement!—forget this injury, which is known to none, and which shall remain eternally buried in darkness and silence! Candaules worships you, admires you; and his fault springs only from an excess of love."

"Were you addressing a sphinx of granite in the arid sands of Egypt, you would have more chance of melting her. The winged words might fly uninterruptedly from your lips for a whole olympiad;—you could not move my resolution in the slightest. A heart of brass dwells in this marble breast of mine . . . . Die or kill!—When the sunbeam which has passed through the curtains shall touch the foot of this table, let your choice have been made . . . . I wait."

And Nyssia crossed her arms upon her breast in an attitude replete with somber majesty.

To behold her standing erect, motionless and pale, her eyes fixed, her brows contracted, her hair in disorder, her foot firmly placed upon the pavement, one would have taken her for Nemesis descended from her griffin, and awaiting the hour to smite a guilty one.

"The shadowy depths of Hades are visited by none with pleasure," answered Gyges: "it is sweet to enjoy the pure light of day: and the heroes themselves who dwell in the Fortunate Isles would gladly return to their native land. Each man has the instinct of self-preservation; and, since blood must flow, let it be rather from the veins of another than from mine."

To these sentiments, avowed by Gyges with antique frankness, were added others more noble whereof he did not speak:—he was desperately in love with Nyssia, and jealous of Candaules. It was not, therefore, the fear of death alone that had induced him to undertake this bloody task. The thought of leaving Candaules in free possession of Nyssia was insupportable to him; and, moreover, the vertigo of fatality had seized him. By a succession of irregular and terrible events he beheld himself hurried toward the realization of his dreams; a mighty wave had lifted him and borne him on in despite of his efforts; Nyssia herself was extending her hand to him, to help him to ascend the steps of the royal throne: all this had caused him to forget that Candaules was his master and his benefactor;—for none can flee from Fate, and Necessity walks on with nails in one hand and whip in the other, to stop your advance or to urge you forward.

"It is well," replied Nyssia; "here is the means of execution." And she drew from her bosom a Bactrian poniard, with a jade handle enriched with inlaid circles of white gold. "This blade is not made of brass, but with iron difficult to work, tempered in flame and water, so that Hephaistos himself could not forge one more keenly pointed or finely edged. It would pierce, like thin papyrus, metal cuirasses and bucklers of dragon's skin.

"The time,"—she continued with the same icy coolness,—"shall be while he slumbers. Let him sleep and wake no more!"

Her accomplice, Gyges, harkened to her words with stupefaction; for he had never thought he could find such resolution in a woman who could not bring herself to lift her veil.

"The ambuscade shall be laid in the very same place where the infamous one concealed you in order to expose me to your gaze. At the approach of night I shall turn back one of the folding doors upon you, undress myself, lie down; and when he shall be asleep I will give you a signal . . . . Above all things, let there be no hesitancy, no feebleness; and take heed that your hand does not tremble when the moment shall have come! And now, for fear lest you might change your mind, I propose to make sure of your person until the fatal hour;—You might attempt to escape, —to forewarn your master: do not think to do so!"

Nyssia whistled in a peculiar way; and immediately, from behind a Persian tapestry embroidered with flowers, there appeared four monsters, swarthy, clad in robes diagonally striped, which left visible arms muscled and gnarled as trunks of oaks: their thick pouting lips, the gold rings which they wore through the partition of their nostrils, their great teeth sharp as the fangs of wolves, the expression of stupid servility on their faces, rendered them hideous to behold.

The queen pronounced some words in a language unknown to Gyges—doubtless in Bactrian, —and the four slaves rushed upon the young man, seized him, and carried him away, even as a nurse might carry off a child in the fold of her robe.

Now what were Nyssia's real thoughts? Had she, indeed, noticed Gyges at the time of her meeting with him near Bactria, and preserved some memory of the young captain in one of those secret recesses of the heart where even the most virtuous women always have something buried? Was the desire to avenge her modesty goaded by some other unacknowledged desire?—and if Gyges had not been the handsomest young man in all Asia would she have evinced the same ardor in punishing Candaules for having outraged the sanctity of marriage? That is a delicate question to resolve, especially after a lapse of three thousand years; and although we have consulted Herodotus, Hephæstion, Plato, Dositheus, Archilochus of Paros, Hesychius of Miletus, Ptolomœus, Euphorion, and all who have spoken either at length or in only a few words concerning Candaules, Nyssia, and Gyges, we have been unable to arrive at any definite conclusion. To pursue so fleeting a shadow through so many centuries, under the ruins of so many crumbled empires, under the dust of departed nations, is a work of extreme difficulty, not to say impossibility.

At all events, Nyssia's resolution was implacably taken; this murder appeared to her in the light of the accomplishment of a sacred duty. Among the barbarian nations every man who has surprised a woman in her nakedness is put to death. The queen believed herself exercising her right;—only, inasmuch as the injury had been secret, she was doing herself justice as best she could. The passive accomplice would become the executioner of the other; and the punishment would thus spring from the crime itself. The hand would chastise the head.

The olive-tinted monsters shut Gyges up in an obscure portion of the palace, whence it was impossible that he could escape, or that his cries could be heard.

He passed the remainder of the day there in a state of cruel anxiety; accusing the Hours of being lame, and again of walking too speedily. The crime which he was about to commit,—although he was only, in some sort, the instrument of it, and though he was only yielding to an irresistible influence,—presented itself to his mind in the most somber colors. If the blow should miss through one of those circumstances which none could foresee?—if the people of Sardes should revolt and seek to avenge the death of the King? Such were the very sensible, though useless reflections which Gyges made while waiting to be taken from his prison and led to the place whence he could only depart to strike his master.

At last the night unfolded her starry robe in the sky; and its shadow fell upon the city and the palace. A light footstep became audible; a veiled woman entered the room, and conducted him through the obscure corridors and multiplied mazes of the royal edifice with as much confidence as though she had been preceded by a slave bearing a lamp or a torch.

The hand which held that of Gyges was cold, soft, and small; nevertheless those slender fingers clasped it with a bruising force, as the fingers of some statue of brass animated by a prodigy would have done: the rigidity of an inflexible will betrayed itself in that ever-equal pressure as of a vise,—a pressure which no hesitation of head or heart came to vary. Gyges, conquered, subjugated, crushed, yielded to that imperious traction, as though he were borne along by the mighty arm of Fate.

Alas! it was not thus he had wished to touch for the first time that fair royal hand, which had presented the poniard to him, and was leading him to murder; for it was Nyssia herself who had come for Gyges, to conceal him in the place of ambuscade.

No word was exchanged between the sinister couple on the way from the prison to the nuptial chamber.

The queen unfastened the thongs, raised the bar of the entrance, and placed Gyges behind the folding door as Candaules had done the evening previous. This repetition of the same acts, with so different a purpose, had something of a lugubrious and fatal character. Vengeance, this time, had placed her foot upon every track left by the insult: the chastisement and the crime alike followed the same path. Yesterday, it was the turn of Candaules; to-day, it was that of Nyssia: and Gyges, accomplice in the injury, was also accomplice in the penalty. He had served the king to dishonor the queen; he would serve the queen to kill the king,—equally exposed by the vices of the one and the virtues of the other.

The daughter of Megabazus seemed to feel a savage joy, a ferocious pleasure, in employing only the same means chosen by the Lydian king, and turning to account for the murder those very precautions which had been adopted for voluptuous fantasy.

"You will again this evening see me take off

these garments which are so displeasing to Candaules. This spectacle should become wearisome to you," said the queen in accents of bitter irony, as she stood on the threshold of the chamber;—"you will end by finding me ugly." And a sardonic, forced laugh momentarily curled her pale mouth; then, regaining her impassible severity of mien, she continued; "Do not imagine you will be able to steal away this time as you did before; you know my sight is piercing. At the slightest movement on your part, I shall awake Candaules; and you know that it will not be easy for you to explain what you are doing in the king's apartments, behind a door, with a poniard in your hand.—Further: my Bactrian slaves,—the copper-colored mutes who imprisoned you a short time ago,—guard all the issues of the palace, with orders to massacre you should you attempt to go out. Therefore let no vain scruples of fidelity cause you to hesitate. Think that I will make you King of Sardes, and that . . . . I will love you if you avenge me. The blood of Candaules will be your purple; and his death will make for you a place in that bed."

The slaves came according to their custom, to change the fuel in the tripod, renew the oil in the lamps, spread tapestry and the skins of animals upon the royal couch; and Nyssia hurried into the chamber as soon as she heard their footsteps resounding in the distance.

In a short time Candaules arrived all joyous: he had purchased the bed of Ikmalius and proposed to substitute it for the bed wrought after the Oriental fashion, which he declared had never been much to his taste. He seemed pleased to find that Nyssia had already retired to the nuptial chamber.

"The trade of embroidery, and spindles, and needles seems not to have the same attraction for you to-day as usual. In fact it is a monotonous labor to perpetually pass one thread between other threads; and I wonder at the pleasure which you seem ordinarily to take in it. To tell the truth, I am afraid that some fine day Pallas-Athena, on finding you so skillful, will break her shuttle over your head as she once did to poor Arachne."

"My lord, I felt somewhat tired this evening, and so came down stairs sooner than usual. Would you not like before going to sleep to drink a cup of black Samian wine mixed with the honey of Hymettus?" And she poured from a golden urn, into a cup of the same metal, the somber-colored beverage which she had mingled with the soporiferous juice of the nepenthe.

Candaules took the cup by both handles and drained it to the last drop; but the young Heracleid had a strong head, and sinking his elbow into the cushions of his couch he watched Nyssia undressing without any sign that the dust of sleep was commencing to gather upon his eyes.

As on the evening before, Nyssia unfastened her hair and permitted its rich blonde waves to ripple over her shoulders. From his hiding place Gyges fancied that he saw those locks slowly becoming suffused with tawny tints,—illuminated with reflections of blood and flame; and their heavy curls seemed to lengthen with viperine undulations, like the hair of the Gorgons and Medusas.

All simple and graceful as that action was in itself, it took from the terrible events about to transpire a frightful and ominous character, which caused the hidden assassin to shudder with terror.

Nyssia then unfastened her bracelets, but, agitated as her hands had been by nervous straining, they ill served her will. She broke the string of a bracelet of beads of amber inlaid with gold, which rolled over the floor with a loud noise, causing Candaules to reopen his gradually-closing eyes.

Each one of those beads fell upon the heart of Gyges as a drop of molten lead falls upon water.

Having unlaced her buskins, the queen threw

her upper tunic over the back of an ivory chair. This drapery, thus arranged, produced upon Gyges the effect of one of those sinister-folding winding sheets wherein the dead were wrapped ere being borne to the funeral pyre. Every object in that room, which had the evening before seemed to him one scene of smiling splendor, now appeared to him livid, dim, and menacing. The statues of basalt rolled their eyes and smiled hideously. The lamp flickered weirdly; and its flame dishevelled itself in red and sanguine rays like the crest of a comet:—far back in the dimly lighted corners loomed the monstrous forms of the Lares and Lemures. The mantles hanging from their hooks seemed animated by a factitious life, and assumed a human aspect of vitality; and when Nyssia, stripped of her last garment, approached the bed, all white and naked as a Shade, he thought that Death herself had broken the diamond fetters wherewith Hercules of old enchained her at the gates of Hell when he delivered Alcestes, and had come in person to take possession of Candaules.

Overcome by the power of the nepenthe-juice, the king at last slumbered. Nyssia made a sign for Gyges to come forth from his retreat; and, laying her finger upon the breast of the victim, she directed upon her accomplice a look so humid,—

so lustrous,—so weighty with languishment,—so replete with intoxicating promise, that Gyges, maddened and fascinated, sprang from his hiding place like the tiger from the summit of the rock where it has been crouching, traversed the chamber at a bound, and plunged the Bactrian poniard up to the very hilt in the heart of the descendant of Hercules. The chastity of Nyssia was avenged, and the dream of Gyges accomplished.

Thus ended the dynasty of the Heracleidæ, after having endured for five hundred and five years; and commenced that of the Mermnades in the person of Gyges, son of Dascylus. The Sardians, indignant at the death of Candaules, threatened revolt; but the oracle of Delphi having declared in favor of Gyges, who had sent thither a vast number of silver vases and six golden cratera of the value of thirty talents, the new king maintained his seat on the throne of Lydia, which he occupied for many long years, lived happily, and never showed his wife to any one; knowing too well what it cost.

# ADDENDA.

("*One of Cleopatra's Nights.*")

A.—There is no correct English plural of "necropolis";—the French word *nécropole* is more normal. As the Greek plural could not be used very euphoniously, and as I have tried throughout to render an exact English equivalent for each French word whenever comprehensible, I beg indulgence for the illegitimate plural "necropoli," used to signify more than one necropolis, as an equivalent for the French *nécropoles*.

B.—In the opening scene of "*One of Cleopatra's Nights*," the reader may be surprised at the expression "the *chuckling* of the crocodiles." Our own Southern alligators often make a little noise which could not be better described,—a low, guttural sound, bearing a sinister resemblance to a human chuckle or subdued, sneering laugh. A Creole friend who has lived much in those regions of Southern Louisiana intersected by bayous and haunted by alligators, comprehended at once the whole force of the term *rire étouffé* as applied to the sounds made by the crocodile. "*Je l'ai entendu souvent*," he said, with a smile.

("*Clarimonde.*")

The idea of love after death has been introduced by Gautier into several beautiful creations, sometimes Hoffmanesquely, sometimes with an exquisite sweetness peculiarly his own. Among his most touching poems, there is a fantastic,—*Les Tâches Jaunes*,—so remarkable that I cannot refrain from offering a rude translation of it. Though transplanted even by a master-hand into the richest soil of another language, such poetical flora necessarily lose something of their strange color and magical perfume. In this instance, the translator, who is no poet, only strives to convey the beautiful weirdness of the original idea:—

*With elbow buried in the downy pillow*
*I've lain and read,*
*All through the night, a volume strangely written*
*In tongues long dead.*

*For at my bedside lie no dainty slippers;*
*And, save my own,*
*Under the paling lamp I hear no breathing:—*
*I am alone!*

*But there are yellow bruises on my body*
*And violet stains;*
*Though no white vampire came with lips blood-crimsoned*
*To suck my veins!*

*Now I bethink me of a sweet weird story,*
*That in the dark*
*Our dead loves thus with seal of chilly kisses*
*Our bodies mark.*

*Gliding beneath the coverings of our couches*
*They share our rest,*
*And with their dead lips sign their loving visit*
*On arm and breast.*

*Darksome and cold the bed where now she slum'ers*
*I loved in vain,*
*With sweet soft eyelids closed, to be reopened*
*Never again.*

*Dead sweetheart, can it be that thou hast lifted*
*With thy frail hand*
*Thy coffin-lid, to come to me again*
*From Shadowland?*

*Thou who, one joyous night, didst, pale and speechless,*
*Pass from us all,*
*Dropping thy silken mask and gift of flowers*
*Amidst the ball?*

*O, fondest of my loves, from that far heaven*
*Where thou must be,*
*Hast thou returned to pay the debt of kisses*
*Thou owest me?*

---

("*Arria Marcella.*")

Gautier doubtless obtained inspiration for this exquisite romance from an old Greek ghost story, first related by Phlegon, the freedman of Hadrian. Versions of it were current in the twelfth and sixteenth centuries; and Goëthe reproduced it in his "Bride of Corinth." We offer a translation from the brief version of Michelet, who accuses Goëthe of bad taste for having introduced the Slavic idea of vampirism into a purely Greek story.

***

A young Athenian goes to Corinth to visit the house of the man who has promised him his daughter in marriage. He has always remained a pagan, and does not know that the family into which he hopes to enter has been converted to Christianity. He arrives at a very late hour. All are in bed except the mother, who prepares a hospitable repast for him, and then leaves him to repose. He throws himself upon a couch, overwhelmed with fatigue. Scarcely has he closed his eyes, when a figure enters the room: it is a girl, all clad in white, with a white veil; there is a black-and-gold fillet about her brows. She beholds him. Astonishment! Lifting her white hand, she exclaims:

"Am I then such a stranger in the house? Alas! poor recluse that I am! But I am ashamed to be here. I shall now depart. Repose in peace!"

—"Nay, remain, beautiful young girl! Behold! here are Ceres, Bacchus, and, with thee, Love! Fear not! be not so pale!"

—"Ah! touch me not, young man! I belong no more to joy. Through a vow made by my sick mother, my youth and life are fettered forever. The gods have fled away. And now the only sacrifices are sacrifices of human victims."

—"What! is it thou!—thou, my beloved affianced, betrothed to me from childhood! The oath of our fathers bound us together forever under the benediction of heaven! O, virgin, be mine!"

—"Nay, friend, nay!—not I. Thou shalt have my young sister. If I sigh in my chill prison, thou mayst, at least, while in her arms, think of me, of me who pines and thinks only of thee, and whom the earth must soon cover again."

—"Never! I swear it by this flame, it is the torch of Hymen. Thou shalt come with me to my father's house. Remain, my well-beloved!"

For marriage-gift he offers her a cup of gold. She gives him her chain; but prefers a lock of his hair to the cup.

It is the ghostly hour. She sips with her pale lips the dark wine that is the color of blood. Eagerly he drinks after her. He invokes Love. She, though her poor heart was dying for it, nevertheless resists him. But he, in despair, casts himself upon the bed and weeps. Then she, flinging herself down beside him, murmurs:

"Ah! how much hurt thy pain causes me! Yet shouldst thou touch me,—what horror! White as snow, cold as ice, alas! is thy betrothed!"

—"I shall warm thee, love! come to me! even thou though hadst but this moment left the tomb." . . .

Sighs and kisses are exchanged. . . . Love binds and fetters them. Tears mingle with happiness. Thirstily she drinks the fire of his lips; her long-congealed blood takes flame with amorous madness,—yet no heart beats in her breast.

But the mother was there; listening. Sweet vows; cries of plaint and pleasure. "Hush," says the bride; "I hear the cock crow! Farewell, till to-morrow, after nightfall." Then adieu, and the sound of kisses smothering kisses.

Indignant, the mother enters. What does she behold! Her daughter! He seeks to hide her—to veil her! But she disengages herself; and waxing taller, towers from the couch to the roof.

"O, mother, mother! dost thou then envy me my sweet night? dost thou seek to drive me from this warm place? Was it not enough to have wrapped me in the shroud, and borne me so early to the tomb! But there was a power that lifted the stone! Vainly did thy priests hum above my grave. What avail salt and water where youth burns? The earth may not chill love. . . . Thou didst promise me to this youth. . . . I come to claim my right.

"Alack! friend, thou must die. Here thou must pine and wither away. I possess thy hair; to-morrow it shall be white. . . . Mother, a last prayer! Open my black dungeon; erect a funeral pyre; and let the sweetheart obtain the repose that only flames can give. Let the sparks gush out,—let the ashes redden! We return to our ancient gods."—[*La Sorcière*, pages 32–4; edition of 1863.

Printed in the United States
2168